March 8 2025

Return to Red Winds

Ronda and Tommie,

Hope You enjoy
Return To Red Winds

Donna

Return to Red Winds

By
Donna Eimer Villani

Strategic Book Publishing and Rights Co.

Strategic Book Publishing & Rights Co., LLC
USA | Singapore
www.sbpra.com

For information about special discounts for bulk purchases, please contact Strategic Book Publishing and Rights Co. Special Sales, at bookorder@sbpra.net.

ISBN: 978-1-63135-883-8

Other Books by the Author

The Capture of Art
Sole Mate
The Portal (available on Amazon Kindle)

With the exceptions of actual personages identified, historic events and places as such, the characters and incidents in the fictional story of Return to Red Winds are entirely the products of the author's imagination and have no relation to any person or event in real life.

Dedication

Thanks to the blessings from God; through the intercession of His son Jesus and the mother of Jesus, Mary, who through the love of my father, August John Eimer, Jr., and my mother, Rosemary (Cookie) Eimer (née Schuler), gave me life; and His blessing to my life of Frank and Juanita Villani (née Powell), and the love and inspiration from my family and friends.

A special thanks to Denny and Carol O'Brien (née Villani) for editing input.

Thanks to Connie Voss (née Eimer) and Ken Schmitt for technical and artistic advice.

Finally, for my husband Ronald Frank Villani, who lives to inspire me to keep my feet on the ground and my head out of the clouds!

Tribute

We were blessed with the following Mothers and Fathers and recently lost them. But believe this; they are together smiling and forever showering their love down on us.

Rosemary (Cookie) Eimer (née Schuler)
Betty Ann (Bee) Grobe (née Schuler)
William (Bill) Schuler
Pamela Ann Timmermann (née Denny)
Glenda Joy Huskey (née Hicks)
Richard T Brown
James R. Timmermann

Acknowledgements

Thanks to the smile of actor Harrison Ford!

Maternal Grandmother, Marie Schuler for her saying: "If a bean's a bean ..."

Thanks to Maxine Smutzer for the Grandpa poem used in this book.

Thanks to Dorothy Doyle as told to her daughter Evelyn Ortwein: "You only lose when you quit trying!"

Thanks to the following for Christmas spirit ideas:

Rosemary "Cookie" Eimer (née Schuler): Santa behind closed door making Christmas exciting, family love, and the birth of Jesus.

Bob and Maryclare Stephens (née Eimer) and family: snuggle together in front of the fireplace; multi-colored lights are jolly, while blue lights are peaceful.

John and Cathy Eimer and family: family togetherness

Bill and Peggy Eimer and family: family togetherness

Jim Eimer: mysterious Santa turns on the light and plays the music.

Jim and Sherrie Eimer and family: family togetherness

George and Diane Hotard (née Eimer) and family: family togetherness

Tom and Karen Toti (née Eimer) and family: playing the guitar and singing Christmas music

Henry and Victoria (Gotchie) Pattrin (née Eimer) and family: three kids in a tub and Santa behind closed doors, kids, and love.

Ken Schmitt and family: making cookies, and playing cards

Constance Voss (née Eimer) and family: watching the snow fall, being with family, and putting up the manger

Joseph and Liz Eimer and family: family togetherness

Juanita Villani (née Powell): perfect mantel decoration, and my family's love all around me

Charles and Mary Villani and family: per Stephanie—an understanding of family love and togetherness

Denny and Carol O'Brien (née Villani) and family: decorations, baking cookies, family love, and getting together

Toby and Kim Palmer and family: getting a Christmas tree and, dipped frozen yogurt, and spirited excitement of the season

Jeff and Kelly Wagner and family: peppermint schnapps and family togetherness

Chelsea Wagner: fudge and hot chocolate

David and Vicki Villani and family: family love and getting together

Shirley Bush and family: love of family touches the heart

Bill and Clare Trelc-Lang (née Eimer) and family: warm atmosphere that is in the air and coming from the hearts of family and friends, as well as the wonder in the eyes of the babies and small children

Bill and Mary Trelc (née Vodicka) and family: coming from a small family and excitement of going to a large family Christmas party, family love, and togetherness

Fern Timmermann and family: family togetherness

Pete and Debra Rothrock and family: no-bake cookies.

Martin Timmermann and family: getting together with loved ones

Darrin and Charlene Shoemaker and family: blue Christmas tree bulbs and getting together with family and friends

Tracy and Chris Timmermann and family: phone calls to the family

Jesse Martin and family: getting together with family

Bob and Terry Gray (née Langford) and family: to be able to hold lost loved ones in our arms again

Clara and Joseph Lark Lamkie and family: the love and closeness of family and friends

Bill Denny: wishing his grown daughters were kids again so he can watch them open their gifts

Laura Denny's cousin, Debbie Eggman: call up to heaven and talk with deceased loved ones

Michael and Christy Fisher and family: gifts for less fortunate and looking into their children's eyes and seeing joy and happiness

Jesse Broadbent: gifts and, of course, the birth of Jesus

Tonette Thurman: VFW candlelight vigil for deceased veterans

Ronald Villani: making Christmas cookies for family and friends, decorating and, "Glad when it's over . . ."

Chapter One

She patiently sat alone near the bay window. Methodically, she turned and looked out the left side of the floor-to-ceiling picture window. She could see the gray sky and the cool mist in the air. Unfortunately on this particular autumn day, the leaves on the trees at Red Winds did not display their usually cheerful blazing red colors, mixed with glimpses of flaming sun yellows. The afternoon drizzle dulled their brilliance and made the day look completely gloomy to her as she rose from her chair and neared the bay window. Slowly, she parted the heavy drape and gazed out front, remembering with pure joy in her heart that Christina was coming to visit.

Twelve-year-old Christina loved her nickname Christy because she had picked it herself. Her energetic personality could instantly lift anyone out of a dismal mood when her sparkling, light hazel eyes looked at you with mischief lurking behind them. She loved to wear plain, soft cotton shirts and, depending on her mood, various colors of denim overalls with white socks and sneakers. She was a tomboy and didn't care who knew it. She enjoyed knocking around outside with Josh and Adam, who she preferred to call brothers but who were actually her two uncles, slightly older than herself.

Farm chores never bothered her, the dirtier the better, but when visiting Grammy—just down the road from where they lived on the Red Winds Estate—she loved to have tea parties and "gossip" about the past, something she knew Grammy loved as well.

Thank God, here she comes. Oh goodie, pink overalls, my favorite, Grammy thought when she spotted Christy skipping down the drive. She noticed Christy's long black ponytail swaying back and forth from her trotting action. "She sure reminds me of me at that age," she said aloud, laughing to herself.

She opened the door to greet Christy. "My little Sunshine," Grammy said.

"Morning, Grammy," Christy said. Lovingly, they hugged each other. "Not your kind of day, *huh,* Grammy?" Christy asked, half smiling. She hung her jacket on the hook by the door, and they both walked to the kitchen with an arm around each other.

"No, not my kind of day until my little sunshine gets here," said Grammy. They looked at each other with a hint of sadness in their eyes. "But it's just another day, right!" Grammy stated. They didn't like to talk about sad times, but they both did like to "gossip" as they called it.

"Right, just another day," Christy agreed. "But I think, even though it's not so nice outside, the yellow leaves still shine with the reds." She knew that talk about the trees at Red Winds always had a happy effect on Grammy.

"Now that you mention it, they do have a glow about them." Grammy looked out the window. "It always amazes me the way some people describe the leaves." She had a faraway look in her eyes. "And sometimes, depending on what kind of mood I'm in, they look different to me too." She slowly turned toward Christy. "Over the years I've heard all kinds of different opinions about the colors, but today I think it's your little bit of sunshine that makes them show off their colors." She gently lifted Christy's chin. They looked at each other, smiled sweetly, and walked hand in hand to the dining room.

Besides being a dismal day, this was the first anniversary of the death of Christy's grandfather. They both had made a pact that they would never have sad talk or thoughts on this day, so although they knew what day it was, they would only allow it to be just another day.

"I'll get the lace tablecloth for today, okay Grammy?" Christy asked without hesitating. She opened the well-polished, walnut drawer of the buffet. "This pretty thing is just what we need today." She walked to Grammy with the delicate cloth carefully hung across her arms.

"Yes, it's just what we need. The only thing prettier is you." She caressed Christy's rosy cheeks and took the cloth from her. "I put the kettle on if you want to start setting the table after I put down the cloth." She watched as Christy happily turned and went to get the fine china dishes and silverware.

"Oh, Grammy, how wonderful—Reggie made Grandpa's favorite buttermilk cake." She walked past the tall cake, sprinkled with powdered sugar, in the glass cake canister on the buffet in the dining room.

"Reggie is such a treasure; I couldn't have asked for a better helper." Grammy always referred favorably to her trusted companion. She watched as Christy carefully carried the elegant porcelain from the hutch to the buffet. "I thought we would enjoy the cake." She finished placing the tablecloth. "It seems it even takes longer putting down the cloth. These old hands don't work as fast as they used to." She looked at Christy and they both just smiled.

"Grammy, do you think I can pour today?" She knew Grammy was always apprehensive about her handling the hot liquid.

"We'll see." Grammy had a look of skepticism in her eyes while they continued to set the table with the cups and saucers.

Just then the teakettle started to whistle. "You forgot the silverware, honey," She watched as Christy quickly went into the kitchen ahead of her. "All that energy," Grammy snickered softly. "It should be canned and saved for later in life." With a chuckle, she carefully headed for the stove and turned off the gas.

"Can we start at the beginning again?" she asked, as she watched Grammy scoop the tea into the strainer.

"You never seem to tire of all the old gossip." Grammy smiled. She loved telling the tales—especially to someone who truly seemed interested.

"I just love gossip," Christy said. Grammy scooted her away from the stove as Christy watched her pour the hot water over the strainer into the teapot. "Maybe I'll write a book about it someday," she added.

Grammy placed the pot on a pushcart and slowly walked behind it toward the dining room with Christy right behind her. "Honey, I forgot the cream. Can you get the pitcher from the fridge?" Finally, she reached the table and placed the teapot on it as Christy came in with the cream and sugar. "Oh good, you remembered the sugar too." Grammy shrugged her shoulders. "Don't get old baby." She winked.

"But like you always say . . ." Christy began as Grammy said it with her. "It's better than the alternative." They hugged and laughed.

"Honey, if you ever really do write a book don't forget . . ." Grammy was saying when Christy interjected.

"I know. I know. Like you always say: don't forget the disclaper . . . disclemer . . . I don't . . ." Christy was stammering the word she wanted to say.

"The word is *disclaimer*. Go get a piece of paper and a pencil from the drawer. I'll write it down for you." She watched Christy as she energetically went for the items. "Here you go. *Disclaimer* means that the names may be familiar, but to protect the innocent the story is fiction."

Grammy wrote down what she believed to be very important about the "gossip" if Christy really should write a book about it someday.

"Honey, you're young. Even though you act like an old soul, you have a lot of living ahead of you, and if you should write these tales . . . well . . ." She knew she really didn't have many more years or even hours left on this Earth to explain how she believed they should be treated.

"Grammy, don't worry, it will be done just like you want. I'll do my very best. I'll make you proud." She gave Grammy a quick hug, and then started to dance around the table like a ballerina. Grammy laughed and seated herself at the head of the table near the window, so they could look outside while they enjoyed their tea and conversation.

"You're such a hoot." She gestured for Christy to take a seat next to her.

"Please Grammy . . ." She watched as Grammy placed her hands on the teapot.

"Not this time, honey." Emphatically, she glanced at her. "I'll know when you're ready." Feebly, she poured the amber liquid into the cup in front of her and passed it to Christy.

Slowly, she put the pot down. "Heavy thing." She graciously smiled at Christy and then placed her slow moving, wrinkled hands on the handle of the teapot. Again, while displaying grace and great care, she poured herself a cup of the hot brew. "Don't fret, my little sunshine, your day will come and many more after that." She noticed Christy looking a bit forlorn when she finished the pouring.

"I know, Grammy, I just wanted it to be today." She frowned.

"Please pass me the cream pitcher," Grammy asked.

"I feel like I could do it." She noticed Grammy's stern look, immediately changed the subject, and started to smile. She didn't want to mess up her day with Grammy. "I'm sure I could cut us a piece of the cake." Her young, eager eyes looked at Grammy.

"That sounds yummy, and I know you can manage the sharp instrument." She had a calm look in her eyes as she demurely placed her worn hands on her lap. She could feel Christy's excitement, as she watched her move about. She couldn't help but wonder how Christy really saw her, now that her gray hair was thinning and her eyes were losing their luster. *Why does she love to be around an old hag like me?* she thought. She straightened her cotton print dress and fluffed the long sleeves that covered her now sagging arms while she watched Christy neatly cut the cake like a pro.

"Didn't lose a crumb." Christy proudly replaced the heavy glass lid over the cake.

"No, not a crumb, and now as you asked, I will start at the beginning," Grammy said when Christy returned to the table with their treat. "It was not like this day, gray and gloomy. It was a day full of sunshine and happy feelings," she began.

Christy munched on her cake and stared at Grammy. Patiently, she focused her attention on every one of Grammy's words as she began the gossip.

***

Red Winds came into Olivia's view. It had not changed in all these years. Cal and Rachel had seen to its upkeep. It was 1950 and Olivia was forty-one. In all her dreams she never believed this day would ever come. She thought she felt her heart skip a beat. Reminiscing, she looked out the car window. *Just like they always have*, she thought. She was watching the wind blow the leaves on the trees. The colors were as she remembered them, glowing vibrant reds with hints of lemon yellows. They created a dazzling picture against the bright blue sky. She was home. She had finally returned to Red Winds.

"Are you okay?" asked her husband, Ronald—the treasured love of her life. He gently took her hand in his, and she turned to look at him. "Okay?" His dark eyes looked deep into hers and she suddenly felt her heart melt as it had always done before. She thought that looking at him was like looking in a mirror that reflected the love they shared.

"I'm fine, honey. It's just . . ." Suddenly, she felt warm tears on her cheeks. She believed she was releasing feelings that had been pent up for many years and that she was washing away many years of hurt and disappointment. She felt safe and found it easy to cry in front of him. She quickly stopped her crying; she wanted this to be a happy occasion.

"I'm here for you." Ronald said. He held her close while she composed herself.

From the front passenger side of the car, their son, Byron, turned and looked at them. "You're home, Mom." He felt an odd twinge in the pit of his stomach. He thought it was a weird feeling because he was still trying to get used to calling her *Mom*.

"Yes, home . . ." Olivia took a handkerchief from Ronald and wiped away her tears. She then gently squeezed the hand of her daughter, Alyssa, who sat on her other side in the backseat of the car.

"Cal, I can never thank you and Rachel enough for all you've done to keep Red Winds in shape," said Olivia as

Cal drove. As they neared the house, she noticed the barn and corral where Olivia's childhood horse, Jargon, used to stay. "More memories . . ." she said. Ronald noticed she was looking at the corral. He tenderly squeezed her hand.

Cal parked the car, and Byron immediately jumped out and opened the backdoor for his parents. Ronald got out, and Byron hurried to his mother. "Here, Mom, let me help you." He extended his hand to her.

His mother slowly accepted his hand. "Always the gentleman, just like your father. And those eyes—such a deep brown, almost the same color as your hair." She stopped, hardly able to take her eyes off him. "Tall and slender, just like your dad when I first met him. I can't say it enough: you're him all over again." She was almost afraid to blink for fear he would be gone.

"Mama, your home is just lovely," Alyssa said— getting her mother's attention, while Ronald, Alyssa's father took his daughter's arm in his and escorted her to her mother.

"Our home, honey—Red Winds is our home," Olivia said, with a loving tone in her voice. Looking at each other, they silently walked through the front door of the enclosed porch, and finally entered the newly designed, spacious living room.

"Welcome home," Rachel said. She approached Olivia and gave her a slight hug.

"Thank you, Rachel. You can't know what this means to me," Olivia said. Warm tears glistened in her dark, slanted eyes.

"The children helped me. We aired out the house and gave you all clean linens. I took the liberty of making your first meal and stocking the pantry, but we intend to leave you all to get settled in," Rachel said, in a mannerly yet hurried way. She didn't know her blonde hair appeared to be standing on edge, or that her blue eyes were sending signals to Olivia that sent a chill to her bones.

"Please stay, Rachel," Olivia said. She had not been in touch with her dearest, lifelong friend, since she left her in New York some weeks earlier. She wanted to make this an easy, pleasant transition.

"We actually have chores at home. With the veterinary clinic and all, we still have a lot to do. Besides, we have the rest of our lives to visit," Rachel said. She had a bit of sarcasm in her voice that cut Olivia and those within earshot to the quick.

"Yes, we do have the rest of our lives to visit. I just thought . . ." Olivia noticed Rachel getting her belongings together. Like a mother hen, Rachel gathered her children around her and headed for the door.

"Coming, Cal?" Rachel looked sternly at her husband, with raised eyebrows.

"Yep, on my way," Cal said, using his always-trying-to-keep-the-peace tone. He neared his wife. "I'll stop by in the morning. There's a cow I've been tending." He was always the attentive local veterinarian. He followed his wife onto the porch and out the front door.

"Okay, Cal, see you in the morning," Ronald said. He went to the door and watched them go to their car.

"That was a bit curt," Cal whispered to Rachel. She was helping their four-year-old twins, Alyssa and Andrew, into the backseat.

"Dad, can I drive?" asked their oldest son, Cal Junior, CC for short.

"I guess that's okay." Cal saw Rachel give him the "I don't give a care" look as she got in back with the twins. Cal then got in front on the passenger side.

As they left, only Cal waved to Ronald, who still stood in the doorway of the house.

During the drive home, Rachel's curious daughter asked, "Mama, why do I have the same name as their Alyssa?"

When she spoke Rachel tried to curb her bitter feelings for Olivia. "When you were born we didn't know Olivia had named her daughter Alyssa. So, all I can say is that Daddy and I loved that name and that's why we chose it for you." But deep in her heart Rachel believed it was actually a sign of the closeness she once shared with Olivia.

"Okay." Satisfied with her mother's answer, Alyssa replied and dropped the subject.

***

"Grammy, I never can understand why Rachel was so mad at Olivia. It wasn't her fault she wasn't around. I think she really believed she had to stay away," said Christy.

Grammy then stopped the gossip. "Well, Rachel was hurt to the core." She looked at Christy. "You see, for many years she thought Olivia was dead. It took a long time for her to find it in her heart to forgive Olivia, because as it turned out, for years Olivia was living only miles away from her family, but she never let them know she was alive. Back then, it took a bit of a miracle for Rachel to come to grips with her love and feelings for the woman she always thought of as a sister." They continued to drink their tea and eat the delicious buttermilk cake.

As she was enjoying her cake, Christy glanced over at Grammy. She realized during her visits that in some instances when Grammy related parts of the gossip, she was inclined to pause in her chitchat and let her mind wander off on its own about the gossip. These instances were becoming more frequent, and Christy was becoming accustomed to them. She believed they were things that happened to older people. Just then, she noticed Grammy's eyes become transfixed, and Christy knew Grammy was having another one of those mind-wandering moments.

Yes, Grammy was having her own thoughts about the gossip—thoughts that she believed, at that time, she could not relate to the young mind of Christy. At times, Grammy knew that when she was with Christy, she would nod off and think of the gossip. Later that night she would dream of the gossip. Sometimes, just like at that very moment, a memory of the gossip would fill her head, and her mind would start to daydream about the remembered gossip. Right then, Grammy consciously knew, but did not care, when her thoughts reflected back to the gossip of Olivia's return to Red Winds and her first night alone with her husband.

> The room was lit with a yellow and orange glow from the fireplace; the amber glow flickered against the walls and ceiling. The strobe light relaxed Olivia into almost a trance-like state as she sat in a soft, wingback chair near the warmth of the fire.
>
> She had closed her eyes and Ronald thought she might be asleep as he watched her from his matching chair across from her. He thought she looked cute in her identical to his silk pajamas that their kids had given them, but he knew that looking cute was the furthest thing from her mind.

"I'm not asleep. I'm just getting my thoughts together," Olivia said. He believed she must have read his mind. "I'm truly frightened." She knew, after all these years, this would be their first time together as man and wife.

He saw her place her hand on her cheek, and in the limited light, he could see tears falling onto her cheeks from her strange looking, dark eyes. "You're home." He knelt next to her chair. Purposely, he did not reach for her although his heart truly wanted to. Instead, he held back to give her some time and space to readjust.

"Does the shape of my eyes upset you?"

"They're you, and I love all of you," he answered.

"I know you love me, but Mikail insisted I get them altered, I did—for our son." She put her hand by her eyes. "If they offend you, I will get them fixed." She bowed her head, but she could still feel him looking at her.

"When I look into your eyes, I only see you and your love, and when I see the shape, I remember that you sacrificed your life and your physical appearance for our son. Unless it's something that you want, I will never ask you to take away one ounce of who you are or what your eyes represent." It was hard for him not to hold her in his arms, so he continued to kneel next to her and hold himself back.

"You're the man I've always loved, and telling you all of these things is hard for me," she whispered.

"Trust in our love. We will survive anything you have to say." He took a deep breath, and so did she. He noticed she slightly relaxed in the chair.

"Ronald, after Rachel discovered that I was still alive, I know she didn't tell you anything that I told her when I first met her at the hotel in New York." She deliberately did not look at him. "I know it shocked her to see me. Learning that I had your daughter, Alyssa, gave her another shock." She was remembering the look not only on Rachel's face, but also on his when he realized Alyssa was his daughter.

"She was breathtaking that evening at the Yasieu Gallery when she played 'Beautiful Dreamer' so perfectly on the piano," he said. "I knew in an instant she was our daughter." He saw her glance at him.

His tears, like precious diamonds, sparkle in his eyes, she thought.

"Looking at her that night was like looking at you when I proposed to you so many years ago," he said. He rose to his feet and went back to his chair.

"She was my sanity. Without her I never would've survived." It felt like she was opening an old wound. The fear and loneliness she experienced all those years ago when Mikail Yasieu took her far away from her loved ones to the Japanese Seto Islands, flooded her mind and hit her psychological scars like a sharp knife. But then, she remembered the joy she felt when she realized she was going to have Ronald's baby; and when their beautiful baby girl was born, how caring for her gave her the strength to live. "But now, I have to tell you something. I hate to tell you this, but I must." She hung her head and started to sob.

"Olivia, all I care about is that you're here and alive. My life was completely empty without you. I had Byron and he was my savior in life, but I was out of my mind without you. You can tell me anything. I don't care if you murdered someone. I can take anything you have to say." She looked at him so deeply that he thought he would sob. "Just say it," he said softly, and then saw a fear in her eyes that gripped his heart.

"One night, I came to you," she said. She seemed to be in a dream state. "When Mikail first took me away, he never approached me sexually. That baffled me, because when he first talked about his crazy scheme to fake my death and take me as his wife, I thought sex was all he had on his mind." She feared the words would never come from her mouth if she didn't get them out fast. "And when I met with him at his office all those years ago, I thought for my son's life that I could live with that knowledge. I even asked him to take me right there and then." She hesitated for just a moment, but knowing she had to get it all out continued. "I thought he could just get me out of his system, but that was not his way." She looked, with a heavy heart, at the man she had loved for so many years for any sign of hatred toward her.

"What do you mean you came to me?" He only acknowledged that part of what she had just said. He eased forward in his chair, propped his elbow on his knee, and rested his chin on his hand.

"One night, Mikail came to my bedroom. He demanded that we have sex. He said he would not alter our baby Alyssa's eyes to look Japanese, the way he had done mine, if I gave him his own baby." She had to turn her face away from his stare. "In my heart and soul I was gone. Except for when I took care of my baby girl, the Olivia you knew was gone. My life was all messed up, and I truly became that turned around name that I gave myself. In Mikail's presence Olivia was gone. I existed as Aivilo Yasieu, a completely different, uncompassionate, unloving woman." She again faced him.

"I can understand that. I can also understand why you went on with his farce of a life. You did it so our son could live. At the time, we didn't know Mikail made the doctor available for his operation. All we knew back then was that Byron would have died without it. Now we know that because of your sacrifice he was saved." He hoped she knew he completely did not blame her for what she did to save their only child at that time. "But I have to say I never remember you coming to me." Then something in him started to open up, and he began to remember a time long ago—a time when he believed he had a wonderful dream.

"Mikail hated Aivilo. He wanted me as Olivia, and maybe that night, for one miraculous moment, I did become Olivia." She had a calm, mysterious look on her face.

"In my heart I traveled to you. In my mind I was with you instead of him. I was in our bedroom. We made love as we always had. I opened up to you, and I felt you in my arms and in my body. It was you I loved. It was you I kissed and caressed." She saw him look at her with understanding in his eyes. "I had sex with him, but I made love to you." She again hung her head and tried to wipe away the many tears that fell.

"Oh God," he whispered. He went to her again. "I felt it. I was with you. We were in our bedroom. The lights were dim, and I imagined you came to me. I thought I was dreaming. It was only that one time, but I truly felt you, and we did make love." He also was remembering that one time he felt her with him after he thought she was dead.

"It was real. I truly felt it, and now I know it was real for both of us," she said softly.

He held her hand as she rose from her chair. They both sat on the plush carpeted floor next to the chair. She snuggled between his legs and rested her head on his chest. "It was real. As I sit with you now and hold you in my arms, I know it was that real," he said. They both reveled in the realization of that time.

"But, I have to tell you," she said slightly hesitating. "That one time with Mikail produced twin daughters." She thought he might tense up, but when he didn't, she felt more reassured to continue. "Mikail promised me that if I gave him his child he would never again lay a hand on me, and thank God he kept his word." She knew this news would shock him, and not wanting to see it in his eyes, she purposely did not look at him.

"You have twin daughters? Where are they? Did they die?" Knowing her as a mother to their son, he believed if humanly possible she would always care for her children.

"I couldn't look at them or mother them. They were his children. They looked like him; they had his slanted eyes. He took them, and they lived together on another side of his island until the war. Then he sent them to Switzerland, so they would be safe," she related. "I've never heard from them or seen them since then. They were born after we had been on the island for about two years. Alyssa is seventeen, and they're fifteen." She did not feel one bit of remorse for Mikail's children. "They were borne from me, but they were not of me. I don't know how else to explain it. I know this sounds hateful and not like me, but I couldn't bring myself to love them." She continued to lay her head close to his chest. "I felt as if they were little Mikails, and I truly despised the man. You knew that. I told you many times how I felt about him.

I even told your sister, Mary, when we worked together at Mr. Ti's laundry, the way I felt about him and how the first time I met him he gave me the creeps. You must remember how I felt all those years ago when you worked for him at the Yasieu Gallery." She was trying to explain her feelings and why she acted the way she did back then.

He could feel her body go rigid. "I remember how he gave you the creeps," he said. "I read that he died in Hiroshima." Trying to calm her, he rubbed his fingers along her arms the way he did so many years ago.

"Yes, he died, but I have to say after my last meeting with him that he seemed a changed man. He almost seemed human, not the manipulating monster I always thought him to be. He told me, at that last meeting, about the Japanese bombing of Pearl Harbor, and that he had been asked by the Japanese emperor to serve. He enlisted, which threw me because he had always been the pampered one." She noticed he only mumbled an acknowledgement that he was listening to her.

"He had arranged passage for me, Alyssa, and her nursemaid, Hattie, back to the United States." She looked up at him as he held her close in his arms.

"He said that because of the love he had for his children something opened up in him. He said it was love, and when I looked at him that evening, for the last time, I think I actually saw some kind of a feeling in the man's eyes. He asked for my forgiveness, and I gave it to him. I had mixed emotions. I hated him and felt sorry for him all at the same time." She tried to suppress her sobs. She went silent and buried her head in his chest.

"You were brave. You had to endure all that time in the Japanese-American internment camp. I can't even imagine the horrors." He felt her body relax so he knew she could continue.

"I had a lot to live for." She did not look at him. "But now I have to tell you something that I don't know if you'll ever be able to forgive me for." She accepted his handkerchief.

He released his gentle hold on her, and she rose to her feet. "I told you—you can tell me anything." He remained seated on the floor.

She went to the foot of their bed, slowly got her bearings, and sat on the edge. "All those years ago, I took Rags." She saw a look of disbelief in his eyes.

"You took Rags?" he almost shouted. Hastily, he ran his fingers through his graying hair and took a deep breath. "Oh my God, I have to tell you Byron was devastated. We all were beside ourselves with worry. We searched and put out flyers for months and months," he said, in a louder than usual voice.

"Oh dear God, I'm so sorry but I lost all of you. I didn't know right then that I was pregnant with Alyssa, and it felt like I was losing my whole life. Can't you understand, Rags had been a part of my life for so many years." She wiped her eyes. "When I was young and I lost my parents and my baby brother in that horrific storm, Rags was always with me. She gave me love, and I had to have something to hold onto, so I made Mikail help me steal her." She felt as if a great weight had been lifted from her. "I saw that Martha was watching Byron in the backyard, which meant my baby boy was going to live, so I kept my end of the bargain to stay with Mikail." She saw a change in Ronald's eyes.

"You could have bolted right then. We could have figured it all out. Byron was safe and survived his operation." He got up from the floor and started to pace in front of her.

"I felt as if I couldn't take that chance. I lost and won at the same time, but I had to have a part of my family so I took Rags." She saw a hint of gloom in his dark, once loving eyes.

"Byron cried himself to sleep every night for over a year. He lost you and then his puppy. I'm telling you . . ." Sadly, he shook his head. He looked at her and saw a small, childlike woman looking back at him.

"Ronald, when you say that I could have bolted, it sounds so simple, but back then I couldn't take that chance. I was scared out of my wits. I didn't know what that man was capable of. Can't you understand that?" she whispered. She was hoping he would try to comprehend what she went through.

"Oh God, I can't tell Byron. That's something . . ." he spoke with sorrow written all over his face. He sat back down on his chair. What she said hurt him, but he knew it would deeply distress their son.

"I'll find the right time to tell our son," she said, knowing it would be a hard task. She knew, even though he was only three when it happened, that he loved and remembered her childhood dog Rags that they adopted as their family pet.

"I truly didn't know what that man was capable of. Oh God, Ronald, my blood curdled when he showed me the body of my Aunt Junietta." She shivered when she remembered the last time she saw her maternal aunt. "In life, Junietta and I did look similar, but she was always such an obnoxious, hard-core woman." She again envisioned the sight of her aunt at the morgue. "Seeing her all crumbled up like that made me think of what else he might do to my family," She knew he also had to see Junietta's body, thinking it to be her, his wife's body. "I didn't know how she really died, and to this day I'm still not sure she wasn't murdered." She looked at him with fright and wonder evident in her eyes.

"I know it was horrible," he said. He looked at her and felt a deep empathy. "I am so sorry you had to go through that, and also for your time lost with us. I will never forget what you did for us." He went next to her on the bed and they embraced. "Honey, we will work it all out. Let's stop all this talk of the past and try to make this a happy time. We have a lifetime to talk about all these things." He stood in front of her. "I want you to always feel safe and know I will never let you go." He took her hands, and she came into his arms.

"In your arms I always feel safe. I will never go. Only when I die will I go." She caressed his unshaven cheek and stared into his soft brown eyes. "You gave me this ring all those years ago." She put her hand with the ring on it in his hand. "When you placed it on my finger again, it felt like it was welded here forever." She could almost feel it burn her finger when she remembered throwing it at Mikail, relinquishing it to him to use as proof of her demise. Ronald had the 18K gold engagement ring, with a solitaire diamond centered between two entwined hearts, personally fashioned for her.

"I love you," he whispered. He lifted her ring finger to his lips and kissed it. Then he lowered his lips to hers. "You taste like honey." He could feel the building passion of his deep love for her flowing throughout his body. "I

RETURN TO RED WINDS

have never forgotten the softness of your lips." He fully, yet gently, kissed her.

"My lost heart has finally been found," she whispered in his ear. She stepped back from his embrace and started to undress in front of him.

"Your beauty is incredible," he whispered. He too undressed and came to her. "You're trembling." His hands softly outlined the shape of her breasts. "Do you remember our wedding night?" he whispered in her ear and then gently nibbled it.

"I remember we were both very nervous," she whispered back. She put her supple lips on his neck and found the spot that she knew made him whimper.

"Do you remember what I said to you?" He gently held her at arm's length, admiring her petite body with a desire in his eyes that showed he had yearned for her all those lost years. Displaying a bit of hesitation, he looked into her always-loving eyes and knew she did recall.

"Yes, I remember, but I would love to hear it again." She stood on her tiptoes, hugged him, and felt his manly form on her body.

"Now that I have you . . ." he began, and they both said in unison, "I don't know what to do with you." They giggled while she tenderly kissed his neck. He picked her up and gathered her into his arms.

"You're my forever," he said and carried her to their bed.

"Forever and beyond," she whispered.

They could not take their eyes off each other. Life to be shared was again theirs, and only death could physically separate them. Later, they slept in each other's arms dreaming only of new tomorrows.

Chapter Two

"Grammy, Grammy . . ." Christy was trying to rouse Grammy from her daydream. She stared at Grammy who, for only a few moments, seemed to have fallen into a deep trance.

"Yes, honey," replied Grammy. She acted like nothing had happened.

"I think you're remembering some gossip that you don't want me to know," Christy said. She closely scrutinized the older woman.

"Oh, you little whippersnapper, don't you know old people have wandering minds! Sometimes I sleep with my eyes open. Don't you worry about it," she said teasingly.

"Well it looked like you were thinking . . ." Christy started to say, but then changed the subject. "Oh well, can we talk about the time Rachel and Olivia tried to find each other and be like sisters again?" She tried to pass over Grammy's little divergence with the gossip and gave her a look of anticipation so she would continue.

"You always like the sad parts," Grammy said. She took a sip of her tea, which had slightly cooled, and it made her wince.

"May I warm that for you?" Christy asked and started for the teapot. She stopped when Grammy gave her a commanding look.

"Trying to kid a kidder?" Grammy asked, with a slight smile. She lifted the teapot, filled her cup, and then gestured if Christy wanted some too. Christy shook her head, her smile fading. "I still remember things I've said," Grammy added, with a slight grin.

"I know. I just thought . . ." Christy shrugged her shoulders wishing she could have poured the tea.

"In due time, in due time," Grammy repeated. She watched as Christy sat back in her chair and reached for her cooled cup of tea.

"So let me see, oh yes that was a time for many memories or should I say more gossip." She saw Christy's eyes light up as she again started the gossip.

***

Rachel had decided to take a horseback ride. Cal knew his wife's ways and could understand why she headed for the cemetery on Red Winds. It was a time for reflecting and thanking, and it was the anniversary of the deaths of Olivia's family and Cal's parents during that violent tornado twenty-five years earlier.

On that same day, Olivia rode a horse to the cemetery and reflected on fond memories of her beloved girlhood Appaloosa, Jargon. She chuckled when she remembered back all those years ago how Cal took her mind off thoughts of her mother, who was having problems giving birth to Olivia's brother Jay. She and Cal were riding to the Anderson farm, so Olivia could stay with Rachel until her mother was okay and her father could come for her.

"I've always admired your Appaloosa." Cal said. "He has strong lines and well defined raindrop spots." He looked over at her. "He's a fine horse." He openly marveled at the animal's good traits, and she later realized that he was just trying to take her mind off her mother's predicament.

When Cal asked her why she named her horse Jargon, she said, "Well, when Daddy gave him to me, I couldn't stop talking about how beautiful he was and how much I just loved him. I went on and on, and my dad said I was full of a lot of jargon, so . . ." Cal had smiled at her as they continued to ride. That was also the first time she understood why Rachel was so in love with Cal, even though Cal was thirteen years older than she and Rachel. He was a very open and caring man and still is to this day. She smiled to herself and stopped her horse when she reached the cemetery. "Old memories . . ." she pondered. "Always on my mind!"

Her mood changed as she dismounted her horse. She could feel the spongy earth beneath her feet, and then she noticed that the wild strawberry plants were meticulously manicured over the burial grounds. Tombstones stood like silent reminders of a terrible time. She felt the wind in her face and it chilled her to the bone, but she could not close her eyes or forget the sadness that filled her heart all those years ago.

"Oh God, you all would love Ronald," Olivia spoke aloud. "Daddy, to me he has something about him that reminds me of you. I think it's the way he makes me feel safe." she said as if her family were right in front of her listening to her.

"I think you would have understood why I went with Mikail. Next to my husband, Ronald, your grandson, Byron was my life, and when I thought I would lose Byron . . ."

She went to a wrought iron bench and sat down. "I know Cal and Rachel must have put this bench here. Cal probably made it." She was running her hand along the cool, flat iron of the seat when something caught her eye. "Oh my God," she said in a louder than usual voice. She went to a tombstone she had never seen before.

"Olivia Anne Webster-Brown. Dearly beloved wife of Ronald Brown, mother of Byron Brown, Daughter of Elizabeth and Jason Webster sister of Jason Junior Webster, and dearest beloved sister and friend," she read aloud. Her knees buckled, and she fell to the ground. "God help me," she cried. She lay prostrate on her aunt Junietta's grave. "They thought you were me," she cried out as the scared birds flew from the trees. "I had to do it," she whispered. She began to crawl toward the graves of her parents and her brother. "I know you can understand it." She pulled back the leaves of the strawberry plants and touched the cold earth.

"Mama, Daddy, you have to know . . ." she was saying aloud. "I can feel that you understand." Tears fell from her eyes and onto their grave as she sobbed. With her eyes closed, she pressed her fingers over the smooth stone. She felt their engraved names: Jason, Elizabeth, and Jason Junior (Jay). Finally, she touched the deep impression of Beloved Webster Family. "It makes me feel good knowing you're buried together with my sweet little Jay in your arms. I love you all still." She felt a close connection with her departed loved ones. She did not notice Rachel ride up and tie her horse to a tree a short distance away and witness her.

"Oh Jay, I can still see your sweet smile and the way you wanted me to stay with you that day before the carnival. I told Rachel I should have stayed with you." She got up and went to the side of their grave. "I can feel you in my arms," she said. Rachel watched her caress herself as if she were actually holding her brother in a loving embrace. "You have a nephew and a niece. You would have been a wonderful uncle." She was remembering his big blue eyes and his toothless grin. "My baby brother, my godsend," she whispered. She could not stop the mournful tears from flowing through her closed eyes.

"Mama and Daddy, you would be so proud of your grandchildren," she said, almost inaudibly. She then opened her eyes and looked down at their grave. "Thank you, God, for keeping them close in my heart." Finally, she heard Rachel approach her.

"Not every day you see your own gravestone," Rachel said, with a cold heart. She did not care if she hurt Olivia with her words.

"No, not a pleasant sight," Olivia whispered.

"I think you missed one," Rachel then said. She pointed to a small stone next to what was named as Olivia's grave marker.

"No, I didn't see that one. It's so tiny." Olivia slowly walked to the smaller stone. A flush filled her body, and she could feel a clammy perspiration under the pits of her arms as she read the name aloud. "Olivia Anne Yarborough." Without warning, her knees gave way, but this time she fainted.

After some time, she awoke to find she was covered with a blanket and her head was on Rachel's lap. "You're lucky my husband taught me a lot about first aid," Rachel said, with a look of relief in her eyes.

"What happened?" Olivia whispered, with a crackle in her voice.

"Quick as anything you passed out." Olivia tried to get up but fell back down on Rachel's lap. "You better lay still a bit," Rachel said, with care in her voice.

"I remember riding here and sitting on the bench. Did you and Cal put it here?" She peered into Rachel's blue eyes.

"Yes, Cal made it and we put it here, after . . ." she hesitated.

"Rachel, I know it's going to be hard for you to forgive me, and I guess I can understand why, but you have to know I did it for my baby, don't you?" Olivia asked, with hope in her eyes. She felt a damp cloth on her forehead and reached for it.

"Better leave it on for a while." Rachel said. She pulled the blanket up closer to Olivia's chin.

"You should've been a nurse," Olivia said, with a slight smile.

"I have enough nursing to do with the twins and helping Cal at the clinic. Somebody always seems to need some kind of care," Rachel said. She was starting to feel a place in her heart start to open up, but she quickly closed the gap and would not let it flow. "I see Ronald gave you the necklace." She stared at Olivia's neck. "It was with your belongings and Ronald gave it to me." She remembered the tears in Ronald's eyes as he placed the gift she had given Olivia as her maid of honor when she married Cal. "Of course, I gave it back to Ronald when . . ." She could not look at Olivia remembering back to the days they found out Olivia was alive.

"Yes . . ." Olivia's voice was a whisper. She placed her hand on the three entwined hearts with the sapphire in the middle. "It is as special to me today as it was then." She saw a flash of hate in Rachel's eyes.

"After Ronald gave it to me, whenever I touched it I remembered my wedding day and the look in your eyes when I explained its meaning." She glared at Olivia.

"My family . . ." Olivia barely said.

"Yes, your mom, dad, and little Jay . . . your baby brother, all represented by the hearts." She could not keep from staring at it. "And . . ." She did not want any tears now. She backed away.

"And my birthstone in the middle." Olivia ran her fingers over the endeared pendant.

Rachel blurted out, "Well, you might be able to sit on your own now." She did not want her deep feelings to pour out.

"Thanks for this Rachel." She took the cloth from her forehead and sat up. She could tell Rachel wanted to change the subject. She again noticed the tiny gravestone. "That's when I fainted," she said, looking at the stone. "Rachel, who was . . ." Olivia began. Rachel hurried to her feet. "Please tell me." She could feel a deep dread gripping at her heart.

"My baby daughter. We named her after you," said Rachel. Tears that she tried to hold back filled her eyes. "I was pregnant when we got the news about you. I collapsed and lost our baby girl." She had to turn away from Olivia.

"Oh God, Rachel, my heart goes out to you." She knew Rachel loved her very much to have named her daughter after her, and now to find out that she had really been alive all those years ago made Olivia understand her animosity toward her now.

"Rachel, when we were young we were like two peas in a pod. We knew each other's innermost thoughts." Olivia hesitated slightly. "And now I can understand why you feel the way you do about me." She took the cloth and tried to wipe her warm face.

"We were one in thought, and when I lost you, something in me died too," Rachel finally said. She neared her baby's tombstone. "I was in my eighth month. We kept it from you and Ronald because we were going to come to New York for a visit. We were bringing our new baby with us to surprise you the way we did when I was pregnant with CC." She dabbed at her eyes, but did not look at Olivia.

Olivia remembered how happy they were when they came to visit her in New York. It was the night Ronald had first kissed her and told her he had learned to love her. "It was a happy time when you came to visit that winter. We all were so happy to see you both, and then to see that you were going to have a baby. I know Martha was beside herself, and I remember that she made so many of her famous cinnamon rolls." Olivia said.

Rachel knew she was just trying to change the subject. "And Martha tried to help Ronald with Byron. She was more than a nanny or housekeeper. She was like another mother to you and them, but it was not the same after you . . ." Rachel stopped before she said *died*. She felt a cold flush fill her veins as a dark gloom filled her eyes.

"Rachel, like I was saying before, we were like two peas in a pod . . ." Olivia again started to say.

Rachel exploded. "Shut up . . . Olivia . . . just shut up." Rachel raised her hand toward Olivia. "You don't have to tell me how we were . . . we were sisters . . . we knew it like that. We were not good friends . . . we were soul mates in every sense of the word, and then you were gone." She bowed her head and tried to control her building emotions. "I tried to understand my feelings." She coughed and brushed the hair away from her face.

"You were gone—the one person, besides my husband that I could tell it all too." Her voice quivered. "I even tried to talk about my feelings with Byron. You were gone for many years, but he was still trying to get his feelings straightened out." She looked at Olivia. "In fact, it was the day of his first interview with you as Aivilo, at the Yasieu Gallery." Her face was burning. "But, what you don't know is that before he met with you for his interview, he told me there were times when he thought he felt you."

She noticed Olivia squirm a bit, but not caring how Olivia felt, she continued. "And I told him that I felt you at times too." Her blue eyes looked like they were on fire. "Little did we know that we truly did feel your presence," she blew her nose into a tissue, "because you were not only in the room with him when he interviewed you, but in that same building, only a few rooms away from me." She coughed again and felt a bit queasy and went to the wrought iron bench to sit down.

"Rachel, when I saw Byron that day, when he interviewed me about being in the Japanese-American internment camps, I knew I did the right thing. He would have died without that operation. He wouldn't be here today had I not faked my death and left with

Mikail. You know I hated that man, but to save my baby I would have walked on fire." She truly believed the Rachel she grew up with would be able to understand why she did what she did.

"When you knew that Byron was okay you could have somehow let Ronald know about what that bastard, Mikail was doing to you. We all could have gone to the authorities! We could have done anything else. For you to fake your death and go off with him and just leave us, my God, it tore us to pieces." Her tears started to flow again. "I don't know what you can say to make me understand." She could not stop her tears.

"Rachel, all I can say is . . . like I was saying . . ." Olivia was about to bring up about the two peas in a pod again, but hesitated. "Well, I feel we were the same back then and we are still the same now. I can feel your pain. It hurts. But in my place you would have done the same thing." She saw a pained look in Rachel's eyes and tried to prepare herself.

Rachel shot her a look that almost put her to the ground. She shouted, "I would never . . ." She got up and started to pace. "Never . . . damn it . . . never . . . maybe you really don't know the real me."

"Yes, you would. If CC had needed you like Byron needed me, you would have been there like I was in a heartbeat," Olivia said.

Rachel stopped pacing. "Don't you think I thought about that? Thank God I took the tour at the Yasieu gallery and saw the painting with your familiar Olivia signature in the mirror. Sure, you took care to sign the painting on the wall AivilO, but when I turned and saw it in the mirror on the opposite wall it was backwards and the big O and big A were just like I remembered." She could feel her arm pits start to itch. "Oh God, your name . . . you would still be dead to us if your name, OliviA, hadn't screamed out to me." She took a deep breathe. "I couldn't do that to my family . . . you know me so well, huh?" Rachel hung her head.

Olivia could feel Rachel's building rage. She went silent, but then tried to make Rachel understand why she had done what she did all those years ago. "It wasn't as easy as just getting the operation for my baby. Mikail was evil, and when I saw Junietta's body I knew he was capable of anything. I was also protecting those I loved. I thought if Junietta was dead he could also do harm to my family," said Olivia. She then saw something in Rachel's eyes she had never seen before.

"I would have killed the bastard," Rachel said, not fearing any words that came out of her mouth. "Before he would have done any of the things you said, I would have choked the life out of him." She went next to her baby's grave.

"He held Byron's life in his hands. He had the doctor who could save my baby's life on the phone. Only his words could save his life. And, like I said, I didn't know what else he was capable of doing. I was certain he had others, somewhere, lurking around to do his dirty work. I didn't know." She tried to quiet her shaking body. "Do you think we can ever get past this?" Olivia whispered. She tried to get up, but could not.

"I don't know. My heart cracked in places that I don't know can ever be mended. I truly feel for Cal. He's lost a lot too. It took me a long time to be intimate with him again. You know our twins are only four," Rachel said. She was not looking at Olivia, but at her daughter's grave.

"You haven't asked about my family," Rachel said. She went back to the bench.

"Oh God, Rachel," was all Olivia could say. She saw Rachel point to another side of the cemetery. "I can't look," she cried. She lay down on the spongy ground.

"Mom died in another one of those terribly tornadoes and Dad a few years later. We think he just died from missing and loving her. Must run in the family," Rachel said, not looking at her. "My brothers left and live all over the country. We get together here at least once a year," she said, not caring if she heard her or not.

Finally, Olivia rose and walked to the bench. "I might feel the same as you do if . . ." Olivia said.

Infuriated, Rachel shouted, "If what? If I'd done what you did? Don't you listen? I would never have done it, period." She noticed she had startled the birds in the distance. She tried to compose herself. She let Olivia sit near her on the bench.

"You know, I guess we never really know what we're capable of until we're put to some kind of ultimate test," Rachel said. She scratched her brow. She was truly trying to understand Olivia's rationality. "We really were not those peas in a pod like you were saying." She got up from the bench.

"Maybe not, but I know I always loved you," Olivia whispered. She bowed her head.

"You know you really never could understand my love for Cal," Rachel said. She was remembering how Olivia always tried to talk her out of her feelings for Cal until she just quit telling her about them.

"I remember," was all Olivia could say.

"When the night gets cold, don't leave Ronald to sleep alone ever again. He's had too many of those," Rachel said. She knew the loneliness the man had experienced for so many years.

"He understands. Or, at least he's trying," Olivia said. She was hoping Rachel would try too.

"I think we better walk our horses back to Red Winds. You feel up to it?" Rachel asked.

"I guess so," Olivia replied, but then thought, *No we're not the same young, naïve girls from yesterday*, as she rose from the bench and they went to get their horses.

***

"More, Grammy more." Christy asked, excitedly after Grammy finished that part of the gossip.

Grammy was getting up from the dining room table. "Honey, tomorrow's another day," Grammy said and went to the kitchen. "Don't mess with those dishes. Reggie will take care of them," she said.

Christy came into the kitchen. "Grammy what's an expletive?" She remembered Grammy had used that word in place of any profanity in the gossip.

"Go ask Reggie for the dictionary," Grammy replied. She headed for the front porch while Christy ran to Reggie.

"Got it," Christy said to Grammy. "Let's see. It says expletive: Filling up space, extra, redundant, a word or thing inserted to fill a vacancy, interjection, profanity," she read aloud. "Oops! The profanity. I'm thinking like the 'F' word. My brothers use the 'F' word sometimes when they don't think I'm around." She saw Grammy give her a look.

"You always bring that up, and we always look the word up after some of the gossip, so I guess you have to use your own imagination," Grammy said. They both just laughed a little. "Should I speak to your mother about the guy's use of language?"

Christy started to blush. "I don't want to be a tattletale, Grammy," Christy said, with pleading eyes.

"Well, we'll just keep that between us for now as long as the 'F' word doesn't go any further," Grammy said. She watched Christy shake her head no.

"Olivia was thinking that Rachel had changed. People do change, don't they Grammy?" Christy asked. They were sitting in matching rocking chairs on the heated front porch.

"Baby, I don't think we really change. I believe a person can be challenged to the point of finding something in them that was always there." She looked at Christy. She then reached for her and gently pinched her cheek.

"I believe an idea, or change as you put it, is always a deep part of a person's personality that has never been tapped before. And then, because you become aware of it, it becomes a part of your conviction." She saw a puzzled look on Christy's face. "Look it up." She watched, with a smile, as Christy again picked up the dictionary.

"C-o-n," Christy started to spell, "v-i-c-t-i-o-n: the act of persuasion; the state of being convinced. So you're convincing yourself to believe something?" she asked Grammy.

"But it was something that was always in you; it just had to be found. Get it?" Grammy asked, trying to explain her theory.

"I guess," Christy said. "It was there when something happened to trigger it, and it popped up and hit you in the face; you always believed it anyway." She looked at Grammy, who smiled at her. They both started to laugh. "Maybe I'll be a therapist instead of a writer," Christy said and rocked in the chair.

"Did you know your granddad made this window for me?" Grammy said, with love in her words. She was pointing to the bay window. She also started to rock in her chair.

"Yeah, and it's sure neat," Christy replied. She was used to Grammy repeating herself.

"I'm glad when you tell me I've said something to you before. Some people just let me rattle on and on, and I get tired of the same old stories because I think I'm telling them for the first time," she said, and they both laughed.

"And I know he made these chairs too," Christy said. "Grammy, next time I come over, can we go to the chalet by the lake that Ronald built for Olivia?" She noticed Grammy let out a sigh.

"It should be renovated. You know the whole idea of the place was a start for retirement housing for Olivia's family." Grammy looked at Christy. She knew they had talked about the chalet many times.

"I know, and it's such a pretty place, even if it never was used like it was supposed to be. Maybe this winter I can ice skate on the lake," Christy said with a smile. "I guess nobody ever had time to retire." She looked at Grammy. She noticed she had a faraway look in her eyes.

"I'm guessing there was just too much fast living to retire," Grammy replied with a half smile on her lips. "It's just a buzzard's lookout now," she continued. "Last time I was there the turkey buzzards were migrating and circling overhead and looking down like they wanted to pounce."

"But to me it's still neat to go there, and if I see any buzzards I'll shoe them away," Christy said. She got up from her chair and kicked into the air.

"My word, you're such a hoot. I think you really could kick those little buggers to kingdom come," Grammy chuckled.

"No buzzards safe with me around," Christy said. She made a fist to make her point. "Pounce, you buzzards!" she shouted. She saw a look of love in Grammy's eyes. "I love you, Grammy." She went to Grammy and gave her a hug.

"Me too," Grammy added. She watched the young girl sit back down on her rocker. *So precious*, Grammy thought and smiled.

They rocked and looked out the window in silence.

"Oh look, Grammy, a dove is feeding," Christy said, breaking the silence. They both watched the bird eat from the outside feeder.

"The other day I watched a male cardinal feed a female cardinal. They were so cute. The female kissed the male to thank him for feeding her," said Christy. She looked at Grammy to see if she thought she was being overly sentimental.

"Oh, that's sweet. You know I love to watch the birds. The world could learn a lot about peace and harmony from watching birds," Grammy said.

"And sometimes even survival," Christy added.

"Yes, you're right, even survival, but not in a mean, vindictive way." Grammy said. She saw another look of puzzlement on Christy's face as she again reached for the dictionary. "You're going to wear that book out. It means hateful or spiteful," she said. Christy eased back in her chair with a sigh.

"Thanks, Grammy. I learn a lot from you too," Christy said and chuckled. They again sat in silence.

Finally, Grammy whispered, "We'd love for you to spend the night." They were watching the setting sun. They both looked over at his chair on the other side of the room.

"Love to," Christy said. She scooted her chair closer to Grammy's and took her hand in hers.

"Your room's just like you left it, except cleaner," Grammy said with a chuckle. "Christy, I want you to always remember you have a home here. Red Winds will always be home to you, okay?" She reached across and patted Christy's hand.

"Okay," Christy whispered. She was about to say something else, but when she looked at Grammy, she saw a distant look in her eyes as she stared out the window.

Quietly, they both sat and watched the red blushing sky turn dark. Reggie came in and lit a candle on a table near them and like a church mouse left them.

"More gossip in the morning, Grammy?" Christy asked. She heard her stomach growl.

"Yes, more in the morning. I'll call home, I'm sure they knew you would spend the night. Now, I think we better get some vittles in us," Grammy said. But they both still continued to sit and think of the tales they had talked about that day. Oh how they just loved to gossip.

Chapter Three

It was two in the morning. She could not sleep. Slowly, she slipped from beneath the warmth of her blankets. *Will it ever stop raining?* She made her way to the kitchen with her walker.

"Here we go—a little honey and a dash or two of apple cider vinegar. That should do it! Get the water nice and hot. That's how I like it," she whispered to herself. "Don't want to wake anyone. This gossip with Christy always keeps me up." She downed her sleep aid. *Yep, that should do it!* She kept hold of her walker with one hand and filled her glass with hot water and left it in the sink. *Reggie will know I was up again. Oh well, poop happens.* She thought and laughed as she started back to her bedroom.

"King size beds are wonderful. All this space." She snuggled between the sheets and brought her blanket up to her chin. "I can feel it working already." Feeling sleepy, she finally drifted off to dream of past times of gossip.

***

"I'm telling you brother I have the woman for you." Alyssa said to Byron. They were eating lunch together at a café near the university.

"Allie, I love you, but please no more blind dates," Byron said. He took a bite of his French fry.

"Oh, honey, don't be so old fashion," Alyssa said. She always loved to use endearments with him, and he loved to hear them. "It won't kill you to just meet . . ." She studied his body language. "You don't want to die an old bachelor now, do you?" She chuckled when he turned red.

"If I go first, I'm going to haunt you till the day *you* kick the bucket." He took a bite of his sandwich. They both laughed.

"And if I go first, I'll be sure to let you know if there really is a Heaven." They always teased each other about death, Heaven, and what would happen should the other die first. She also knew that thinking his mother had died gave him ideas of what death and life are all about.

"So you think you're going to Heaven?" He gave her a sly look.

"Quit—I'm a good girl." She gave him a demur look. "Besides, we're not dead yet, brother." They both laughed. She took a sip of her latté.

"I just don't think we have the same taste in women." He frowned and sighed knowing she would not rest until she fixed him up.

"I'm telling you she's a beauty." She stared at her big brother with a devious look in her eyes. Now that he was in her life, she wanted to keep him as close to her as she could and she wanted him to always be happy. "Her name's Madison Yames." She looked up as her friend neared their table.

"Hi," Madison said. She stood next to Byron and looked directly at Alyssa.

"Oh my God, Madison, we were just talking about you." Alyssa rose from her seat. She went to her friend and they hugged. "Can you join us?" She noticed Byron gave her a raised-eyebrow look thinking this was not a coincidental meeting.

"I have about a half hour until my next class, so I guess I could get a cappuccino to go." Madison said. She seemed to almost glide past Byron and he could smell the tang of her perfume.

"I'll get it," Alyssa said. She quickly rose from her seat. "Here take my seat." She pulled out the chair. "Oh, by the way, Madison, this is my brother Byron. He's in his last year here," she said, with excitement in her voice. "I'll be right back," she then added and hurriedly left them.

"I think my sister set this meeting up," Byron said. He was truly taken aback by Madison's beauty.

"I think you're right. She's been talking about you for some time now, and I kept telling her I don't like blind dates." Madison said. She took her seat and smiled shyly.

"Me either" was all Byron could think of to say. He thought she was so beautiful and could not take his eyes off of her. She was not like the other women at the college; she had a mature, sophisticated air about her. "But maybe in your case I was wrong." He saw her blush in a shy sort of way that intrigued him.

"You're staring at me," Madison said quietly. She looked around the café and could see others watching them.

"I'm not the only one," Byron said. "You're incredibly beautiful." He wondered how he got the nerve to say something so personal. "Gosh, I'm sorry. I'm not usually that forward, but you must get that a lot—I mean, people telling you how beautiful you are." He saw her slim figure slightly squirm with a modest acknowledgement of his compliment.

"We're having dress rehearsal in my drama class, and you're right, I do get the looks when I'm all dolled up like this," she said coyly. She tried to divert his eyes and his attention from her. "Here comes Alyssa. We'll have to tease her a bit I think. Can you go along with me?" she asked hurriedly. She saw him wink and nod as Alyssa sat down at the table.

"What a hunk," Madison said excitedly. She scooted her chair next to Byron's. "You told me he was cute, but this . . ." She openly ran her hand down the front of his shirt and purposely rubbed his arm. "I was not expecting such a sexy man." She licked her overly made up red lips.

"*Huh*" was all Alyssa could say. She watched the two of them almost make love with their eyes. "You two sure got acquainted while I was gone." Her dark eyes opened wide and she gawked at them—so did everyone else in the café.

"Well, darlings, I'm off to my drama class. Thanks for the cappuccino," Madison said pertly. She quickly got up and accepted the drink from Alyssa. "Nice to finally meet you Byron. Later." She winked at Alyssa, and then left.

"Holy crap, I was pretty scared there for a second," Alyssa said. "I thought she was serious." She looked at her brother with a relieved look in her eyes.

"Don't you think I'm sexy enough for a beautiful woman to fall head over heals for me at our first meeting?" Byron asked. He gave her one of the most enhanced, cocky smiles that he could muster up.

"Quit! I would like for you two to get to know each other, but I have to say she's a good actress." She squirmed slightly in her seat. "Look, everyone's looking at us. They probably think you're my guy and she was making a play for you," She bent over toward him, grabbed one of his fries, and bit into it. "Crap, cold as ice. Oh well, I have to get to class anyway." She hurriedly rose from her seat.

"Are you free for happy hour tonight?" she then asked. She saw that he looked uneasy.

"Allie, I like her, but can I do it on my own." Byron grunted.

She came next to him and bent down to whisper in his ear. "Sure, you can do it on your own, but if you want to join us, we're going to O'Shey's. You can have beer there." She winked at him.

"Don't you have to be twenty-one to get in there?" He looked serious.

"So, you're over twenty-one, and I have a fake ID," she said and saw another one of his fatherly looks. He always seemed to want to protect her. "God, Byron, everybody does it, so don't look at me like it's the end of the world for Pete's sake." She took a last sip of her drink and kissed him on the cheek. "Around seven, if you're interested." She ran off.

Boy, she's sure changed from the calm, naïve girl I first met. I guess college and being away from home can do that to some people, he thought and left the café for his internal affairs business class. *I might just go tonight. What else do I have to do?* He wondered if he was trying to convince himself. *What the hell, I'm all caught up with my studies and everybody always says I'm a bookworm, so why not get out.* He had always felt a bit guilty knowing he was not the party type like the rest of the guys at the dorm. *Those eyes—almost a jade color and so mysterious—I could have fallen for her act had I not known it was an act,* he walked slowly to his class. *I don't think I've ever seen such big, round, green eyes before. She sure can get one's attention.* He had her on his mind when he stumbled on the petite, blonde girl in front of him.

"Hey," she shouted. Her books went flying, and he caught her just before she fell to the ground.

"I'm so sorry," he said. They both got their bearings. He knelt down to pick up her books. "My mind was elsewhere." He continued to kneel as he handed her the scattered books.

"Obviously," she said curtly. "Most men's minds usually are." She seemed rushed as she squatted down in front of him and reached between his parted legs. Supposedly by accident, she brushed his private parts.

He could see right away, when her short skirt hiked up, that she was not wearing a stitch of underwear. "Excuse me," he said. His eyes opened wide. "Here let me ..." He tried to move back, but she was so close and it all was happening so fast. He then noticed she had a brazen look in her eyes. She seemed to enjoy him staring at the exposed breasts that nearly fell from her tight-fitting, silk blouse.

"Nice," she whispered in his ear. "This subject is really hard for me." She emphasized the word *hard.* "So I wouldn't want to lose it." She giggled. She retrieved a journal he had missed, and to make a point, waved the journal in his face. "Thanks for the help," she blurted out and winked as she hurried off.

"Holy crap, not much to wonder about with her," he mumbled. He hurried to get up. *That was fast. Did she really get a quick feel,* he thought. He could feel himself start to perspire. He looked at his wristwatch and realized he was running late for his class. *She looked familiar. Maybe she's in one of my classes.* He watched her hurry away. *Cute little blonde, big blue eyes, but not my type; she can't keep her hands to herself.* He tried to picture her in one of his classes. *It'll come to me,* he thought, but then memories of Madison again came to his mind. *Get with it man.* He tried to focus on his class as he entered the hall just seconds before Professor Striker.

***

I know I'm early, Byron thought later that evening. He looked around the noisy clubroom, ordered a glass of beer at the bar, and took a seat at a table. *Not really my kind of entertainment but . . .* He saw them come into the barroom. *Wow, she's worth it, and can she dress.* He noticed that the tight red dress, with the slits at either side, showed off her long, slim legs. *Get a hold of yourself man.* He could feel his heart pumping. *Her long, dark hair flows with her body. I bet she has red lips just like before.* He saw Alyssa wave to him. They started toward his table.

"I guess this table's okay, but not very close to the stage." Alyssa said.

Byron went to Madison and pulled out a chair for her. *Not the same tangy perfume as this afternoon, or lips,* he thought, and then pulled out a chair for his sister.

"Thanks," Madison said. She saw a look of surprise in his eyes.

"You're welcome, Madison. That is you Madison?" he asked.

His sister interjected. "Yes, it's Madison. She had makeup on this afternoon that hid her eyes. She's of Japanese descent," Alyssa said. She lightly smacked him on the arm. "Don't look so shocked," she added. She waved to a waiter and ordered three pitchers of beer for them.

Byron sat next to Madison. "Allie this makes me nervous," Byron said. He pointed to the beer he had already been drinking as she reached for his glass and downed the last half of it.

"I've been drinking beer ever since I started at the university. I can handle it, so don't make such a big deal about it." She tried to divert his stares of disbelief at her actions when the waiter brought their beers.

"I'm not really into beer myself," Madison said. She put her hand up next to his ear when she spoke because of the loud music.

"It's just the age thing," he whispered to her. He again looked at Madison with a baffled look in his eyes.

"Does my heritage bother you?" Madison asked and took a sip of her drink.

"No, not really, I was just shocked. I never realized that the shape of one's eyes could alter their appearance so much." He saw his sister give him a startled look. He felt himself flush and thought he must look beet red. *How could I say such a stupid thing . . . Mama?* he thought. *I'm so sorry, Mama.* He felt ashamed. He saw Alyssa roll her eyes and shake her head as she was finishing another glass of beer. Just then the master of ceremonies came onstage.

"Welcome, welcome everyone." he shouted. The spotlight came on and the music subsided. "We have a special treat tonight." Alyssa slid closer to her brother.

"You're lucky you're here tonight. I heard this is a great show," Alyssa whispered.

The lights started to flicker and a snorting sound came from the side curtain. "May I introduce our Lady Godiva!" the master of ceremonies shouted. A white horse slowly walked out and up a ramp to the stage area with a beautiful woman mounted fully astride on the animal's back.

"What the heck," Byron blurted out. He looked at his sister and then at Madison. "I think she's really naked." His eyes were as big as saucers.

"He doesn't get off the farm much," Alyssa said to Madison. She then laughed and took another gulp of her beer.

"Miss Godiva." the master of ceremony continued. He helped her slide off her stallion and into his arms. He then led her to the pole in the middle of the stage. The lights dimmed and the music started to roar as did the crowd.

Miss Godiva played with the pole like a lost lover. Her long, red hair was placed in just the right spots to only reveal a teasing part of her flesh. She danced with the pole and then played with the MC. Finally, she took the MC's hand and they both went to the horse. She kissed the horse's nose. After a few more seductive dance steps with the MC, he playfully assisted her in mounting the horse. This time she sat sidesaddle, and the crowd went wild.

Byron could hardly contain himself as Madison looked at him with a calm, curious look on her face. *He fascinates me,* she thought. She wet her peach-tinted lips with her tongue.

"I know my brother's a virgin," Alyssa whispered in Madison's ear. She watched as Byron stood up and applauded while the actors left the stage.

"And you're not," Madison whispered back.

"Hell no, what fun's that." Alyssa said. She noticed a familiar, tall, handsome man at the bar eyeing her. "Hey, I'll be back in a bit," she then said to Madison.

Byron sat back down. "Wow, I've never seen anything like that before," he said, almost breathless. He took a swig of his beer.

"So you think you've been missing out," Madison asked in a low voice. She started to rub his leg in an affectionate way nearer to his personal areas than he was used to being touched by another. Just then, a flash of the girl with the books came into his mind.

"Whoa," he said. He had never experienced such a suggestive touch by a woman he was attracted to and definitely not one who so openly acted like she wanted to be intimate with him.

"Let's get out of here and go someplace a little more private. How about my apartment?" Madison suggested. She cupped her hand near his ear as the loud music started and said, in a low seductive voice, "My roommate's out this evening."

"*Huh*! I don't know. Where's Allie?" he asked. He noticed she was not at the table.

"She said she would be back, but I saw her leave with someone," Madison said. She hoped he would take that as his cue to leave with her.

"What? Is she nuts?" Byron looked at Madison and shouted. He bolted out of his seat and went outside to look for his sister.

The parking lot was dimly lit, but he could hear his sister giggling from the far side of the building. Nearing her, he could not believe his eyes; she was all over a tall figure of a man. In the limited light, he could see that the top of her dress was down around her waist. He saw the man licking her breasts and fondling her with his hand up her skirt.

As he hurried to her, Byron watched his sister wiggle and squirm in the strange man's grip. "Wait until I get my hands on you, you bastard," Byron shouted. He watched her bend over while arching her back.

All at once, she saw her brother coming toward her. "Holy shit," she yelped. She quickly raised her head, not realizing her indecent lover was so close, and she cracked him right in the nose with her head.

"Fuck!" her stunned, sex-crazed partner cried out in surprise. She shocked him with her movement and she fell from his hold on her.

Byron hurriedly caught her before she hit the hard pavement. "Professor," Byron said when he recognized the man. He watched as the professor immediately took his handkerchief from his pocket and tried to stop the blood streaming from his nose.

"Damn it, Byron, get the fuck away from me," Alyssa shouted. She watched as the professor ran to his car and sped off while she was trying to get away from her brother.

"Are you crazy? Do you know that was my business professor from the university?" He had a stunned look on his face. He saw Madison come out and walk toward them.

"You're causing a scene," Alyssa said. She hid behind him and was pulling the top of her dress back on.

"I'm causing a scene? I'm thinking you've lost your frigging mind," he whispered through clenched teeth.

Madison stood next to them. "Can I help?" she asked in a seemingly caring way.

"I think my sister had a little too much to drink. I know it's an inconvenience, but could we possibly go to your apartment?" he asked with a look of embarrassment in his eyes. "I think she needs to sober up before she goes back to her dorm."

Madison took out her keys and dangled them in the air. "My casa's your casa," she said and headed toward her car.

"Thanks, Madison. I'll bring Allie, and we'll follow you." He grabbed his sister's arm and pulled her to his car. He opened the door, and she flopped inside.

He put his head in the car, and as she tried to situate herself he shouted, "Where the hell's your bra?" He looked at her, and she rolled her eyes.

"I don't wear underwear. God, you act like it's the end of the world. And could you quit looking at me like that and just get into the fucking car!" Alyssa shouted. She saw the shocked look on her brother's face. "You're not my daddy," she snorted.

"Oh boy, how cute would that be?" He shrugged his shoulders. He looked at her and finally saw a hint of embarrassment in her eyes. Making sure she was secure in the car, he slammed her door and went to the driver's side.

They followed Madison to her plush, two-bedroom loft in a classier part of the city. *She surely comes from money,* Byron thought. He followed Madison through the door and led his nauseated sister into the spacious loft.

"Wow!" was the first thing that popped out of Byron's mouth. "Classy." He could not help but look around the room.

The smell of incense burning made his sister sick to her stomach. "Bathroom!" she shouted and ran to the familiar room.

"I see she's been here before," Byron said, with raised eyebrows.

Madison escorted him through the comfortable living quarters. "We became instant friends when she started at the university, and we have several classes together," Madison said, in a matter-of-fact way. "She really doesn't do this kind of thing all the time. I think she's just wound up after our study fests. When we study, we really do cram. She's a smart girl." She hoped he would not be too disappointed with his sister.

"Until tonight," he added. She pointed to an overstuffed sofa where they both sat down.

"You really have a nice place," Byron said. He looked around at the beautiful artwork and modern furnishings.

"My grandmother takes care of . . . me." She rose from her seat. "Can I offer you a drink? I have wine or if you prefer a beer," she said.

He thought she looked somewhat nervous. *I'm guessing she's twenty-one if she has alcohol or maybe the roommate is.* "I feel like we're invading your privacy. I probably shouldn't have asked to come here,"

She started for the kitchen. "Don't give it another thought. Come on let's see what's in the fridge," Madison said.

He followed her. "You said your grandmother takes care of you. May I ask about your parents?" He thought since she already brought up something that personal, it would be all right to ask.

"Well, my father died when I was young and my mother at my birth." She went to a tall, freestanding cabinet and withdrew a large wine goblet. "I'm for some wine. How about you?" she asked. She turned toward him with the one glass in her hand.

"Sounds nice," he answered. "I guess Allie's okay in there." He watched Madison carelessly grab another crystal goblet and reach for a bottle of wine from a rack.

"I'll check on her if you open this bottle," she said. She gave him a corkscrew and left the kitchen.

After a few minutes she returned. "She's resting on my bed. She said the room's kind of spinning, so I gave her a cool cloth for her head." Madison sat next to Byron on the sofa in the living room where he had placed the glasses of wine on a table in front of them.

"Here ya go." He handed her a glass of the wine.

"Thanks."

"I really feel weird sitting here with my sister all tanked up in your bed." He could feel a warm flush fill his body. *Could be the wine*, he thought.

She scooted next to him. The skirt of her tight dress clung to her body and exposed more of her long, bare legs. "I'd prefer it if it were us," she whispered. She gave him a seductive look as she licked the wine from her lips.

"You're a very beautiful woman, and I'd have to be dead if I said I didn't think about those exact things, but I'm kind of a one-girl guy." He took another gulp of his wine.

"Oh," she cooed. She started to rub his leg again the way she had at the club. "And you think maybe I'm not a one-guy kind of girl." She left his side. She propped herself up in front of a soft pillow on the sofa and crossed her legs beneath her.

"I guess that's my point. I don't know anything about you, but I would like to," he added. *She has to think I'm crazy. I must look like I'm out of my mind to be turning down such a willing beauty,* he thought. He squirmed a bit in his seat. "What kind of a guy would turn down a gorgeous woman like you?" He grabbed the bottle of wine he had placed on the table and refilled his glass. "You?" He tilted the bottle her way.

"I'm fine," she said, looking completely relaxed. "I'm not a slut, if that's what you're thinking." She took a tiny sip of her wine.

"Oh no . . . I never thought that . . . It's just . . ." he stammered. He didn't know how to explain that he had decided a long time ago that his first time would be with the woman he loved.

"I'm guessing you're a virgin," she said. She knew she was correct when he turned ten shades of red. "There's nothing wrong with that. I think it's great. And I'm guessing you're saving yourself for that one and only woman." Now it was her turn to reach for the bottle and add just a swallow of the wine to her glass.

"Well, yeah . . . something like that." He stared at her and felt very uneasy.

She took the last swig of her drink and popped up off the sofa. "Excuse me a minute would you?" She saw him nod okay. "These clothes are really bothering me. I'll be right back." She went to her bedroom and a minute later came out. Then, without a word to him, he watched her quickly go to the other bedroom.

Wow! These paintings look like originals, he thought. "I hope comfortable doesn't mean what I think it means," he whispered. *She has to know Allie could come into the room at any time. Get a hold of yourself man.* He started to fidget in his seat as he waited for her to return. He started to take a closer look around the room and took it upon himself to take a tour of the assorted arrangements on the walls. *Such beautiful, prominent, fall colors,* he was thinking when she came back into the room.

"Now I feel human." She came next to him. She had bare feet and instead of the tight dress, she was now wearing a soft pink cotton top and loose fitting, gray sweatpants. She seemed more comfortable.

"You do look more comfortable," he said. He also noticed she had the same tangy scent of perfume that he remembered when he first met her. "Smell good too," he said as a compliment.

She seemed a little nervous and started to walk away from him. "Let's make eggs. When I can't think of anything else to do, I love to make eggs." She motioned for him to come with her. She waited for him to catch up with her and then grabbed his arm. "Come on, I promise I won't hurt you or come on to you or whatever."

He thought the effects of the wine were making her giddy. "Eggs sound good," he said. He let her lead him to the kitchen.

"Get the eggs from the fridge and grab the cheese, will ya?" she asked with a light air about her and got out the bowl and whisk. "I'm thinking I'll make the works. Will you trust me?" she asked and winked. She reached for a hanging frying pan and placed it on the range top. "Butter—lots, and lots of butter." This time she just pointed to the refrigerator.

"I'm in your hands," he said as he watched her. "You look like a professional chef," he commented.

She laughed. "Actually, I am. I graduated from culinary school, but that didn't interest me, so I entered the university. I really love the drama class, and I'm also taking a business course to become a legal secretary. But I don't know what I really want for a career." She was chattering on. As the butter melted, she added a bit of extra virgin olive oil. "I'm sure my grandmother thinks I'm going to make a career as a student," she said and they both laughed.

"This is fun," he said.

She asked him to get the silverware and some plates from the cupboard. "And you know what—we're getting to know each other," she said.

He saw her in a different light: not so seductive, but open and friendly. "I do feel better too," he said. He noticed she seemed a little bit shy and blushed slightly when she smiled and looked at him.

Alyssa walked into the room. "I'm famished if you can believe that," Alyssa said. She felt right at home and sat on a barstool by the counter that separated the main living room from the kitchen. "You two seem to be having fun." Byron and Madison started to laugh. "Please not too loud," she said and held her head in her hands.

"Come on we have plenty of eggs for all of us," Madison said.

Alyssa went and stood next to her by the range. "Would you mind if I made some toast?" Her red eyes pleaded with Madison. "I'm thinking some carbs would help my stupid hangover," Alyssa added. Madison nodded an affirmative and Alyssa went for the bread and toaster.

"You make yourself at home, don't you sister?" Byron asked. His sister only nodded.

"She has always been welcome. We have a lot of study fests here, and on Fridays—well Fridays are usually our downtime," Madison admitted.

Alyssa took the toasted bread and accepted a plate of eggs from Madison. "You're the best," Alyssa said. They all went to the dining table in the main room.

"This is a neat setup," Byron said. He sat down after he seated the ladies.

"It really works out nicely for . . ." Madison started to say.

Byron interjected. "Oh yeah, you said you have a roommate. I'm guessing you share the same clothes too." he said, knowing she came from the other bedroom after changing.

"Well, I just went to my room for my clothes. I didn't want to wake Alyssa, so I went to the other room to change. You see my roommate's working tonight and also attends the university," she said, and then added, "Come on now, don't make me beg. How are the eggs?" She looked at them both with an inquisitive look on her face.

"Excellent as always," Alyssa said.

"I don't know when I've tasted anything this good," Byron added and kept eating.

"Your appetite explains it all," Madison said, with a satisfied grin. They all became silent and enjoyed the omelet.

***

"Grammy, Grammy it's late." Christy said. She woke Grammy from her dream state.

"Holy cow! What time is it," Grammy asked. She looked at the other side of the bed, all neat and tidy, and then reached for her cane.

"It's after nine. Reggie wouldn't let me wake you any sooner," Christy said. She sat in a chair near the bed.

"Blessings, I'm full of blessings that someone would make sure I get a good night's sleep," Grammy said. She went toward the bathroom. "Honey, let Reggie know I'm up." Before closing the bathroom door, Grammy watched as Christy immediately went to do as she was told

What a dream: so real. All that gossip has me dreaming of things I surely can't tell Christy. Maybe someday, but not just yet at her tender age, she thought.

Reggie knocked on the door. "Christy went outside. She waited until you got up for breakfast," Reggie shouted to Grammy through the bathroom door.

"What a sweetheart," Grammy shouted back. "I'll be ready in a bit."

Reggie went and sat on a chair to wait until Grammy called for help with her quick shower.

I just love the barn, Christy thought after she left Grammy to the capable hands of Reggie. She knew it would take awhile for Grammy to get ready for the day.

"Hey there, Bandit, how you doing, buddy?" Christy skipped toward their Shetland sheepdog. The happy dog ran to her. "That's a good boy." The dog sat in front of her and let her pet him. "Wolfgang around?" She spoke aloud to the dog.

Just then Wolfgang howled like a wolf and came out from one of the stalls he was cleaning. "Right here, missy," said the black handyman, sporting his usual big grin. He was dressed in his work overalls, cotton shirt, and rubber, high-top boots. And, like always, his short, curly, graying hair was neatly cut, with every hair in place. "Looking for some barn chore fun?" he asked, with a chuckle. He knew she loved to help in the barn.

"*Hooowwll*" she wailed back: their way of greeting each other. "That's what I'm here for. You know me," she said, with enthusiasm.

He gave her his pitchfork and went for another. "Never can understand why you love horse manure so much," he said. His dark eyes sparkled and he kept laughing as they both cleaned the stalls.

"Grammy says it must be in my blood," she said, teetering in her tall, rubber boots.

"Well, I'm always happy for the company," Wolfgang said. They heard the whine from the Appaloosa stallion in the outside corral. "I think he knows you're in here."

Christy pitched her last load of manure onto the pile in the trailer, and they headed for the corral. "Hi, Fella," Christy said. The horse came to the fence and she petted him. "Good boy." She felt a pang hit her heart. "One day." She scratched him under his chin.

Wolfgang stood next to her. "Yeah, baby girl, one day—one day you'll ride like the wind," he sang to her. His big grin seemed to get even bigger.

"Yeah, can't pour tea and can't ride horses. Sure hard to be so little," she said, looking downcast. She jumped from the fence.

"Let your grandmother know the car's ready whenever she is," he said.

Christy started back to the house. "Sure will." She howled a good-bye to him, and he did the same while she turned and waved to him.

***

"I could've walked home, Grammy," Christy said. She sat next to Grammy in the Bentley.

"I know it's not far, but now I'll know you made it safe, honey," Grammy said. She gave Christy a questioning look.

"Sorry, Grammy, must've been from the ham and beans last night," Christy said, with an embarrassed look on her face.

"Oh well, part of the works," Grammy smiled.

"Somebody should make a human gas muffler. You know, silence it, and cover up the fumes," Christy laughed.

Wolfgang looked at them both in the rearview mirror and started to chuckle. "I'd buy some stock," he said.

Christy added. "Maybe I'll invent it someday. It could be used like when you go to church or have an important meeting. You know stuff like that." They pulled into her driveway.

"Or after you've had ham and beans," Grammy said. They all laughed. "I hope I live long enough to see what you really do when you grow up."

Christy accepted a kiss from her and a loving pat on her cheek. "Whatever I do, I'll make you proud, Grammy. And you know what? Maybe next weekend you might think I'm ready to pour," she said.

Wolfgang opened her door and was helping Christy out of the car. "We'll see," Grammy only said. She then watched as Wolfgang escorted Christy to the door and she went inside.

"Before we go by the florist and make my other stops, I have an appointment at the law firm on the other side of town." Grammy gave Wolfgang her itinerary when he returned to the car.

"Yes Ma'am," he said as he slowly drove off.

***

Later that afternoon she sat with her husband and softly massaged his hand. "I put flowers down again today," she whispered. "My heart just misses so much."

"I'm sorry I can't be there for you," he said. A tiny tear ran down his cheek.

"I know." She held his hand. "Christy's been stopping by more."

"She can bring life back into the house," he said. He looked at her with only love in his eyes. "The doctor says I might be coming home soon." He looked at her for a sign of hope.

"I'm praying." She kissed his hand and held it to her breasts.

"You can always make me feel good," he said. "And you always bring me flowers with buds, so I can watch them open." He smiled. He watched her put the miniature roses mixed with gardenias into the vase. "You're my tonic, and not bad to look at either." He winked at her.

She gave him a rather sexy glance. "You'd better watch yourself, mister," she teased. He started to caress her breasts. "Somebody will see." She looked toward the door.

"Oh, who cares!" He gave her a sly look. "Besides, they'd never think I'm doing what I'm doing. They'd think we're too old to make out." He acted like he wanted to get out of bed.

"Hold on, we don't want the buzzer to go off again." She tried to change the subject. "Christy and I have been into the gossip again." She knew the mention of her name always calmed him.

"Any good stuff?" he asked.

She helped him readjust himself on the pillow in the hospital bed. "Of course, you know I can't really get into all the gossip with her. But now that she's getting older, I sometimes think she's putting things together herself," They just looked at each other.

His mood seemed to change. "Sometimes it's really hard . . ." He seemed to be in a trance. "Please, just give me a moment." He raised his hand to her. "I just wish I could be there . . . I try to adjust." He looked into her eyes.

She watched him close his eyes, and she closed hers. They sat without saying a word. They could feel their deep emotions mingle and could understand each other's innermost feelings. Finally, he reached for her hand.

He did not have a tear in his eyes. "He sure can give me strength," he whispered. "And I can always feel His mother right next to me." He squeezed her hand.

She gently squeezed back. "I know what you mean," She placed her head on his shoulder and hugged him.

They stayed close and quiet for another moment, but then she spoke. "Last night, I dreamt how the gossip went when Byron believed Alyssa was getting out of control at the university. You remember when he first met Madison?" She looked at him.

He frowned. "That almost became a Greek tragedy," he said. He slowly put his hand behind his head.

They looked at each other; while daydreams came to mind, they privately reflected on the time many years passed and how they believed the gossip must have gone on.

***

It was wintertime back then, and surely the loft must have been warm and cozy. The two of them carelessly talked about what was going on in their lives while they relaxed on the plush sofa drinking large goblets of wine.

"He's cute, but he acts like a nerd," her roommate said to Madison. "He just doesn't seem like your type. I always thought you'd go for a big, tall football guy. You know a hunk with wavy blond hair and those big Caribbean blue eyes you always talk about."

"I don't know what to say," Madison said. She looked at her roommate, who she felt she could tell any of her innermost thoughts. "He brings something out in me that I never knew was there before. I really think he's my soul mate," she confessed.

Her roommate's eyes rolled. "God Madison, do you honestly believe something like a soul mate is real?"

Somewhat let down, Madison turned her head. She felt this might not be the time, place, or person to divulge certain deep feelings. She took a big gulp of her wine and then refilled her glass.

"You've been drinking a lot more lately too," her roommate added, while relaxing back on the soft pillow with legs tucked under.

"I can drink as much as I like. I'm not going anywhere. My drama class starts at ten tomorrow, so I can sleep in," Madison said. She openly enjoyed another swallow of the tart liquid.

"Have you slept with him yet?" her roommate asked blatantly.

Madison almost spit up her last drink. "Boy, you go straight for the jugular, don't you?" She coughed and gave her roommate a stunned look. She then grabbed one of the cheddar cheese crackers they had made to snack on.

"What if he's a bad lover?" her roommate asked, with raised eyebrows.

Madison cut off the conversation. "I can tell he's great. We've done some stuff—just not all the way. Not that it's any of your business, but I truly respect him for wanting to wait," Madison said, holding her ground.

"And now you're going home with him for the Thanksgiving holiday to meet the family. Oh God, girl, you really got it bad this time. It seems to me if you're that close to him, you should be completely honest, right?" Her roommate flashed Madison a curious look. "Looks like trouble to me," her roommate added while grabbing a snack and going for another bottle of wine.

"I'm not worried about telling him my whole life story right now. I'll know when the time's right," Madison said. She was not really concerned about complete honesty until she was truly certain where she stood in his life. She wanted to know how serious he was about their relationship.

"Well, since you're going to tie one on, I might as well join you. I never could get the hang of this damn thing." Awkwardly, as if with a mind of its own, the corkscrew slid around the top of the bottle.

"You just don't have any patience," Madison said. She took the bottle, and easily twisted the screw into the top, and pulled out the cork with a pop.

"Holy shit, it just came to me. If you marry the guy, you're going to leave me," her roommate said with a put-on look of panic.

"Well, yeah, if it ever happens," Madison said. She thought she had never seen her roommate act so scared. "But . . ." Madison began.

"God, girl, I'm pulling your chain. I'd love to have this place to myself. Of course, I'd have to get another roommate, and I think I have just the right person in mind." They both just looked at each other and started to giggle from the effects of the wine.

"Yeah, I'm sure you do. I'm not even out the door and you already have my replacement," Madison said. She downed another one, and they continued to talk and drink well into the wee hours of the morning.

***

The taxi driver followed the winding road to Red Winds. The snowflakes were starting to fly around them, and the opaque sky looked like it would burst.

"You should see this place in autumn. The leaves have such bright, vibrant colors," Byron said. He was riding in the taxi from the train station with Madison and his sister, Alyssa.

Alyssa interrupted him. "Oh yes, they're *just* beautiful," she said mockingly. "But now that I've had a taste of the 'real' world, I can't believe I agreed to come back here with you two lovebirds, just to be stuck out here in the sticks." She looked out the window from the front seat of the cab. "Look at that—as far as you can see there is nothing but bare trees, and now the snow will probably keep us from going anywhere." She fretted like a spoiled child.

"It makes me feel all warm and cuddly inside," Madison said. She patted Byron's knee, while she sat close to him in the backseat.

"That's because you're in love," Alyssa said, emphasizing the 'in love' part.

"Allie, aren't you happy for me and Byron? You introduced us, and now you act like you don't even care about my friendship with you anymore." Madison gave Byron a curious look and shrugged her shoulders when Allie did not reply. Just then, the cab pulled into the driveway to Red Winds.

"We're here," Byron said.

Madison looked out the window and could see the house through the bare trees. "Oh my!" she exclaimed.

"Finally," Alyssa snorted. She shrugged her shoulders and stretched her arms as the cab driver pretended not to be concerned about their conversation.

"Oh Byron, your home is such a beautiful estate. Look, smoke is coming out of the chimneys, and the snow is swirling all around. It looks so homey; it reminds me of a Currier and Ives print," Madison commented.

Byron gave her a gratifying look as the cabby parked the car. "I hoped you'd be happy here. I know I love it," Byron said. He looked at her, and she snuggled into him.

"For pity's sake, it's just a farm. It's not some kind of romantic estate," Alyssa said, sounding disgusted.

They all got out of the cab and got their bags from the trunk. Just then the front door of the house opened.

"Welcome home," Olivia and Ronald shouted as they came out of the house and approached the trio.

"Here, I've got that," Ronald said. He reached for his wallet when his son started to pay the taxi driver.

"Thanks, Dad," Byron said. He went to his mother and received a kiss on the cheek and a hard hug.

"Mom, Dad, this is Madison Yames," Byron said as the cab pulled away and they all started for the house.

"It's so nice to finally meet you, Madison. Our son has spoken to us about you so many times that I feel I already know you," said Olivia. She and Madison greeted each other with a hug instead of shaking hands.

Olivia started walking toward her daughter to embrace her, but Alyssa hurried in front of them all, entered the house, and went straight to her bedroom.

"I see your sister's in a mood," said Ronald. They set their bags down in the foyer and hung their coats by the door.

"She's been in a mood for some time now," Byron said. He felt Madison squeeze his hand. "But let's not dwell on that right now. I would really just like to settle in and let you get to know Madison."

They went to the living room. "Your home is just beautiful. I feel right at home. Almost like I've been looking for this exact home all my life," Madison said. She looked around the room.

Olivia offered her a comfortable seat on a long sofa where Madison and Byron sat next to each other. "Thank you for the compliment. This was my parents' home. Has Byron given you any of the history?" Olivia asked. She felt somewhat sensitive about her past and hoped Byron had already informed her about most of it.

"A little," said Madison. "I know you're not truly from Japanese decent." She could not help but look at Olivia's slanted eyes.

"Yes, that's a long story," Olivia said and reached for her eyes. "One day I'll tell you all about it, but I would truly like to explain how blessed we are to have such a beautiful home."

Ronald went to stoke the fire while Olivia sat across from Bryon and Madison on a matching sofa.

"I would love to hear it," Madison said. She felt so completely relaxed with Byron's parents that she did not feel she had to hide her feelings for their son, so she lovingly placed her head on his shoulder and snuggled in next him. *This must be what it feels like when you're about to be told a bedtime story,* she thought. She noticed Byron give his mother a loving look.

"Many years ago, I believe it was when Rachel and I first went to New York . . ." Olivia started her tale. She looked at Ronald and he shook his head. "Yes, it was after the deaths of my family that I received my legacy," she explained to Madison.

"Byron told me about the loss of your family, and I'm truly sorry," Madison said, with deep compassion in her voice.

"Can I assume he also told you about the money stored under the kitchen floor?" Olivia then asked. She saw a confused look on her son's face. "I didn't think so." She resituated herself on the couch.

"Honey, I'm going to get the drinks and sandwiches," Ronald said, excusing himself to get them refreshments.

"My husband is always ready to take care of us; I'm sorry, I should have asked when you first arrived if you wanted to freshen up," Olivia said. She noticed they declined her offer.

"Mom, what's this about money under the floor? I knew you inherited Red Winds, but I never knew about any money," Byron said. He and Madison perked up.

"There was a fortune in gold left there by my parents. You see, after I moved to New York, I wanted to be my own woman and make my own way of life," said Olivia. She thought that was how her daughter was acting out now. "When Rachel and Cal married and moved back to Kansas, Cal phoned to remind me about my legacy after I turned twenty-one."

Ronald returned with their snack. "Honey, I think I'm going to check in on Alyssa. The Yarboroughs are coming over soon and I want her to be . . ." He didn't finish what he wanted to say but just shrugged his shoulders. He knew from the way she was acting that they all understood he wanted to make sure she would be on her best behavior.

"Okay. We're at the legacy part," Olivia said. She did not want him to have to sit and listen to the story he had already heard.

"I'll be back in a bit," Ronald added. Byron and Madison smiled at him, and he left the room.

"You heard him say the Yarboroughs are coming?" Olivia asked, looking at her son.

Byron rolled his eyes. "They have kids." He looked at Madison. "Don't get me wrong, they're good kids and I love kids but it's just . . ."

Olivia helped her son out. "Their daughter Alyssa—she's seven—has the same name as our daughter, and that's another story for another time. Anyway, now we call her Lyssa, and she's got a huge crush on Byron."

Madison looked at him and smiled. "Oh, how cute." she noticed Byron turning red. "I think red is Byron's favorite color." She started to tickle and tease him.

"I think you two like to see me embarrassed." They all laughed. "Now come on, Mom, we're getting off track. What's this about a fortune?" Just then the doorbell rang. "I'll get it," Byron said as he quickly rose from his seat.

"He's such a sweetheart," Olivia said. She smiled and Madison smiled in return.

"Oh God, I didn't know you guys were coming," Byron shouted in surprise. "Mom, it's Aunt Mary and Grandma Martha." Olivia and Madison came into the foyer.

"When there's a commotion you can always find me," Mary said. She was hugging her nephew. She then turned to Olivia. "How you doing, sister?" Happy tears filled her eyes when she and Olivia hugged.

"Especially good, now that you two are here safe and sound." Olivia replied.

Ronald and Alyssa came down the stairs. "Sure glad you built on the upstairs with all this company," Alyssa said. She had a rebellious tone in her voice.

"I'm sure glad too. I'll be close enough to pester you," Mary said. She went to her niece. "Come here and give your Aunt Mary a big hug," Ronald's younger sister said to Alyssa. With outstretched hands, she took her niece into her arms.

"God," Alyssa said. She rolled her eyes back and held her arms limp at her sides.

"We're going to have so much fun," Mary said. She squeezed Alyssa in her arms. "With all the snow coming down, we made it here just in time." She continued to hold her niece in her arms. "We saw Cal and Rachel right behind us," Mary added. She felt Alyssa slowly break free from her hold and saw her cold look.

Just then, there was another knock at the front door. "Happy Thanksgiving! We brought sleeping bags." Cal said when they came in. He quickly shut the door behind them. "Good grief the flakes are as big as pancakes." His family, bearing many bundles, left all of their belongings on the enclosed front porch. "I think we're in for a big one. I'm glad CC decided to stay at the university. He says he's cramming, but I think he's got a girlfriend," he added about their oldest son.

They all came inside and Rachel, his wife, gave him a stiff look. "I think I'll go check on the mare," Cal said. "She was about due this morning." He and Ronald went out the back way to the barn.

"Martha, how nice to see you," Rachel said. She went to Martha and received a loving hug. "I don't know if CC really has a girlfriend. I wish he could've made it, but . . ."

Martha interjected. "Oh well, he's at that age when family seems to take second place." She continued to hug Rachel, and then noticed Alyssa and Andrew standing silent. "Your twins are getting so big."

Rachel looked at the twins. "You remember Martha—cinnamon rolls Martha! You know the best . . ."

It looked as though a light appeared in the twins' eyes. "Oh yeah, I remember," Alyssa Yarborough said.

"Me too," her brother Andrew chimed in.

"So good and yummy for the tummy," Alyssa sang. Everyone laughed, and she backed off with a frown on her face. She thought she must have sounded like a child, something she surely did not want to do in front of the man of her dreams—the man she knew she would marry one day.

"Please, let's go to the living room. We have a big fire to keep us warm," Olivia said.

They were following her when Lyssa approached Byron and Madison. "Hi Byron," seven-year-old Lyssa said to her dreamboat, which was how she thought of him.

"Hi Alyssa," Byron said.

Lyssa looked at Madison and scowled when she saw Madison holding Byron's hand.

"This is Madison," Byron explained to the cow-eyed, young girl.

Lyssa stood in front of Madison and looked her straight in the eyes. "I'm going to marry Byron one day," the young girl said brazenly. She tried to stand as tall as she could when she looked up at Madison.

"Oh," was all Madison could think of to say. "Does he know that?" She had a sincere tone in her voice. She squeezed Byron's hand.

"He will. Oh, and by the way, everyone calls me Lyssa now," the young girl said. She then turned and happily skipped away from the pair.

"I'll try to remember that!" Byron, irritated with her attitude, shouted.

"She sure doesn't hide her feelings," Madison said.

They started for the living room. "I know, and sometimes it's kind of annoying," Byron said. He scanned the room and sat as far away from the young, infatuated girl as he could.

"This was just supposed to be a short visit this evening, but I think . . ." Rachel began.

Olivia cut her off. "We have plenty of room. You know that's why we built this house so big." She noticed Byron look at her and nod toward Madison. "Everyone, may I introduce Madison, Byron's dear friend."

"Hi Madison," everyone said happily. Lyssa shot her a menial look.

"We have plenty of time for everyone to personally introduce themselves," Olivia said.

Everyone got comfortable. "I guess we can continue that conversation another time, Mom," Byron commented.

Everyone was seated on sofas, plush chairs, and even the carpeted floor near the fireplace. "Well son, actually Cal and Rachel played a big part in the fortune that was under the kitchen floor. And, may I add, also saved a very important relationship," Olivia said.

Rachel sat next to her on the arm of the sofa and put her arm around Olivia just as Ronald and Cal returned from outside.

"The mare gave birth and all is well," Ronald said. He and Cal seated themselves.

"I was about to continue with the legacy again and how important it was for . . ." Olivia began.

Rachel interjected. "Who would've thought that something with monetary value could not only save a life but also something as dear as a relationship. Would you mind if I started it?" Tears glistened in her eyes. Olivia nodded. "It was right after Olivia's return to Red Winds. I'm sure most of you remember how bitter I was back then,"

"Sure do," Lyssa shouted. They all laughed. "But if some people didn't feel like they had to go all the way to New York to go to college, they would've known all about how Aunt Olivia saved my life." She looked Byron straight in the eyes.

This was all new to Byron. He just stared at his mother as he listened while his sister, Alyssa, however, appeared to be in another world.

She cowered in her chair wearing a blank look on her face and was unknowingly biting her fingernails. She did not hear anything that was going on around her.

"Wow, I don't think I've heard this one either," Mary said. Martha nodded in agreement.

"Well about the money . . ." Rachel continued. "It was after that deadly tornado that took Olivia's parents, Jason and Elizabeth Webster, and her baby brother, Jay." She had a sad tone in her voice. "And for those who don't know, we also lost Cal's parents—May and Calvin—in that same storm." She looked at her husband and he smiled.

"Back then, Olivia and Cal stayed with my family for a time. Later when Cal returned home, he found evidence among his parents' possessions that Olivia's parents wished to leave all of their worldly possessions to their children, Olivia and Jay. Of course, no one knew what fate had in store for them." She looked at Olivia and then at her husband. "So Jason and Elizabeth never fathomed that Olivia would live alone." Olivia looked at her and Rachel patted her dear friend on the shoulder.

"Well, her parents' last will explained that the money was under the kitchen floor: the money being gold left to Jason by his parents. From what we learned, Jason's father prospected in South Dakota and struck it rich, but Jason's parents, like Olivia's parents, were people of simple means. They didn't need a lot monetarily to be happy in life, so they saved the money for their posterity," Rachel said. She resituated herself on the arm of the sofa. She noticed the room was still and quiet.

"In their will, Olivia's parents asked May and Calvin to be guardians for Olivia and Jay if something happened to them until Olivia turned twenty-one and could then take over the estate and care for her brother," Rachel continued. "After that deadly storm, my parents took Olivia in, and she became a part of our family. We were sisters in every sense of the word." She squeezed Olivia's shoulder.

Olivia then continued with the story. "I could've stayed in Kansas and received my inheritance when I turned twenty-one, but I felt as if I had to get away. I was twenty, and I felt like the walls were closing in on me. I felt almost desperate and from the way Rachel was acting, I thought she was desperate too," Olivia explained. She looked up at Rachel and saw only love in her eyes. "It took a miracle for the love I now see to come back to me." She patted Rachel's hand.

Ronald got up from beside Olivia and motioned to Rachel to take his seat.

"Back then, I was so crazy in love with Cal when I left for New York that my head wasn't on straight," Rachel said. She looked at Lyssa and saw her daughter roll her eyes. "Just part of Mama's love story, honey."

Lyssa got up and sat on the floor across from Byron. She wanted to keep a close eye on him and, of course, Madison. "I know, Mama," Lyssa said. "I've heard it a million times." She watched Byron start to wiggle uncomfortably in his seat when she stared at him, while Madison gave her a baffled look.

"Well, when Cal and I married and returned to Kansas, my parents asked Olivia about her inheritance once she turned twenty-one. At that time, she trusted our family with the money. So we surprised Olivia with some minor repairs to Red Winds. She asked if Cal and I would use the money to continue to care for Red Winds until the day she could get up the courage to come home again," Rachel said. She reached for Olivia, and they held hands.

"And I did get the courage to return on our wedding day," Olivia added. She looked at her husband. "After the deadly tornado that took my family and almost destroyed our home, I was the lucky one to have such a wonderful, new family. If Cal, Rachel, and her family had not renovated Red Winds and changed the appearance of the rooms, I never would have been able to stay in the house for our honeymoon night. I felt I was home, but all the terror was gone because they made it so. I will never forget . . ."

Martha interjected. "I remember. It was the most beautiful wedding I have ever attended. The leaves on the trees looked almost like they were on fire against the bright blue sky."

Mary chimed in. "And to get married on the hillside was incredible. The way the wind blew Olivia's veil made it look like a wisp of many angels were flying around her. It was just unbelievable." Mary knew she was not really a sentimentalist but that day had always been etched in her memory. "It was my brother's wedding day, and a day I was also given a sister." She winked at her brother and smiled at Olivia.

"So, what you're saying is that the fortune was spent on renovating Red Winds?" Byron asked.

Rachel continued. "That was just a drop in the bucket. The ingots assayed with high gold content and were cashed in when the market was high for the metal. There is a fortune, that if used wisely will last a long time," Rachel said. She looked at Olivia and put her head on Olivia's shoulder. "But back then Olivia still wanted to be her own woman and stand on her own . . ."

Olivia then added. "It was also a time when the inheritance could have been used to help Ronald's family, but at that time another anonymous benefactor, who we won't go into now, came through for the Brown family." She did not want to mention that Mikail Yasieu turned out to be that benefactor and quickly changed the subject. "You see I had my own lucrative dress boutique. Many of the New York elite scrambled for my new fashion designs."

Mary joined the conversation. "Oh golly, remember Mr. Ti?" She looked at Olivia. "Normally, the Japanese merchants hire or bring their own family into their business, but Mr. Ti was so impressed with Olivia's dress designs and, of course, her sewing abilities that he asked, actually asked both of us, to go into business with him." Mary seemed to be reminiscing. "Of course, I was becoming a great stage actress back then," she said, with a slight smile.

"And you did become one, my dear," Martha added.

Mary hugged her and added, "You should be my agent." They all laughed.

"Well, as you can see, Red Winds has also turned into a great mansion, but only because of the help of Cal and Rachel," said Olivia.

Again, it was Rachel's turn to add to the story. "But the best part of the story is how this money that had been stored under the kitchen floor for so many years also saved another life." Rachel looked at her daughter.

"Guilty," Lyssa shouted. "I wasn't obeying my parents' wishes, but as it turned out I helped my mom get over what she called her love hate ..." She glanced at Madison and then completely turned her body away from her view.

"God, she hates me," Madison whispered in Byron's ear.

"Just ignore her," Byron whispered and squeezed Madison's hand.

"Yes, Lyssa, like many times before when you went against our wishes and took a horse out riding. She can ride like the best of them, but I always ask our children to only ride with a buddy," Rachel said.

"But she just loved to be alone," Cal added. He too remembered the terrors of that day. "She was out on her pinto, Gallagher. Everyone knows we teach our children how to respect animals, and I know my girl knows how to ride just as well as her brothers, but it was the alone part that ..."

His daughter interrupted him. "Dad, I think they get the picture. I was a bad girl," Lyssa added and grimaced. She folded her arms in front of her.

"Gosh," Madison whispered in Byron's ear. "Never thought she'd actually admit it." Byron looked at Madison. They both tried to muffle a giggle as Lyssa turned and shot a hateful look at Madison. "Golly, if looks could kill ..." Madison began. She and Byron choked back their giggles.

"Well, Gallagher returned to his stall without Lyssa," Rachel began again. "It was well into the afternoon before we noticed Lyssa was not around the house. Gallagher was in his stall, but the gate was open. Lyssa always knew to close the gate on his stall, so we phoned Red Winds to see if she happened to be there." Her face started to redden.

"Back then Rachel and I were not close." Olivia jumped in. She looked at Rachel, and they tugged each other's hand. "As soon as we all knew for sure that Lyssa was missing, Cal called the sheriff, and I'm thinking most of the county came out to help us look for her." Lyssa came closer to her mother and Olivia and sat on the floor between their feet. She continued to fold her arms in front of her and closed her eyes.

"It was nighttime, and I was beside myself with worry," Rachel said as tears glistened in her eyes.

"We all rode our horses in different directions. Ronald and I separated near the big oak where Rachel and I used to meet when we were children, and that's when I heard her," Olivia said. She lovingly patted Lyssa's head. "I called for Ronald, but he was already out of range. We had it set up that we would meet back at Cal and Rachel's. I had everything I needed, so I got my saddlebags and pulled out my blanket and canteen. She was moaning, but unconscious." She remembered the fear in her heart when she thought she might not be able to save Lyssa.

"I hurried and lit my lantern, hoping Ronald or someone else would see it and come help, but no one did. Then it started to rain." Olivia looked at Rachel and knew she was also remembering the panic she experienced that night.

Rachel added, "Everyone but Olivia returned to our house. Ronald told us where he last left her so we all went there, but she was nowhere to be found. I think that's when I passed out."

Cal took over. "I'll say she passed out; I thought she was dead." He chuckled nervously. Lyssa gave him one of her looks as she continued to sit with her legs crossed and her arms still folded in front of her. Her blonde curls seemed to pop straight out as her light blue eyes sent daggers toward her father. "Honey, I'm just trying to make light of it now. I know it was tragic back then, but just think, now you'll have something big to talk about with your grandchildren."

Everyone who knew Cal understood what he meant. It was always in Cal's nature to try to make the best of every situation: a lesson he learned after the deaths of his parents. "Well, we had to stop the search," Cal said, with a bit of hesitation in his voice. "But we resumed it again in the morning. We were lucky the rain stopped," he added, with a little less humor than before. "Rachel couldn't get up from the sofa, but she was the one who remembered about the haunted, abandoned shack." He had an eerie tone in his voice.

Olivia said, "With all the rain, I knew I wouldn't be able to get Lyssa back to Rachel's that night. Then I remembered the abandoned shack that my parents tried to keep us from exploring by telling us it was haunted. Although I was an adult, the thought that it was haunted was planted so deep that I almost decided to just stay out in the rain and cover us with my rain poncho."

Lyssa started to squirm by Olivia's feet. "From what they tell me, that's when I woke up in the shack. I remember I was cold and shivering, and I didn't know I had been thrown from Gallagher. I sure was glad to see Aunt Olivia." Shyly, she looked around at the eyes that were upon her.

"Early next morning after we found them at the shack, we rushed her to the hospital. That's when we found out that she had to have the pressure relieved on her brain. It was a costly operation, way more money than we had at the time, but Olivia never even flinched when she gave us the money from her inheritance," Rachel said as she put her arm around Olivia. "I will never forget how you saved my baby's life. I guess it was then that I realized and truly believed that a parent would do anything in the world to save a child's life." She reached for Olivia and both women hugged. Tears flowed from their eyes.

"Gee, Mom, your baby . . ." Lyssa said in her grumpy way. Then she quickly jumped up in front of them. "Hey, don't forget the best part." She put her hands on her hips and slightly tilted her head. "The doctor said being out in the cold that night probably saved my life." She looked over at Byron and saw an outstanding look of adoration on his face. She hurriedly turned her head, thinking she must have looked like the little baby her mother had just described, but she savored his look.

"Yes, that's true. The doctor said it kept the swelling down," Rachel said. She wanted to take her baby girl and hug her but thought better of it when she saw how flushed her cheeks had turned and the way she kept looking over at Byron.

"My wife gave her life for our son too." Ronald said. Everyone fell silent. "I will never forget what she did for our son." He went behind Olivia on the sofa and put his hands on her shoulders.

"And . . ." Olivia began.

Ronald finished her sentence. "You would do it all over again. That's how much she loves you." Ronald looked at their son. "And you too, Alyssa." He turned to Alyssa, but his daughter just gave him a blank stare.

"Alyssa, are you all right?" Olivia asked her daughter.

Mary glanced at her niece. *Holy shit,* Mary thought to herself. "Oh no," Mary then said aloud.

Alyssa darted from her seat. "God, can't you all just leave me the fuck alone!" Alyssa shouted. She ran from their view and back up to her bedroom.

"Wow!" Lyssa and Andrew exclaimed in unison. "Did she say . . .?" Lyssa was going to repeat the curse word.

Her mother stopped her. "Lyssa," Rachel said with raised eyebrows.

"I better go to her," said Olivia.

"Would you mind if I tried?" asked Mary.

Olivia looked at her husband. "Fine with me," Ronald said. "Second room on the left." Then, to take the focus off of his daughter's abrupt departure he added, "How would everyone like refreshments?"

"We brought some things too," Rachel said. She and Cal went to the front porch to get their basket of goodies.

"Because of the snowstorm, we brought everything that we were going to bring tomorrow for Thanksgiving dinner," said Rachel. She and Cal joined Olivia and Ronald in the kitchen.

"Something's wrong with my girl. I've never seen her like this before. Maybe we never should've let her go off so far to college," Olivia said. She, Ronald, and Rachel were making trays of snacks while Cal filled glasses with juice.

"Mary's pretty experienced. She might be able to get to the bottom of this," Ronald said. He remembered his sister had been a high-spirited teenager. "Don't forget that was the reason I came to New York that year I met you." He looked at his wife.

"I remember. Your family didn't want her to follow her acting career at the time, but, honey, this doesn't seem like the same thing. She's not acting out; she's acting. I don't know . . ." said Olivia.

"Weird?" Rachel questioned. She looked over at Olivia and Ronald, and she and Cal started to add cheese on top of crackers.

"Yeah, weird," Olivia agreed.

"Come on, let's get this in there. If I'm hungry, I know the kids have to be starving," said Ronald. Rachel and Cal left with trays of food.

"Mary can help, honey, I know she can," Ronald whispered to his wife as they hugged, and then went to the living room, carrying more goodies and drinks.

Upstairs, Mary did not have trouble finding Alyssa's room. "Alyssa, it's Aunt Mary, can I come in?" Mary asked, after she knocked on her niece's bedroom door.

"Go away!" Alyssa shouted.

"I think I can help," Mary said, to the closed door.

"Get the hell away from me!" Alyssa shouted again.

"Honey, I'm not going anywhere." Mary sat down in front of the door. "I think I know what's going on with you." Tears started to flow from her soft brown eyes and down her cheeks. She was remembering back a long time ago when she acted exactly like her niece. *Oh God, let me be wrong,* Mary thought. She pressed her hand to her forehead and ran her fingers through her shiny, straight blonde hair as a memory popped into her head. *I was about her age, and I know I was in love—or I thought I was.* She remembered a time she wished she could forget.

"I love you." She could hear his voice now as if he were right in front of her.

"I love you too," she had said to him.

"You're incredibly beautiful—even more so than you were when we were together onstage this evening," he had told her. He lifted the satin sheet from her naked body.

She remembered how sexy he made her feel. She could again feel his eyes as he watched her slightly arch her back and squirm in front of him. "You make me feel beautiful," she had whispered. She slid her hand down her slim, taut leg and then up his naked leg where she massaged and fondled his building manhood.

"I knew you would be the lover I was looking for." His French accent melted any inhibitions she might have had.

"I'm yours," she purred as she opened up to him.

"*J'ai du vous*," he murmured. He lowered his thick lips to hers and parted them with his tongue. "I must have you," he whispered in her ear. He nuzzled into her neck and started to kiss her. Gently, he fondled her breasts with his smooth fingers.

"I love you so much," she whispered. She felt him run his fingers across her flat belly and then find the spot he knew, as an expert lover, brought pleasure to women. "Oh, that's it ... that's it ..." she whispered excitedly, with an aroused moan.

He knew that meant she was close to her climax, so he came to her, and their pleasures were met and completely satisfied.

How could I have been so stupid about that one moment that changed my life forever? "I let him take me, and it was my first time." She did not realize she had said it aloud.

"I loved him and I thought he loved me too." She did not know Alyssa was also sitting just behind the closed door listening to her. "He made me feel so special. The other girls in the troupe told me to stay away from him, but I didn't listen to them." she continued, "He wouldn't do that to me, not me. I thought I was his only love, and he was the one and only man for me. God, he looked at me like I was his favorite piece of lemon meringue pie. Then I found out the worst."

Alyssa slowly opened the door and looked down at her aunt where she sat on the floor. "Did you find him with another woman?" Alyssa asked. She helped her aunt up, and they went into her bedroom.

"Worse," Mary said. She looked at her niece with tears in her eyes. "Another man," she whispered. She bowed her head and tried to hide her tears. "I always try to be a strong woman, but that crushed me." Mary accepted a tissue from Alyssa.

"That bastard. If he wanted to be with men, why did he go with you?" Alyssa asked. She sat down next to Mary.

"I found out he likes both; he also had a wife and kids back home in France." She looked at Alyssa. "You look like I felt back then." She started to laugh and cry at the same time. "And you're right; he was a bastard. I mean literally. His mother was an over-the-hill actress with many lovers. If he wasn't so pathetic, I could've felt sorry for him." She got up from the bed. "But as heartbreaking as that was, it wasn't the worst." She turned and looked at her niece. "I got pregnant. After that one time of so-called lovemaking, I was pregnant. I didn't have anyone to talk to. I had lost the only person I could ever talk to:

your mother. She was like a sister to me, and she was gone." She looked at Alyssa, with sadness in her eyes.

"You haven't met your grandmother, your dad, and my mother, Rosemarie. She lives in St. Louis. She's a wonderful woman and mother, but I couldn't tell her something like this over the phone. Besides, after losing my grandma Sarah and my dad—within months of each other—her life was upside down too. So I talked with Martha."

"You're right you know; I think I'm pregnant, but how did you know?" Alyssa asked quietly.

"Like I said, honey, you look exactly how I looked and acted all those years ago." They were now sitting on the bed and Mary took her niece in her arms.

"I don't know what to do. I can't tell my mom; it would kill her," Alyssa said. She turned her red eyes to her aunt and, for a moment, they could only stare at each other.

"This is something time will not let you hide," Mary said. "Trust me, I tried too." Mary got up and again started to pace the floor in front of Alyssa.

"They think I'm their special little princess," Alyssa said. She started to get a queasy feeling in her stomach. "I'm sure I can't tell them their little princess has had sex more than ten times." She also thought she could not tell her aunt that the father of the baby was one of the professors at college and that he was probably twice her age.

"Sweetheart, do you know how far along you might be?" Mary asked.

"I haven't had my period for about two months," Alyssa said.

Her aunt stopped her pacing and took a seat by the small desk in the room. "You have to see a doctor to make sure," Mary explained.

Alyssa looked as if she had jumped out of her skin. "Mama will know then!" She had a look of terror in her eyes.

"You might be surprised to know that your mom will understand," Mary said, with kindness showing in her eyes.

"How come nobody talks about your baby?" Alyssa asked.

Mary hung her head. "I gave her up for adoption."

"Her? You had a girl?" Alyssa looked surprised.

"Yes, a girl. They weren't supposed to tell me, but one of the nurses slipped and said something about her when I first delivered. Martha is the only one who knows. And now you." She looked at her niece with trust in her eyes.

"Only me and Martha," Alyssa said as they both hugged each other.

"Honey, I'm going to get your mother, okay?" Alyssa shook her head. "I'll be right back." She kissed her niece on the cheek and left her room.

***

The heavenly scent of cinnamon rolls filled every room in the house. "What a way to get up," Rachel said to Martha when she went into the kitchen where Martha stood in her matronly dress donned with an apron. Martha's hands were covered in baking flour.

"Ready for some coffee?" Martha asked, in her usual cheerful way. She was generously spreading the icing on the first batch of rolls.

"I'll say," Rachel said.

Just then Byron and Madison came into the room. "We peeked into the living room; the kids are still asleep, but they won't be for long with this smell," said Byron.

Rachel had poured them all cups of coffee and brought them over to where they all sat at the kitchen table. They enjoyed watching Martha continue to make her magic.

"Ronald and Cal saddled up and rode over to the clinic to check on the stock. Thank goodness the snow stopped last night," said Martha and gave each of them a plate with a colossal, sweet smelling roll on it.

"You know, you'll have to teach us how to make these," Rachel said. She looked up at Martha as she accepted the roll and winked at her.

"I suppose it's time," Martha replied, thinking she had always wanted to keep the secret to herself. But now, at her age, she thought it might be time to pass it on.

Madison, holding her plate and cup of coffee, went and stood next to Martha to watch her prepare the next batch.

"Mom's still up in Alyssa's room with Aunt Mary. I'm guessing they're having a good heart to heart," Byron said as a drip of the buttery icing dribbled down the side of his lip. Madison saw it and used her napkin to wipe it for him.

"Awe, isn't that sweet," Lyssa said, in a singsong way. She had just walked into the kitchen and witnessed it.

"Good morning, Lyssa," Rachel said sternly. She was trying not to embarrass her daughter with a blunt reprimand, so she used her motherly tone to caution her about any further rude remarks.

"Morning everyone, isn't it such a beautiful day. And those rolls smell just yummy. I'm sure I can keep 'em in my mouth," Lyssa said, teasing Byron. She skipped in front of him and mockingly pretended to dab at her mouth.

"Lyssa," Rachel said. She gave her daughter her commanding, motherly look.

"I'll be a good girl," Lyssa said, with a sly look in her eyes.

"Like that's possible," Madison said under her breath.

"I heard that," Lyssa said. She again gave Madison one of her looks.

"Keep it up, Lyssa, and these yummy rolls won't be going into your tummy," Rachel said.

Lyssa bowed her head in a submissive way. She then acted shyly as she received a plate with a roll on it from Martha. "Thank you so much, Aunt Martha," Lyssa said, with a sweet smile, and curtsied in front of Martha.

"Is she for real?" Madison whispered in Byron's ear. They both chuckled. Madison joined Martha, hoping to learn more of her baking secrets.

"Sure am," Lyssa said. She also stood near Martha to take in her secret recipe while they all enjoyed their breakfast.

Upstairs another dilemma was unfolding. "Mama I'm so sorry," Alyssa was saying to her mother.

Olivia was brushing her daughter's hair as Alyssa sat by her dressing table. "We've talked about this all night, and I still can't say I'm sorry enough," she said. Her dry eyes were still red.

"I'm glad you told me; we'll get a doctor's appointment next Monday," Olivia said. She glanced at Mary, who was sitting on Alyssa's bed.

"If I can help in any way," Mary said. "You know this kind of thing happens a lot back home. She can stay with Martha and me and still go to college until . . ."

Alyssa almost lost it. "I can't go to college and have everybody staring at me, and what about Wally, he'll know it's his," she blurted out. Her dark eyes glared at her mother's image in the large mirror on the dressing table.

"Why in the hell do you care about this Wally?" Mary asked sarcastically. "He's the one who got you in trouble in the first place, and he should own up to it."

Olivia looked at Mary with raised eyebrows. She knew her sister-in-law never pondered over her words. "You want to drop out?" Olivia asked. She had a look of disbelief in her eyes as she continued to brush her daughter's long, black hair. "You might break the mirror with that look." She felt Alyssa's rebellious stare shoot straight to her heart.

"Mother, I would be mortified!" a completely agitated Alyssa shouted. She abruptly pushed the bench away from the bureau, almost hitting her mother. "I don't feel so good. Can you two just leave me alone for a while? I'll be down in a little bit." Her voice was calmer.

"Fine with me," Mary said, and she and Olivia left the room.

***

Downstairs the atmosphere was more festive. "Look whose ready for some rolls," said Olivia . She was holding Andrew's hand as he groggily walked beside her rubbing his eyes with his other hand. His personality was completely the opposite of Lyssa's. He acted sedate and more laid back than his twin sister.

"Guys aren't back yet?" Olivia asked. She and Andrew took seats at the table.

"No, but they should be shortly," Martha said as she brought them some rolls.

"Martha, you're not to lift a finger for the rest of the day. You've outdone yourself with our breakfast," said Olivia and looked lovingly at Martha as she enjoyed her roll.

"You know I love to cook, especially when everyone enjoys it," Martha said. She was sporting another one of her contagious smiles.

"I would love to help with dinner," Madison said enthusiastically. She saw Lyssa give her what she thought was a jealous look.

"Madison is an accomplished chef; she finished culinary school," Byron added. He noticed Lyssa give him a sad look.

"I can help too," Lyssa said. She sat up straight in her chair trying to look older and boost her own ego.

"There's plenty to do. The turkey's ready for the oven," said Olivia, just as Ronald and Cal came in through the backdoor.

"It's snowing again," Cal said. He and Ronald went next to Martha and stole a roll. Martha pretended to smack their hands.

"I'd walk a mile for one of these," said Cal. Ronald agreed as they got their coffee.

"Everything okay at home?" Rachel asked.

"Yep, Tommy's going to stay and watch the place for us. He said it would be nice to get away from the kids for a while. Tommy's the oldest in a large family and whenever he can have time to himself, he's ready," Cal told them.

"Did you tell him to make himself at home?" Rachel asked. "We have the roast and . . ."

"Yes, he'll be fine," said Cal. He downed his last bite of roll with a gulp of coffee and went for a second roll.

Finally, muffled by a blanket of snow, the house seemed quiet. Everyone was settling in and preparing for the Thanksgiving feast.

***

That afternoon the snow continued to fall, but Byron and Madison found time to be alone. All snuggled in their warm outerwear and boots, they trudged through the snow to the barn.

"I've always loved the smell of the barn. It's kind of earthy smelling," said Byron when they opened the barn door.

"I know what you mean. Makes you think about the good things in life," Madison added.

After closing the door, he took her in his arms. "I've missed you like this," Byron said as she cuddled up to him.

"Me too," she whispered.

"Madison, I hope you know you've become a very important part of my life," he said, with a stammer in his voice.

"I feel the same way. You've made me feel like I can have the kind of life I've always dreamed of." He squeezed her closer to him. She thought about how his family love and involvement was not even close to what she was used to.

"You never really talk much about your grandmother. I would like to meet her one day," he said and noticed how she shied away from him.

"She's not like your family. I don't know how else to say this. She just takes care of . . ." Her tears started to flow down her cheeks. "I don't think she even loves me." She openly wept. He led her to a bale of hay, and they sat down on it.

"But you have the apartment and college," he said.

"Things, just things, that's all she gives." She started to cry, and he gave her his handkerchief. "Once a year she comes around. Even though she lives in New York, not far from the loft, I only see her once a year." Her tears settled down.

"Have you tried to visit her?" he asked. She got up and walked to the stall where the mare was tending the baby mule.

"You know, mules don't come from mules," he said sincerely.

She gave him an inquisitive look. She smirked as she sniffled and wiped her tears with his handkerchief. "Come on, " she said and grinned broadly, thinking he was teasing her.

He smiled at her. "It's true. The mule is the offspring of a mare—you know, a female horse and a male jackass." He blushed. "I'm sorry a male donkey." They both started laughing.

"I've never met someone who can make me laugh the way you do," she said. They started dancing around on the straw-covered floor.

"Oh God, even in that crazy little beret you're beautiful," he said. He could not look away from her loving eyes. "When I first saw you at the café, I was hooked." He winked at her. "I could not get you out of my mind or my heart." He gently pulled her closer to him, and she let him.

"My sweet Madison, will you do me the honor of becoming my wife," he asked boldly.

She stopped the dancing and looked at him with her mouth wide open. "*Huh*" was all she could say.

"My wife, you know for the rest of our lives," he explained. He reached inside his coat pocket, pulled out a ring box, and opened it. "Here, let me make this perfectly clear." His eyes twinkled as he looked at her and then bent down on one knee.

"Oh my God." She covered her mouth with the mitten on her hand.

"Madison, I love you, and I know we will make beautiful babies. Would you like to make beautiful babies with me?" he teased. He looked up at her with love in his eyes. His hand trembled in hers as he held the box up to her and waited for her reply.

"Oh my God! Yes, yes I'll make babies with you—after we're married of course," She pulled him up, and he took her into his arms.

"I love you Bryon Brown," she purred.

He gently brushed a lock of her hair behind her ear with his fingers. "You're the most beautiful woman in the world and you honor me." He took her hand and put the ring on her finger.

"Oh Byron," she squealed as they kissed with hurried excitement.

"Let's tell the family." His excitement showed in his voice.

She looked him in the eyes and could only see love staring back at her. "Oh, honey, before we tell them, I have something important I would like to tell you," she said.

Just then the barn door opened and Lyssa saw them hugging. She noticed the ring on the hand he was holding up to kiss. "Oh man," Lyssa shouted. With a look of horror in her eyes, her tears started to flow. "How could you!" she screamed. She turned and ran as fast as she could back to the house.

"Oh no, Byron. I know she can be a pain in the butt, but she truly thinks she loves you. I feel terrible for her. She must have a broken heart," Madison said. "Did you see the look on her face?" Madison could feel the happiness in her heart turning sour.

"I'll try to talk to her, but we can't let this spoil our announcement," he said. The cold wind was blowing in from the door Lyssa had left open.

"You're such a caring man; I will love you forever," she said as she tenderly caressed his cheek. Looking into his eyes, she saw his love. She could feel her heart melt when he slowly lowered his lips to hers, making her forget everything she was about to divulge to him.

"We will love forever," he said joyfully and winked. He then grabbed her hand and led her from the barn. They giggled and glanced at each other as they quickly closed the barn door and hurried to the house. Their hearts were overflowing with love as the snowflakes flew all around them.

Madison could not help but laugh aloud. She thought, *If this scene were viewed from an artist's point of view—*

with the snow flying around us and him holding my hand as we run from the barn to the house—we would look like a Currier and Ives print. Just like the first time I saw Red Winds. She giggled and opened her mouth to take in some snowflakes. She then saw him turn his head and glance her way. "I love life!" she shouted as they continued to run. At that very moment, she knew these pictures would be etched foremost in her mind and on her heart forever.

***

That evening, after supper, some were enjoying sitting around the fireplace with cups of hot apple cider while Rachel and Olivia drank wine, sang, and played the piano. Martha wandered to the front room and was enjoying a bit of private time when Madison came into the room.

"Am I disturbing you?" Madison asked.

"Oh no, my dear, I just enjoy listening to the family," Martha said. She patted a place for the younger woman to sit next to her on the cushioned seat of the bay window.

"My husband passed away a long time ago, around this time of year, and we never had any children," Martha explained. "But I was blessed when Olivia and Rachel adopted me into their families." Both women smiled and quietly looked out the window.

"I love to watch the snow here. Back home it's not as pretty," Madison finally said, breaking the silence. Martha nodded in agreement.

"Have you always lived in New York?" Martha asked.

"No. Actually I was born in Japan," Madison said. "My mother died when I was born, and my father died in the war." They were getting to know each other.

"That's sad. Do you have any other family?" Martha asked. She patted Madison's hand.

"Yes, my grandmother. She takes care of me and . . . " Madison hesitated for a second and then continued, "I have an apartment near the college. It does make it easier to study away from college. Alyssa comes over and we study together." She felt very comfortable with the older woman.

"That sounds nice, and I'm so happy about your engagement to Byron," Martha said. She motioned to look at the ring again. "Just beautiful. Byron has wonderful taste, and I don't just mean the ring." They both looked at each other and smiled.

"You make me feel special," Madison said. "I hope you didn't mind that I wanted to learn your recipe for the cinnamon rolls this morning."

"It's time I shared, and you learn fast," Martha said. She winked at Madison and saw a slight blush on her cheeks.

"Thanks. I try," Madison said. "And Lyssa was learning too," Madison added.

"Yes, she's one of those old souls in a young body," Martha said and noticed that Madison looked sad.

"She came into the barn right after Byron proposed to me, and she was very hurt," Madison said.

"I could tell she was pretty quiet during super. Not like her at all," Martha said.

"Byron's planning to have a little talk with her. She thinks she's in love with him," Madison said, her cheeks getting pink again.

"First crush, hard to get over," Martha said. They both nodded in agreement. "But then, when the real thing comes along, the first crush is only a smile in the wind," Martha added. They both started laughing.

"Thank goodness," said Madison, and she patted Martha's hand. "I feel so close to Byron. It feels like I've known him all my life, and his family is so wonderful. They opened their arms to me. I feel so blessed." She turned her head to look outside.

"I know how you feel. They did the same for me. Do you have a relationship with your grandmother?" Martha asked. "Family is so important." She looked deeply into Madison's eyes.

"I've told Byron my grandmother really just takes care of me. I know she's my father's mother, but she actually acts like an unconcerned guardian," Madison said. She felt a bonding trust open up with Martha.

"I'm sorry to hear that, but at least she cares enough to help you get a good education and give you a place to stay," Martha said.

"Yes, that's true. I guess she might not have much time left after keeping things going at the art gallery," Madison said. She noticed Martha's puzzled look.

"She works at an art gallery?" Martha asked. She felt her heart starting to pump faster. "May I ask which one?" She had a bit of hesitation in her voice.

"Well, actually she owns it. It's the Yasieu Gallery," said Madison. She saw Martha's face go white.

"Oh! My God! Please tell me your grandmother . . . is her name Yoshiema?" Martha asked, with a look of horror in her eyes.

"Yes, but Martha you're scaring me; are you all right?" Madison sounded worried.

She watched as Martha, unable to speak, clumsily clutched at her chest and stared at her. Then, Martha's mouth opened wide and her eyes rolled back in her head showing only the whites of her eyes. Finally, she fell into Madison's arms. "Help, Byron, hurry!" Madison screamed. They all came into the front room.

"What happened?" Ronald yelled. He went to Martha and Madison.

"We were talking, she clutched her chest, and just fell over!" Madison screamed. Ronald and Cal laid Martha on the floor.

"Call for an ambulance and get a pillow and blanket," Cal said, in a hurried, yet controlled voice.

"Everything will be okay," Mary said in Martha's unhearing ear and gently placed Martha's head on her lap. "Oh God, Martha," she said to the woman she thought of as her second mother. "I'm here. It's all right." Mary carefully combed Martha's gray hair away from her face with her long, red fingernails.

"Here are some smelling salts," Olivia said. She came back into the room and handed the container to Cal. She then helped Mary place a pillow under Martha's head and cover her with the blanket.

"Martha. Martha . . ." Olivia said, trying to rouse her. She knelt at Martha's side with Rachel on Martha's other side.

"Martha can you hear me?" Cal asked, after passing the smelling salts in front of her nose. Martha's eyes fluttered and then opened.

"Lay still, help's on the way," Cal said as he bent over her. He could see the terror in her eyes.

"Ma—Mad's—O's—" Martha was slurring her speech before she passed out again.

"Just keep her warm and comfortable," Cal said. He looked with wonder at Olivia, Mary, and his wife, and shrugged his shoulders.

"I'm guessing she said *Mama* or something like that," said Rachel. Just then Ronald came back after taking the children into the next room.

"Byron, Madison, and Alyssa will take care of the kids," Ronald said. He noticed the tears flowing down his wife's cheeks.

"Madison said they were having a pleasant conversation and then she just collapsed. She feels awful," Ronald told them. They could hear the ambulance in the distance.

"This weather isn't going to make it easy for them to get here," Olivia said, with fear evident on her face.

"She seems to be breathing normally, so that's a good sign," Cal told them. Finally, they heard the ambulance in the driveway.

***

Later at the hospital, Mary, Olivia, Rachel, and Ronald anxiously awaited word on Martha's condition. They decided Cal would stay home with the rest of the family until other arrangements could be made.

"Waiting is the worst," Olivia said. They all just gave her an understanding look.

"She's a strong-willed woman. She'll fight," Mary said. They all shook their heads in agreement as the doctor came out of Martha's room.

"She has experienced a slight heart attack," the doctor said. Olivia yelped and tears filled her eyes.

"She is comfortable right now, and she comes in and out of consciousness," said the doctor. Mary could feel her bowels loosen.

"I have to go. I'll be right back," Mary said, knowing she did not want to hear Martha's prognosis.

"Although it's a slight heart attack, with her age and other complications, it's bad," the doctor said. "Her family should be notified." They all hung their heads.

"We're part of her family. The rest are at home, but we'll get them here right away," said Rachel.

Olivia cut in. "Can we see her?"

"Yes, but like I said she is in and out of consciousness," the doctor explained. They followed him to Martha's room.

Wires and tubes were attached on her arms and chest, and she was wearing an oxygen nosepiece.

"She still seems to be breathing normally the way she did at home," Ronald said. "That seems to be a good thing, right?" he asked the doctor.

"We did not have to aspirate her, which is unusual in her condition, and her breathing is normal at this time," he answered. He looked at the machinery she was hooked up to and said, "I'll be right outside."

Mary came into the room and spoke quietly with the doctor before he left the room.

"I called Cal," Mary said as she stood next to Martha's bed and took her hand. "Cal said the snow stopped and the road has been plowed, so they're on their way." Purposely, she did not ask about Martha's condition.

"Mary," Olivia said, with an understanding tone. "The doctor told us . . ."

Mary stopped her. "I think I already know. You see Martha has had a heart condition for a while. She had a slight heart attack some time ago."

Ronald looked at her in disbelief. "Why didn't you let us know?" Ronald asked his sister.

Mary interjected. "It was right after Olivia's return. You all were . . ." She could tell by their looks that they all understood, and she did not have to continue with her reasoning. "Well . . . anyway . . . to put it bluntly, the doctors back then said another one would most likely be the big one. We both always joked about it, but now that it happened, I wish I was more prepared." She looked at Martha with tears welling in her eyes.

"She's been a very special part of all our lives," Olivia said.

Rachel went to her. "Remember how she accepted us in her life all those years ago? We were like two little hillbillies going to the big city. She made us feel right at home and showed us the ropes. It was easy with her; she has a big heart," Rachel said and hugged Olivia.

"She's been there for me in more ways than I can ever say," said Mary as Martha opened her eyes. "Hi there," Mary said and softly patted Martha's hand. She wiped a tear from her cheek.

"O—Ma—Ma—" Martha muttered. She spoke much the same way she had at Red Winds.

"It's like she's trying to say something," Mary said. She noticed Martha struggling to look around the room, and then she spotted Olivia.

"O—Ma—Ma—" Martha mumbled her garbled words again as she tried to reach for Olivia.

"I think she wants to tell you something," Mary said as she looked at Olivia.

"I'm here Martha," Olivia whispered. She bent over Martha.

"Ma—Ma—" Martha almost yelled.

Olivia looked at Mary with confusion written all over her face. "I'm sorry," Olivia said.

Mary moved closer to Olivia and Martha. "Are you saying *Mama*?" Mary asked.

"*Ugh*," Martha grunted. She started to thrash about in the bed, and the doctor came in.

"You'll have to leave the room," the doctor demanded. The attending nurses aided him as they hurried out.

After some time, the rest of the family arrived at the hospital. "It seems like he's been in there for hours," Mary said and looked at Alyssa, who seemed to be uncommonly quiet. "You okay?" she asked her niece. Alyssa was sitting on one of the benches.

"I don't know. I'm cramping," said Alyssa. Suddenly, she held her stomach and bent over in obvious pain.

"Oh God," Olivia shouted as Ronald went for help. Just then Alyssa stood up and had blood running down her legs. "We need help here," Olivia yelled. A nurse came in and called out orders.

"Yikes!" said Lyssa. They all watched the orderlies take Alyssa away on a gurney with Olivia and Ronald right beside her.

"Byron, please stay here. We'll let you know what's going on," Ronald said to his son. They were hurrying down the corridor. Olivia stayed close to the gurney, next to her daughter.

Just then the doctor came out of Martha's room. "She's stable right now, but she has experienced another heart attack. Like I said before, it's not good," the doctor explained.

"Can we see her?" Mary asked.

"Yes, but please, only two at a time," the doctor replied.

"Mary, you and Rachel go in first," said Cal.

Mary gave him a look of relief and said, "Thanks." She grabbed Rachel's arm, and they went into Martha's room.

Martha looked a lot paler than she had when they were in the room before. Her hair was disheveled and looked damp.

"Oh, Martha, I'm so sorry for your pain," Mary whispered. She sat near the head of the bed and took her hand in hers. "We just never had enough time."

Rachel moved closer to her. "You two have shared a wonderful life. Be happy for what you have," Rachel whispered.

Martha's eyes fluttered, and she seemed to gaze at them. "Love," Martha said. Her hand slightly moved in Mary's soft grip.

"We love you too, sweetheart," Mary said, thinking Martha to be most dear to her heart.

"Tell me the truth," Martha was able to say to them.

"It's the big one we've always talked about," said Mary and constricted her tears.

"Sorry," Martha said. "Wish stay," she added.

With all the machinery and wires in the way, Mary and Rachel got as close to her as they possibly could to comfort her. "We love you," they both said in unison.

They watched as Martha used a sign language. She slowly moved her hand to her chest and crossed her heart with her fingers. She then raised her hand to her lips where she seemed to kiss the palm of her hand and point toward them, but then her hand quickly dropped to the bed.

"Oh God, Martha," Mary cried out. She quickly lowered the bed rail and crawled in next to the elderly woman to show her how much she cared for her.

"We love you too, Martha," Rachel cried.

The machines started to beep. The doctor and nurses rushed into the room and saw the flat line. The doctor slowly turned the machines off, but did not try to rush them out of the room as he had before. Quickly, without disturbing Mary or Rachel, he checked Martha's vital signs. "She's gone," the doctor said. He wrote down the time of death on her chart. Caringly, the nurses worked around Rachel and Mary to unhook Martha from the oxygen apparatus and other machinery.

"Oh God, Martha, what will I do without you," Mary cried. "She was a like a mother to me. I will always love and remember you," Mary whispered. Lovingly, she caressed Martha's cheek after the doctor had closed Martha's eyes.

"We all will," Rachel said. Her tears flowed uncontrollably.

"I'll send in the rest of the family," the doctor said. He and his staff left them alone in the room.

On another floor of the hospital, Olivia and Ronald were awaiting word of their daughter. "I'm sorry, Ronald. This all happened so fast that I never had the chance to let you know what's going on with her," Olivia said to her husband while they sat on the stiff couch in the waiting room.

"For God's sake, what's wrong with her?" Ronald sounded worried. He had that terrible, tragic feeling he had experienced before. He felt his world crashing in around him. "Is she dying," he asked. His fear gripped at his heart and showed in his eyes.

"She told me she's pregnant," Olivia said as tears welled in her eyes. "That's what the all night discussion was about. We were going to make a doctor's appointment Monday, but with everyone there I never got a chance to talk with you privately." She saw a look of horror in her husband's eyes.

"Pregnant!" Ronald said, with complete shock evident in his voice. He shook his head and gave his wife a look of disgust as he rose from his seat. "Who did this to her? I'll ..."

Olivia stood up. "She said it's some guy named Wally. I'm guessing he's a student at the university. Remember, Byron's been saying for some time that she's been acting out," Olivia said as the doctor approached them.

"I'm sorry to tell you that your daughter lost her baby," the doctor said. Olivia could only bury her head in Ronald's chest and grieve for the loss of their grandchild.

"And our daughter?" Ronald asked. He again felt that terrible fear rip at his heart. He felt Olivia go stiff in his arms.

"She lost a lot of blood and the next twenty-four hours will be critical. For now, she's resting comfortably. She's been sedated and ..."

Olivia interrupted. "Can we see her?" she asked, with hesitation in her voice. She turned her head from Ronald.

"Yes, but she will not be responsive, as I said, she's sedated." The doctor escorted them to the intensive care unit.

"She will be in the ICU for this critical time. I want to keep a strict eye on her progress. I'll be right outside," said the doctor. He left them to be alone with their daughter.

"Oh Ronald," said Olivia as she took her daughter's hand in hers.

"I know," Ronald said to his wife. "It's Byron all over again, but, honey, she will be all right. We have to believe that." He looked at her and noticed her red, swollen eyes.

"I believe it. Oh God yes, I believe she's going to be just fine," she whispered. She kissed her daughter's hand and gently caressed her forehead. "You're going to be just fine," she whispered to her daughter. She thought she was also trying to convince herself. "Mama and Daddy are right here," she said, in a low voice. She could feel warm tears on her cheeks.

Life is precious; with the grace of God, to witness it hanging on was a miracle that over time they were forced to understand. Tearfully, they held onto each other. They trusted in their deep faith to keep their hearts from falling apart.

Chapter Four

Over the next ten years, it seemed that no matter how their lives changed or how much they aged, the trees of Red Winds always looked the same and were always a welcoming sight to anyone who came home.

"Slow down, I'm not going anywhere. You're always so excited," he commented smugly and in an uncaring way. He watched her smirk as she hurried to unbutton his shirt. He tried to curb his anticipation, but when she touched him and he saw her girlish, smooth body move, his passions began building to a point of no return.

"Damn straight I'm excited. You know I have a plane to catch so . . ." She pulled her blouse over her head and almost tore off her bra. "I'm hot and ready and if you don't start playing with me I'm going to go mad," she cried out through clenched teeth. She started to rub her taut nipples on his now bare chest.

"I saw that you didn't have any panties on in class again." He seductively eyed her young body. He could feel his raging hormones taking control. "God, you're a wild little thing." He almost fell on the bed when she straddled his naked leg and started to slowly hump him.

"You drive me crazy." Lustfully, she licked her red lips and then his. "You don't know how hard it is for me to sit there acting like the perfect little co-ed. I could explode."

Her eyes met his. Her passion was on fire, and she started to swing her hips. She kissed his lips, and then ran her tongue along his body until she felt she had him under her control.

"Shit your good," he gasped. He fell on the bed, and she crawled next to him. "Oh baby, take it," he shouted. He watched her tongue work a magic of its own. "Now," he huffed. He could feel his body shaking.

"Not yet, lover boy, I want it all," she whispered. "Come on, you can do it," She was crawling away from him on the bed. She shook her hips luring him to reach playfully for her and pull her on top of him. "You know what I want," she purred. "Here, right here. That's it . . . that's it . . . slower . . ." she growled. She had an animalistic look in her sapphire eyes as she flung her long, blonde hair like a hungry tigress.

"Come on professor teach me," she purred and slithered to his side. She took his fingers, and he knew what to do with them as she squealed with excited pleasure. "That's it . . . that's it . . . faster damn it, faster." Her built passion showed in her eyes. "Yes . . . yes . . . that's it!" she screamed, with a commanding grin on her face. Hurriedly, she rolled onto her back and teasingly spread her legs exposing her nakedness under her miniskirt.

"You little witch," he whispered, with a low slur in his voice. He knelt next to her and started to lick his way to her sexy sweetness.

"That's it," she screeched, while panting and squirming up on all fours.

Finally, they lay next to each other, feeling completely satisfied. He had performed in an unprotected way, like he had never done in many years.

Later that afternoon, she was riding in a taxicab to the airport. Suddenly, a sign on a tiny shop caught her attention.

"Cabby, please stop at the next corner," she shouted. She paid him and took her belongings with her. *I have to see if that's really her,* she thought and started to walk to the shop.

Martha's Cinnamon Rolls, she read. *Besides me, only one other person knows how to make Martha's cinnamon rolls.* She entered the busy café.

"Madison?" she asked the attractive women behind the counter.

"Wow, I haven't heard that name in a long time. Do I know you?" Madison asked. She had a friendly business tone to her voice.

"I thought it had to be you. Besides me, you're the only other person who knows Martha's recipe," she said, putting her bags down around her. "It's me Lyssa, Lyssa Yarborough." She saw sadness in Madison's eyes.

"Oh my, time sure flies, you're all grown up. I now go by my real name: Nina." Madison said as a line was forming behind Lyssa. "Can you stay awhile?" she asked hurriedly. "I have to take care of these customers." She nodded to the line and saw Lyssa nod her head and pick up her bags. "Take any table; I'll bring us some rolls and coffee." She started to speak in Japanese to a couple of her employees, and then went for the rolls and drinks.

"Yes, I finally found my niche in life," Madison said, coming to Lyssa's table and placing a tray on it. "I think you're going to like these—just like old times," She put a plate with several rolls on it in front of Lyssa.

"Oh my God, you're right! They're great," Lyssa said after taking a big bite. "Martha would be so proud," She was openly enjoying the roll.

"Are you in town visiting?" Madison asked.

"No. You remember Andrew, my twin brother? Well, we call him Andy now, and we both go to college here." She took another bite of her roll and was eyeing a second.

"I didn't think you two were old enough," Madison commented.

"I suppose we're gifted," Lyssa said and chuckled. "After we were tested, we skipped two grades back home and then went off to college. But Andy's the smart one; I couldn't have made it this far if he hadn't knocked some sense into me. It took me awhile to comprehend that I could do it myself," she said, finishing off her second roll. "I didn't realize I was so hungry; these are fabulous." She took a drink of her coffee and picked up the third roll.

"I'm glad you like them. I had a great teacher," Madison said. They looked at each other.

"So much happened back then: Martha passed away and Allie miscarried, but Byron's family stuck together though all of it. I wasn't used to a family showing so much support and love; it was very refreshing," said Madison. "And it was really hard on Byron. I was glad I was with him. When I thought about it later in life, I believed that fate brought Byron and me together so I could help him through those tough times." She had a sweet smile on her face.

"That was a horrible time back then when Martha passed away. I was young, but I do remember about Alyssa losing a baby when Martha died," said Lyssa.

"Yes, that was sad, and we had been having such a nice time. I know, in the barn, you saw when Byron gave me my engagement ring." She noticed from Lyssa's expression that she did remember.

"Yeah, I saw it. I had such a huge crush on him, but I was young and didn't know what real life was about." Lyssa wiped her mouth with a napkin.

"Byron was going to talk to you about that, but then later that evening when I was talking with Martha about my grandmother, she had her attack," Madison related to Lyssa.

"Like always, I was brooding, and then the next thing I remember is everybody going nuts," said Lyssa. "The ambulance took Martha to the hospital, and we all ended up there later. Everything seemed to change after that." She saw that Madison agreed with her.

"You're right," said Madison. "After that time and over the years, I know my life completely changed. Even though I haven't gone back to Red Winds since then, Olivia has visited me." Madison's eyes lit up. "She's helped me to move on with my life, but it's still hard for me to understand things. Back then, my sister hurt me the most." Madison was saying when one of her assistants came to their table.

"Nina," the assistant said, and then spoke in Japanese.

"I'm not used to the Nina. Is it okay if I continue to call you Madison?" Lyssa asked.

"Sure, no biggy," Madison said, with a smile. "It's almost time to shut down shop. Could you stick around for a while?"

"Absolutely, I think we have a lot to talk about, and I've got some calls to make," Lyssa said, looking around for the public telephone.

"You can use the one in my office," said Madison. She led Lyssa to her private office and went back to take care of her business.

"Andy, it's me," said Lyssa after her brother answered her page at the airport.

"Where are you?" he replied. "You're lucky the flight's been cancelled, snow in Kansas."

"Good, I can't talk now, but I'm with Madison, you know the Madison who was crazy in love with Byron back when Aunt Martha died."

"Oh yeah, I remember her. Hey, hold on a sec" She could hear him talking to someone. "Yes, I'm about ready. Hold on for a minute," she heard him say before he returned to his conversation with her. "That's my cab. I'm going to the hotel by the airport. You know the one where we always stay? I'll let you know the room number when I check in. What's the number there?" he asked. She could hear the commotion of the airport. "Don't miss the flight tomorrow, it's at 9:00 a.m." He was acting the way he always did—treating her like an insubordinate.

"Quit acting like you're the boss, Andy, you control freak. I know you're just acting for the cabby," she said as he went on with his power play.

"And furthermore, if you're late . . ."

She cut in on him. "Keep it up bro; I'm sure you're making a big impression. Must be a hottie around." She laughed into the phone. "Call me when you're settled." She hung up and noticed that the chatter in the café had diminished. She realized Madison had closed the shop.

Madison came into her office and walked to Lyssa. "Through with your call?" Madison asked.

"Yes, and I gave Andy your number here. Our flight was cancelled. I knew it would be. Snow in Kansas. What else is new?" Lyssa said. She shrugged her shoulders.

Madison sat in another chair and placed two fresh cups of coffee down on the desk. "I loved the snow at Red Winds when I was there," said Madison. Lyssa noticed the faraway look in her eyes. Then Madison quickly changed the subject. "Can I get you some more rolls?"

"No thanks, maybe later. I'm about to bust," Lyssa said and they both laughed. "You have a pretty smile," Lyssa commented as they continued their conversation. She took a sip of her coffee. "You were saying your sister hurt you the most."

"Besides Byron and my sister, only Byron's mom and my grandmother know what my sister did," Madison said and resumed her story.

"I was young back then and some of what I heard just seemed . . ." Lyssa said.

Madison interjected. "Crazy?"

"Yeah, out of this world crazy," Lyssa said. She took another sip of her coffee.

"It all started when my grandmother and Olivia were scheduled to meet me at the bridal boutique to help me pick out the dress I would marry the man of my dreams in. I was excited because not only was I picking out my wedding dress, but it was going to be the first time my grandmother and Olivia were going to meet." Madison shared the tale as Lyssa listened to a part of the gossip that Christy would learn about much later in her life.

***

"Oh Grandmother, I'm so happy. Look at all of these beautiful gowns. The fabric is awesome," Madison commented to her grandmother. She ran her hand over the fine material.

"My dear, I'm sure you will choose the right dress." Madison's grandmother showed a hint of pride in her actions and words. She looked completely at home on a padded Victorian chair covered with silk that had been placed in the large dressing room of the bridal boutique.

"I'm sorry I never told you about my engagement before now, but . . ." Madison was saying to her grandmother.

Her grandmother stopped her. "I've never been one to keep in touch with family matters. It's hard for me to be personable. I was like that with your father too. He always did what he wanted, and I never asked or interfered," her grandmother said. She blushed slightly. "I always thought as long as you were taken care of that everything was the way it should be." She had an unconcerned air about her. "Oh well. Now, as it is, I will meet your future mother-in-law and then one day soon, I will meet your fiancé," said her grandmother as the clerk brought in several more gowns.

"Oh my, they're just breathtaking, but we're still waiting for my mother-in-law-to-be," Madison said to the clerk. "I really don't want to try on any gowns until she gets here." She seemed somewhat concerned. "She should've been here by now," she added.

"I will show her in the minute she arrives. In the meantime, can I offer you both some refreshments?" the clerk asked. They both agreed it would be a good idea.

"She might be stuck in traffic. You know how New York gets congested," said her grandmother.

When the clerk brought them their snacks, the bell on the outside door jingled. "I'll check. That might be her now," the clerk said and left the dressing room.

"This is so exciting," said Madison.

The clerk came back into the room. "A lady's here, but she said she just saw her son with his fiancée on the street as she was riding in the taxi to come here."

Madison started to leave the room. "There must be some kind of mistake. I'll be right back, Grandmother. I'll see if it's her," Madison said and left the clerk in the dressing room with her grandmother.

"You made it, how wonderful. I'm so excited," Madison's grandmother heard her say from the other room as Madison and Olivia were walking into the dressing room. "Grandmother, may I introduce . . ." Madison began as her grandmother got up from her seat and turned to greet her granddaughter's intended mother-in-law.

"Yoshiema!" Olivia shouted. She noticed the older woman's startled look as she stared at her. She watched Yoshiema's face turn white and her legs buckle beneath her as she fell back onto the chair. "Oh no, this can't be," Olivia kept saying. She kept looking around the room as if searching for someone.

"Yes, this is my grandmother, Yoshiema Yasieu," said Madison.

Olivia went ballistic. "Where's the other one?" Olivia shouted. "Oh God, that was her with Byron; your sister was with my son." She felt the room spinning. "You're either Mika or Nina," Olivia then shouted.

Madison's eyes opened wide as she stared at Olivia and then at her grandmother, who looked like she had seen a ghost. "What's going on?" Madison shouted. She quickly went to her grandmother and knelt before her.

"Dear God, my child, Olivia's your mother," Yoshiema said to Madison.

"What are you talking about? My mother died when I was born," Madison screamed. Her tears fell frantically from her eyes as she looked at Olivia, who was leaning against the far wall of the dressing room. "No, Grandmother, this is Byron's mother," Madison said. She sat on the floor too stunned to stand.

"Yes, this is Byron's mother and your mother," her grandmother admitted.

"But that would make Byron . . ." Madison hesitated as the shocked clerk finally left them alone in the room.

"Your half brother—my son is your half brother. And from the way they looked when I saw them on the street, he thinks he's with you, but actually he's going somewhere to be alone with your twin sister," Olivia explained. She desperately wished her husband were standing next to her at that very moment. "We have to find them!" Olivia shouted. She looked at Madison, the daughter she had abandoned so many years ago.

"This is scaring me . . . I can't believe this . . ." Madison kept saying. She again looked at Yoshiema. Her grandmother could only turn her gaze from her.

Yoshiema whispered, "You must find him. They must not . . ."

Olivia quickly grabbed Madison and pulled her up from the floor. "She's right," Olivia said. "We have to stop them." She tried to control the fear that was growing in her heart.

"Byron wouldn't do that. We're waiting for our wedding night," Madison said, in an almost inaudibly whisper.

"Come on . . . let's go . . ." Olivia continued to spur her on as Madison picked up her belongings and they left the room.

Her grandmother, completely stunned, continued to sit in the chair. "I should have been a better grandparent. I should have been in their lives more than I was in my son Mikail's," Yoshiema cried. She buried her head in her hands and openly wept for the fate of her granddaughter.

The ride in the cab to the loft was pure torture. Madison could actually feel a tangible reverse magnetic tension between her and the woman she had just found out to be her biological mother. "Why in God's name didn't you use your father's last name? You both would have saved us all a lot of heartache," Olivia uttered in a whisper. She stared at Madison with revulsion apparent in her eyes.

"We were told you were dead," Madison whispered through clenched teeth. She could see she hit a raw nerve. "We didn't know any better. We were babies and have been on our own all these years. Grandmother never gave us any moral upbringing or support. Oh God, why did you leave us?" She tried relentlessly to compose herself.

"It's a long story," said Olivia. She could feel many years of pain come to surface. "Look at me. Your father did this to me. He forced me to change my eyes to suit him, and then he used the love I had for my daughter,

Alyssa . . ." her bitter tears flowed down her cheeks, and she almost choked from sobbing. "Madison this is horrible. You and Byron are so much in love." She looked at her with terror in her eyes, thinking about what was in store for them.

Finally, they reached the loft, hurriedly paid the cabby, and ran into the building.

"He wouldn't do this; we have a pact," said Madison. They reached the apartment, and she opened the door with her key.

Inside, Madison saw many candles as she rushed into the living room. She cringed when she saw their naked, entwined bodies on the large, plush sofa. They almost looked like one, and the smell of sex permeated the room. "Bitch, get off him," Madison yelled. She forcefully yanked the arm of her sister, pulling her off the man she loved.

"What the hell," Byron mumbled with a cough. He looked from Madison to her twin.

"How could you. We were going to wait until our wedding night," Madison said. She felt a cold fear running through her veins.

"I know but . . ." Byron was so confused he forgot about his nakedness.

"But what? What in the hell do you call this?" Madison shouted vehemently. She noticed her sister trying to crawl away from her. "Get back here, bitch!" Madison shouted. She reached for a blanket and threw it at her.

"I wanted to wait . . . but you . . . you . . ." Byron was saying. He was completely confused and continued to look back and forth at both women. "You . . . you wanted

. . ." he tried to say again. He then noticed his mother standing in the room. "Mom . . ." He realized he was naked. "Oh God, what's going on here," he yelled and reached for a pillow to cover himself.

"Oh God, Byron, I should have told you about her a long time ago. It was her idea to keep it a secret, and now I know why. Mika, how could you do this to me?" Madison shouted at her twin sister.

Mika rose to her feet and readjusted the blanket. "You always make a big deal about things. It's just sex. He loves you for pity sake; I just wanted a little romp in the hay so to speak." Mika, seemingly without a care in the world, smirked.

Madison went to her and violently slapped her on the face. "You are not my sister," Madison shouted.

"How many times have you done this?" Madison asked vehemently, looking at Byron.

"Done what? I, we haven't done anything we haven't done . . ." Byron began, and then remembered her saying they were going to wait until their wedding night to consummate their love. "It was you who did not want to wait—not me—and this was the first time we . . . you and me . . . we almost . . ." He was starting to understand part of the situation.

He looked at his mother, feeling completely ashamed of himself. "We are engaged," he then said. He kept looking back and forth between the woman he loved and someone he really did not know but thought was the woman he loved.

"Byron, I found out something terrible today, and, honey, everything is . . ." Olivia was trying to explain to her son.

Madison interjected. "Our lives will never be the same. Oh God, Byron, I'm your sister. Your mother, Olivia, is my—our mother."

Byron sat up straight and edged his way as close as he could to the corner of the sofa. "What do you mean you're my sister?" he asked. He felt completely out of control when he saw what was going on in front of him. A moment ago he was making love with the woman he would share the rest of his life with and now some kind of nightmare was unfolding right before his eyes. He put his hand to his head.

Olivia noticed that his eyes seemed to glass over as he stared at her, looking as if he did not know who she was. She could not go near him. "It's only too real. I gave birth to Mikail Yasieu's twin daughters, these twins," Olivia said, and pointed to the girls.

"It was all those years ago when you were a baby and you almost died." She felt mesmerized. "Their father took me away from you and your dad," Olivia felt frozen to the spot where she stood. "He had a doctor ready and waiting to operate on you to save your life. Otherwise, you would have died. That is the only reason I went with him. The only way he would allow the doctor to save your life was if I left my family and became his wife," Olivia tried to explain. "I had to save you, so I went with him." She saw a deep sadness in her son's eyes.

"Right now, I feel I might've been better off dead," said Byron. He felt his world coming in around him.

"Byron, don't say that. Your life gave me strength." Olivia felt fear in her heart. "My life would have had no meaning." She looked at him and then at Madison. "I am so sorry for you." She watched Madison bow her head.

"You didn't know the man—your father, like I did; he was a tyrant. He wanted to take my beautiful daughter, Alyssa and mar her eyes to look Japanese like mine unless I had his baby. So I let him . . ." She turned her head from them. "It wasn't love. It was degrading, and I thanked God every day that, after that one time, I had his twins—these twins." Olivia said and again acknowledged them by nodding toward the twins. She felt the whole truth had to be brought out in the open.

"Are you insane? You lying bitch! My mother died when I was born," Mika shouted. Naked, she ran from under her blanket and swooped on Olivia. Forcefully, she knocked her down to the floor, but Olivia did not fight her.

"No, she's not lying. Grandmother saw her today at the boutique, and they both knew right away," Madison screamed. She hurriedly grabbed her sister and held her away from Olivia. "She's our mother, and Byron's our half brother," She painfully explained as tears fell from her eyes. A deep sorrow showed in her eyes and she could feel her heart crack as she looked at the man she loved.

"Oh my God," Byron whispered. He abruptly ran his hands through his hair and then almost yanked it out of his head. "I can't believe it. All this time . . ." He got up and pulled his pants on not caring who saw what. "If we had . . . we might have . . ." he added, putting all the pieces together in his mind.

"Mika could've had your baby," Madison explained. She looked her sister in the eyes and pulled her even closer to her. "Get your clothes on and pack up your shit 'cause you're no longer my sister or my roommate . . . just get the hell out of here," She said calmly as she glared at her through clenched teeth. She continued to stare into her sister's eyes with a hate she had never felt before in her life.

"Damn it—it's just sex," Mika said with a laugh. "And he's not the great lover you keep talking about." She commented brazenly. Madison held her sister at arm's length and knocked her to the floor.

"Maddy, honey, . . ." Byron ran to Madison and took her in his arms. "Leave her alone she's not worth it." He coddled her as Madison buried her head in his chest and sobbed.

"None of you are fucking worth it," Mika finally said. She hastily got up from the floor and went to pack her things.

"All this is my fault! Even though I couldn't give love I should have cared for my babies," Olivia said. She slowly got up from the floor and went to sit on a nearby chair.

"I was not myself back then. Mikail took me away from my family. I felt abandoned. Nothing around me was familiar. Alyssa and I—we were on our own. I took care of her the best way I knew how," said Olivia as Byron and Madison continued to hold on tight to each other.

"I am so sorry, Madison, but your father was a ruthless man back then, and even though I feared him I stood my own ground." Olivia looked at her daughter. "I hated everything about him. I know this sounds cold now, but you and your sister were him all over, and I couldn't love any part of him." She felt her warm tears. "I'm so sorry, but knowing how it was back then, I would do it again to save you, Byron." She looked at her son with pleading eyes.

Byron was starting to remember some of what his mother and father had told him about the time when they learned his mother had been living only miles away from them as Aivilo Yasieu, the widow of Mikail Yasieu.

"I'll never forget my high school interview with you at the Yasieu Art Gallery. You were the most incredibly beautiful woman I had ever seen," said Byron.

Madison looked up at him and then held him as close as she could in her embrace. "Byron this might be our last time." Her tears constricted her throat.

"I know," was all Byron could say. He too held onto her as if his life depended on it. "I know," he said again.

They both sobbed bitter tears as Mika ran from her room carrying her bags and, without a word, slammed the front door as she left the loft.

"You both look so much alike," Byron said.

"It's not your fault. It all started when I first met you at the café." Madison told him. "I fell for you right away, but Mika wanted to play again and trade places the way we have done all our lives. So she's the one who met you at the club that night, not me," Madison said.

Byron remembered. "I thought you seemed different that night," he said.

Madison added. "And that really wasn't the first time you had contact with her. She purposely made herself up as a blonde and bumped into you right after you and I first met at the café."

"Yeah, I remember that too. I thought she looked familiar, like maybe someone in one of my classes. You both can sure put on different faces," he said. He saw a hurt look in her eyes. "I'm sorry, Maddy, but it's true."

"You're right, and I should've stopped it, but I didn't: like at the club that night when first you saw Lady Godiva. You know when Allie had too much to drink and 'we' came back here to the loft . . ." Madison tried to explain as Byron held her in his arms and nodded a yes. "She told me she made a play for you at the club. Then she told me you certainly were not her type and even discouraged me from dating you. Well, later that evening we made the switch. Remember when she went to change her clothes?" She saw a look of acknowledgement in his eyes.

"I remember. I thought I'd messed up so much that night that I'd never get another date with you, but then . . ."

She finished it for him. "I made the eggs," she said, with a slight smile.

"Then you're the one I fell in love with. Your sister came on to me like wildfire, but you let me be myself," Byron said. He took her chin and gently stroked her soft cheek. "No matter how this turns out . . ." With care, he tried to wipe the flowing tears from her face and lips. "Always remember it was you I fell in love with," he whispered. His tears continued to flow. "I'll always love you in my heart . . . I will never forget the tang of your perfume . . ." He buried his head into the curve of her neck.

Olivia felt too paralyzed to move. "I am so sorry for you both, but I have to tell you something that's very important, and it's something I want you both to remember for the rest of your lives," Olivia said, in an almost inaudible whisper. She had their full attention. "Mikail had my eyes altered to mark me as his own. Every time I looked in the mirror, I knew I was his property." She looked like she was in a trance.

"Mom, don't," said Byron. He continued to hold Madison.

"I have to tell you all of it," Olivia continued. "Don't think I hate the Japanese. It was the man I despised. His nationality had nothing to do with it. I'm sorry, Madison, but your father was a very arrogant, manipulative man. At least until the last time I saw him, and then something in him seemed to change. I believe it was his love for you two girls that changed him for the better," she said. Purposely, she diverted their eyes.

"I'm so sorry you had to go through that," Madison said to Olivia. She then gazed into Byron's eyes.

"I had many Japanese friends, which mainly included Mr. Ti and his family. He opened up a new world for me in the fashion world, and it was because of him that I started my own business. He was a great man and I loved him dearly," Olivia continued. "The world was a sad place back then and as horrible as it is to even think it, it is even harder to say aloud. Back then I think the Japanese descendants were easy pickings," she said, trying to explain her views to them. "During the war, although many Japanese-Americans were second generation United States citizens, they were thrown into the internment camps because of their looks, and that included me," she continued. "People were scared, but it was wrong. When you lose your freedom, you lose your dignity," Olivia explained. Her warm tears continued to flow.

"Mom, when I first met you back then everybody called you the mysterious Mrs. Yasieu, but I saw you as a strong, very capable woman," said Byron, which was something that Madison was hearing for the first time. "I admired you and I remember I felt like I wanted to protect you." Byron led Madison to the sofa where they sat near Olivia.

"Byron, my heart melted when I saw you that day, but how could I, a stranger, tell you I was your mother?" she calmly asked. "When you sat across from me, I knew I had made the right decision to save you."

"Hattie, your sister Alyssa's nursemaid, left Alyssa with Yoshiema at the Yasieu Gallery until I was freed from the camp and could join her. For two years Alyssa lived without me. She has never spoken with me about that time, but I know she has to have scars." She flinched at the idea of her daughter alone all those years.

"Dad and I lived without you too," Byron said. He bowed his head. He knew he was hurting her but felt he had to say it. "I'm sorry, Mom, but . . ."

Madison butted in. "All I remember is boarding schools for myself and Mika. That was the only way of life we knew until grandmother sent for us and started to take care of us. I don't remember my father, and we were always told our mother died at our birth. There was no reason to question it," said Madison.

Olivia continued to explain. "None of this is your fault. I take full blame. Oh God, how one decision in your life can affect the lives of so many. After Mikail's death I should have at least made sure you two girls were taken care of, but the bitterness was . . ." She could only turn her head and sob into her hands. "I'm so sorry. I can't even look at you both—I'm so ashamed."

They knelt in front of her. "Please don't, I can't bear to see all this pain. I feel awful about this, and

I know we can't change it; we are forced to live with it," Madison said. She took the hand of the woman she now knew was her mother and gently kissed the top of it. "I loved you as Byron's mother, and now I will love you as mine," Madison whispered as she looked into her mother's eyes.

Olivia cradled both of her children in her arms, and they sobbed together until Byron and Madison fell to the floor and held onto each other at their mother's feet. *I should have done it all differently,'* Olivia despairingly thought to herself. She watched them desperately hold and caress one another enough to last a lifetime.

***

"Oh God, Madison, I'm so sorry for you. I know you and Byron were so much in love back then," Lyssa said to Madison. They were still in Madison's office at Martha's Cinnamon Rolls café.

"It was horrible and I haven't been in touch with my sister, Mika since then. She could be dead for all I know," Madison explained about a time in her life that forever changed her. "Now I have a wonderful husband and two beautiful children, a boy and a girl." She took a picture out of her apron pocket. "I keep it with me always," she said, with a bright smile, as Lyssa looked at the snapshot.

"Beautiful family, I'm happy for you," Lyssa said and then added. "I was a brat back then." She again saw that look of sadness in Madison's eyes.

"It was a long battle and it took me a long time to get over Byron," Madison said. She looked at the photograph of her family. "They saved me. Without them, I don't know what I would've done back then.

"You must have met your husband soon after all that happened." Lyssa said.

"Yes I did. You see, my brother is a professor at the university, and he set me up with one of his professor friends. My husband's a straight arrow, nothing like my brother," Madison said, which surprised Lyssa.

"I didn't know you had a brother," Lyssa said.

"I didn't know either, and he's actually my half brother. Grandmother introduced me to him. I guess after my fiasco with Byron, she thought she had better come clean with all our dirty laundry." Madison saw a puzzled look on Lyssa's face.

"I think I remember. Didn't you say you spoke with Martha back then about your grandmother?" Lyssa asked.

"Yes, I was telling Martha about my grandmother and how she was not as loving as Byron's family," Madison said.

"Did you by any chance tell Martha your grandmother's name?" Lyssa asked. She gave Madison a curious look.

"Yes I did, and now that you mention it that's when she had her heart attack. Oh God, do you think she knew then that Olivia was my . . ." Madison had a look of horror in her eyes.

"Maybe, but even if she did, it's not your fault that she died," said Lyssa as the office phone rang.

"Excuse me," Madison said. She calmed herself and answered her private line. "It's Andy for you." She handed the receiver to Lyssa and reached for a tissue to wipe her eyes.

"Oh gosh, I'm sorry; I didn't know it was this late. I'll catch a cab and be there in a little bit," she said. She handed the phone back to Madison. "He's waiting to go to supper with me. Would you want to join us?" Lyssa asked.

Madison got up quickly from her seat. "Oh no, I'm late myself. I didn't know we talked this long either. I'm sure the kids are starving," said Madison.

Lyssa also got up from her seat, and they both picked up their belonging as they walked to the outside door. "I mean it, Madison, don't blame yourself about Martha. Life's too precious to dwell on the past, and I'm sure she wouldn't want you to."

"I know," said Madison. "She was such a sweet, caring person. If she had lived and told us what she knew it would have saved a lot of heartache."

Lyssa nodded in agreement. "If you don't mind, I'll come by and see you again sometime."

Madison unlocked the door to let her out of the café. "I would like that, and if you see Byron, let him know I'm doing fine," Madison said, as they walked outside.

"I will," Lyssa said, as Madison grabbed her and gave her a quick hug.

"I'm glad we had this time together. You've turned into a beautiful young woman," Madison said sincerely. "Have a good life, Lyssa," She had a hint of sadness in her eyes. She thought she might never see Lyssa again and that her words to come back and visit again were simply a sympathetic fabrication.

"You too," said Lyssa. She hailed a cab.

How sad, Lyssa thought. The cabby had put her bags in the trunk and seated her in the cab. *I'm sure if she can let the past go she'll have a happy life,* she thought as she looked out the back window of the cab and watched Madison close and lock the door of the café. Madison was out of her sight when the cab turned the corner.

Chapter Five

Over the years, personal lives changed—as they always do—and during that time the vibrant leaves of Red Winds fell from the trees with an air of sadness all around them.

"I will never forget you, Grammy," Christy cried. She dressed in pink for the funeral. "I don't care what anybody says I'm wearing your favorite color." She looked at herself in the freestanding mirror and adjusted the bright fabric of her suit.

Later that day, it felt as if she were walking in a dream state. She followed with the rest of the family as they carried Grammy's coffin the short distance to the Red Winds cemetery.

"Shed no tears for me. Until we meet again, only think of me at peace with those I love" were the words the minister read at the gravesite. "Remember, man, that thou art dust and to dust thou shall return. So this is my body, but the spirit of my love will always be with you," the minister continued.

Christy did not hear any more of the funeral services, nor would she allow herself to comprehend what transpired before her. She walked throughout the rest of the day in a trance and was happy when the dark of night hid the sorrow and tears in her eyes.

I'm going to miss you so much, Christy thought. She sat in the cold, gloomy room and watched the flicker of the firelight. *We always knew this day would come and you prepared me, but I never knew the emptiness would cut so deep. Thank God you were at home, in your own bed.* She dabbed at her now dry eyes.

Reggie came in and sat next to her. "Grammy left this for you." Christy turned and accepted a large envelope. "You know how she was. She made me promise not to give it to you, and these were her very words, 'Not until I'm in the ground'." Christy received a loving hug from Grammy's long time caregiver and was left alone to open her envelope in private.

"Oh, Grammy, thank you. Now I don't feel so lonely; you really are still with me," she said aloud. She held the envelope close to her heart, reached over, and turned on a lamp.

The letter began:

> My dearest Christina, Yes, I am calling you by your given name. Just like Christy, Christina is a beautiful name and was given to you by your mother. We knew your mother possessed a renegade spirit, but I must tell you she loved you with a true mother's heart.

"Holy shit, don't tell me some family gossip is finally going to be revealed," Christy commented and continued to read.

> Remember all those years ago when we first started the gossip? Well, after we would drop you off at home and before driving me to the hospital to make my visit, Wolfgang would sometimes drive me to the other side of town where I met with Sean Linder of the Linder Law Firm.

Christy, now curious, stopped reading and thought, *Now what's she up to.* She looked around the room, feeling she was not alone. "God it feels like you're right here talking gossip," she said with a slight chuckle.

Sean Linder has been commissioned by me to deliver a communication to you from me regarding a specific event in your life. I'm not saying he's following you all the time, but he will keep in touch with you at special times in your life—like when you graduate from school, on commemorative birthdays, on your wedding day, and for other events that will explain themselves.

God she's wonderful and so mysterious, Christy thought and read on.

With that said, let's talk about husbands.

Christy raised her eyebrows. "God I'm fifteen and she's got me married off already." She got up from her seat and started to pace around the room. *This is almost as thick as a book. It must have taken her forever to manually write all this down,* Christy thought. She put the treasured correspondence back in the bulky envelope and went to her bedroom. *I'm glad everybody's leaving me alone. I guess they know I need some space,* she thought, as she showered.

She then got ready for bed. "Okay here we go—all nice and cozy in my pj's with one of Grammy's old quilts." She adjusted the bed lamp as she snuggled into the blanket. "Let's see what this husband stuff's all about." She picked up the envelope from her bedside table and began to read. In this way, she could continue the gossip with Grammy.

Honey, remember when my husband finally came home from the hospital after all that rehabilitation he needed because of his heart attack? Okay, I know you always called him your second grandpa, but remember how happy he was when you just called him plain old

Grandpa? So with that in mind, I'll abide by that and that's what we'll call him: Grandpa.

As Christy read, she thought back to that time with an understanding of great love and respect for life. Christy remembered how the natural warmth of the sun on that particularly cold February day had filtered through the blinds on the porch and filled the room with a welcomed heat. *I don't see why I couldn't have gone with them;* she remembered how she felt about that time so many years ago.

"Yeah, yeah, kids aren't allowed in that hospital. Crap! When will I ever be old enough to do anything?" She was saying to herself when she heard the front door open.

"We're home." She heard Grammy's voice as she ran from the porch to the front room. "Honey, let Reggie help you out of your coat," Grammy told her husband when he spotted Christy.

"Pumpkin," he called out. He released one of his hands from his portable walker to hug Christy.

"Grandpa," she said. She thought he looked so much older than when she last saw him. When she hugged him, she saw a twinkle of a tear in his eyes.

"Oh, Pumpkin, you called me Grandpa," Feeling pure delight, he hugged her.

"I know I always called you my second grandpa, but now ... since ..."

He cut her short. "I know," he commented. He gently caressed her small, smooth cheek and could see in her eyes a remembered lost love. "I love it, Pumpkin." Reggie helped him off with his coat, and they all walked to the family room.

"I guess one of these days I'll be using one of those things," Grammy said. She pointed to her husband's walker. "But until then this will work." She cautiously raised her wooden cane.

As her husband slowly made his way, he said, "The doctor said I need it mostly when I'm unsure of myself or until I get used to things around the house. Oh to be home again. I never thought I'd see these walls again." They all sat down on the plush, comfortable sofas, and Reggie left them for some private time.

"I kept the fires going," Christy said. She stood by the fireplace, holding the poker.

"You did a fine job, Pumpkin," Grandpa said and patted a place for her to sit next to him. "Have you been keeping up with your writing?"

"Sure have. I'll let you read some later. I'm spending the whole weekend so we don't have to rush into it," Christy said, as her grandpa hugged her.

"Grammy says you've been a lot of company to her while I was at rehab," said Grandpa.

"I don't know what I would've done without her company and all the fun we have with the gossip," Grammy said.

Reggie came back into the room. "Supper's ready. All your favorites, but made the healthy way," said Reggie. They all went to the dining room.

After supper, Christy and Grandpa were sitting together in the living room. "I sure missed these times," Grandpa said, as Christy snuggled up to him.

"They wouldn't let me visit," she said, as she wriggled in his arm.

"I know, Pumpkin, but I knew you were thinking about me. I could feel your prayers for my recovery." For a moment, they privately reflected on their own thoughts. "Is that one of your poems?" he asked, pointing to a folder on the coffee table in front of them.

"Yes, if you're ready. They're mostly about how I felt when you were in the hospital, but this one's for today," Christy said and handed it to him.

"Let's see what we have here." He gave her a sly look.

"Today is a good day for me; my grandpa's coming back. He was in the hospital, because his heart had an attack. The doctors fixed him up, and said he is okay."

He gave her a wink and continued to read.

"So now we can get back to the games we used to play: Old Maid and Chutes and Ladders, Whoever wins it never matters.'

He finished reading and opened his arms to her. "You're right, Pumpkin, it doesn't matter who wins as long as we're together." He hugged her, and they both had happy tears in their eyes.

"What'll it be Old Maid or Chutes and Ladders?" he asked. A big smile lit up his tired looking eyes.

"What would you say to a game of chess?" she asked. She squinted up her nose and her eyes opened wide.

"Oh yeah, sounds to me like somebody's growing up enough to make such a challenge. I'm game if you are." He watched her go for the game board.

"Did my poem really make sense to you?" she asked sincerely when she returned. Her innocence showed in her eyes.

"Pumpkin, you have a gift. Keep on writing. You make me proud and so happy," he said. She sat down next to him. "See this part?" He pointed to her poem. "You wrote, 'this is a good day for me', well it is for me too, because I'm so happy to be back with you." He was trying to remove his handkerchief from his pants pocket. "And what you wrote in the essays you sent to me at the hospital; you used such grownup words. I think there's an old spirit in there somewhere." He lightly tapped the top of her head and then used the handkerchief to blow away the tears that were flowing.

"I didn't want to hurt your feelings." She looked at him with caring eyes.

"No, you didn't, baby; you touched my heart. One day you'll be a good parent and understand how you would do anything for

RETURN TO RED WINDS

your children. And hopefully, with God's blessing, the love you share with your children will always be expressed with great big hugs," he said and opened his arms to her.

"Grandpa, I could feel your hugs while you were in the hospital." With love in her eyes, she looked up at him.

"I felt them too, Pumpkin." She continued to sit next to him, and for the moment they forgot the chess game. Quietly, they snuggled, while the firelight flickered and gave them a calm feeling of peace.

***

"Okay, okay I get it, and, Grammy, I do hope one day I find a wonderful man," Christy said to herself. For the moment, she put down Grammy's dissertation to her.

Grandpa was a wonderful, loving man, and he deeply loved you, Grammy, she was thinking. She then remembered the sad day when Grandpa's seemingly resilient spirit departed his physical body. That was another sad day, but thank God he was home. She thought of that day as if it were yesterday. Grammy called the family to their house. Memories of that day came rushing back to her.

"Christy, Grandpa wants to see you," she remembered Grammy saying. Christy had just entered the living room where the family waited. Quickly, she hurried out of the room to Grandpa's room. "He's been holding his own for now. All he's talked about is seeing Christy," Grammy told the family when Christy left the room.

"Grandpa," Christy said softly. She saw his eyes flutter and then open. He was lying on his side of the king-sized bed.

"Pumpkin, I don't want you to mourn me, baby," he said almost inaudibly. "Will you do me a favor?" He motioned for her to come next to him.

"Anything," she whispered. She kept her ear close to him as she took his hand in hers.

"Plant a big oak tree, okay?" He looked directly into her eyes, and she noticed they looked glassy. "It will give you something to hug, baby." He squeezed her hand slightly. "Remember?" he whispered hoarsely, his eyes pleading. He wanted her to know, like they had always talked about, that his hugs could always be felt.

"I will Grandpa . . . I will." She crawled next to him and they hugged each other.

The room was dimly lit and for a split second, when she opened her eyes, Christy thought she saw something that resembled a clear, warm looking liquid ripple in front of her. Then, for a second, the room seemed to brighten. She felt completely close to him, and for an instant believed she felt his spirit passing through her into a bright tunnel. She could see the end of the tunnel and many people standing next to a great figure she believed was Jesus. They all had open arms that seemed to welcome him; then, everything darkened. It was at that very moment that she knew his spirit had departed his physical body.

***

"Oh my God, I don't know how long I lay there before Grammy came into the room, but I know I felt his spirit leave. Thank you, Grandpa, and thanks for the hug tree. You'd love it too." She then remembered planting it.

It was a warm spring afternoon. The trees were still bare, but little buds could be seen starting to pop out at the ends of the branches indicating it was the right time to plant.

"I think he'd love this spot," Grammy was saying to Wolfgang. They all had ridden in the pickup truck to the Red Winds family cemetery to plant the 'big oak tree' and maple saplings. "He always loved to make things special," Grammy said as Wolfgang helped her out of the truck and onto the wrought iron bench.

"Can I start the first hole?" Christy asked.

Wolfgang said, "Be my guest," and happily gave her a long, sharp post-hole digger. With a chuckle and a wink of his eye, he went back to unload the truck. "I'll start the smaller holes for the saplings."

"Could you hold on for a bit?" Christy asked. She went next to Grammy. "Look around, where do you think is a good spot for the new red maples?" She thought the location would be an important one for future generations.

"Just like my son—always caring for others," Grammy said. She caressed Christy's cheek and then looked at their surroundings. "I think the first one over there and then sporadically in that direction," Grammy said, pointing out her decisions.

"Perfect! That's close to where I was thinking too. And for the oak, do you like where I started to dig?" Christy asked. She pointed to where she had left the digger.

"Yes, near enough to both of us," Grammy said. She had a faraway look in her eyes as she thought of her husband.

"Oh Grammy," Christy said, with sadness in her voice.

"Honey, the numbers don't lie. We only have so many of them in our lives, and like Grandpa said, now you'll have something to hug."

Christy hugged her. "I'm going to get as many from you as I can." She hugged her again and then turned to wave an okay to Wolfgang, telling him they could begin planting the trees.

"So many memories," Grammy said to herself. She looked at all the grave markers. *Soon,* she thought. She watched Christy do her best to dig the hole for the oak tree. "She's really going to make a difference in this world," she whispered to herself. She watched Wolfgang go to Christy and start to help with the big hole for the oak. She pulled the hood up on her warm coat, as the soft breeze seemed to call her name. Grammy then nodded off and had a dream.

"Oh my God," The television news reporter continued to repeat in her dream. "The World Trade Center has been hit by what appears to be a plane," the reporter relayed over a breaking news report. "Unbelievable! I can't believe my eyes! The tower's collapsing." The panic was evident in his voice.

"I have to call him," Grammy remembered saying in her dream. She went to the phone and dialed her husband.

"I saw it. I'll be home as soon as I can," her husband said.

She continued to watch the news. "I'm just happy you're safe . . . but what about . . ."

"I don't know; we haven't been in touch since last night," her husband, sounding worried, related to her.

"Stay there and keep trying. I'll stay here. I love you and please be safe," she finally said. She hung up the phone and then watched in horror as the second of the twin towers collapsed. "Oh dear God, help us," she blurted out.

Christy then shouted, "Look Grammy," which woke Grammy from her horrific nightmare.

"I see," Grammy said. She tried to shake off the nightmare. *I seem to dream more lately,* she thought, *but I sure wish I could dream of happier things.*

Christy sat next to her on the bench. "It looked like I woke you up from a nap just now."

"Yes, us old folks . . ."

Christy interrupted her. "I know, you have to take a break every now and then." She chuckled.

"Remember that when you get old," Grammy said and they both laughed.

"What do you think?" asked Christy. They both watched as Wolfgang put mulch around the base of the oak tree.

"Looks beautiful," Grammy said. "Someday it will take three people to stand around it and hug it."

Christy looked at her, a smile lighting up her eyes, and then went to help Wolfgang.

***

"I'll never forget all those memories. One day I truly want to put them down, just like I said I would," Christy said to herself. She took Grammy's letter and placed it back in the envelope and put it on her nightstand.

Thanks again, Grammy, we'll continue the gossip tomorrow." She sighed deeply, pulled the quilt up over her head, and drifted off.

Chapter Six

The opaque light was starting to filter into the room. *Oh God, please let it be true*, .Christy thought and sat up straight in her bed. Quickly, she reached toward her nightstand.

"Thank you, God, and thank you, Grammy." She took the envelope and held it close to her chest. "Oh Grammy," she whispered, "I miss you so, but at least I have these." She caressed the envelope. Her tears fell from her cheeks. "I thought I might have dreamt that you left these for me." She opened the envelope and again started to read.

> My dearest Christina, now for some heartbreaking gossip and something that has to be told and remembered.

"I'm getting used to her calling me Christina. So from this day on that's how I'll be called," Christy, now taking on her given name, said to herself. "I guess I'm growing up if she feels I can hear some of the heartbreaking gossip." She opened her eyes wide and lifted her eyebrows, and continued to read.

> This is the tragic gossip about Olivia and Ronald's daughter, Alyssa Brown. To make it clear why this happened, you have to understand Alyssa's formative years. The gossip goes that for many years, to hide their

true identity, Alyssa and Olivia remained sequestered from the outside world in the upstairs living quarters of the Yasieu Art Gallery in New York City.

Christina thought, *Holy crap, now I'm going to get some of the good stuff.* She continued to read.

I'm sure you have already heard bits and pieces of this over the years, but let me say that Olivia truly believed that by remaining incognito as Aivilo and not revealing her true identity, she was protecting her children and Ronald.

Yeah, I heard a little about that, Christy thought and read on.

After Olivia's horrendous two year internment in the Japanese-American camp, she joined her daughter, Alyssa, who had been living under the strict, uncaring custody of Mikail Yasieu's mother, Yoshiema, at the Yasieu Art Gallery. It was then that Olivia's strong, capable personality changed and a deep depression turned her into an unmoving recluse.

That was one little bit of gossip I never heard about, Christina was thinking. Amazed, she continued on.

But then, at the Yasieu Art Gallery, after a shocked Rachel spotted Olivia's painting at the gallery and confronted a very alive Olivia, Rachel left. Olivia's daughter, Alyssa, overheard Yoshiema and her mother arguing about Yoshiema placing Olivia's unique painting for public viewing. It was then that Alyssa became aware that Olivia had been living the lie as Aivilo Yasieu, and her real name was Olivia Brown, with an estranged family. Alyssa knew nothing about it, even though she lived only miles away from them. Finding it hard to believe that her mother could keep such information from her, a traumatized Alyssa forced her mother to come out of hiding and, with Rachel's assistance, again find her place with her family. Unfortunately, the family did not know how living a secluded life had affected Alyssa. And, at this point, Christina, I must say these following words are harsh and very graphic, and I apologize for that. So, if you think you might not be old enough and want to wait and read this at some other time that is perfectly okay.

No way, not when I finally get to choose for myself if I'm old enough. Christina chuckled and read on.

It was the day before Christmas and the streets of New York City were covered in snow, but the airport was open. Byron, now a professor at the university, Alyssa—a student going for her master's degree in psychology— and Lyssa and Andy Yarborough were scheduled to meet the following morning and fly home together to Kansas. Fate, however, had a different agenda planned for them.

"Oh God, that's Lyssa over there with him," Madison blurted out. She was serving a customer at her café, Martha's Cinnamon Rolls. "Here take over," she said in Japanese to one of her employees. She then hurried to the front door of the café.

"Lyssa!" she yelled and waved, "Lyssa!" Lyssa did not see or hear her, and Madison could only watch as Lyssa and Madison's half brother, Walter Striker, ran to his car and they sped away. *I have to get in touch with Byron.*

Walt's too wild for her, and is probably old enough to be her grandfather,' she thought. She went into her private office and closed the door.

"Byron!" Madison said, with shaking hands, after waiting for over an hour to finally reach him by telephone.

"Yes," she heard him say. Her heart melted at the sound of his voice.

"It's me, Madison." She could almost feel his surprise from his silence.

"It's been a long time," he said.

She heard a hint of sadness in his voice. "I wouldn't have called, but something of great importance has just come to my attention. Could you possibly meet me here at my shop?" she asked.

"Yes, and I know where it is. Lyssa told me some time ago," he said. "I can be there in about an hour." Their last kiss flashed in his mind.

"That would work. The shop will be closed and we can talk privately," she then said. She quickly hung up the phone without saying good-bye.

God, what can this be about? Byron thought. He looked at the buzzing receiver in his hand as he slowly hung it on the hook and left his apartment.

"Hey brother, just the man I was looking for," he heard his sister Alyssa say when he was about to get into his car. "What's the hurry?" she asked. She saw a familiar look in his eyes. "It's a woman . . . you're going to see a woman, I can tell." she teased. "Well it took you long enough." She wanted to tease him some more until she saw that familiar look of hurt in his eyes.

"It's Madison. She called and asked to see me," Byron said.

She went to him. "Oh God, Byron, are you sure you should go? It can only lead to more heartache." She knew they had not kept in touch with Madison since that tragic time when they found out she was their half sister.

"I know she's gone on with her life. She married and has a family. I know that's important to her and something she would never jeopardize." He saw the caring in his sister's eyes. "She said something of importance has come to her attention that she thinks I should be aware of so . . ." He dangled his keys and started for the driver's side of his car.

"Well, maybe seeing her again can put some closure on all of our 'family' business and you might find someone for yourself," said Alyssa, as her brother started to chuckle.

"Always trying to figure everybody out, aren't you sister? And what about you, when are you going to find someone?" He was teasing her until he saw a sad look in her eyes.

"I learned that lesson a long time ago; besides, I would only hurt some big galoot." She tried to smooth over the hurt she felt, as she watched him get behind the steering wheel. She motioned for him to call her when he got back from his visit with Madison.

As he approached the door of the café, he saw that the lights were dim and the closed sign was lit in the window.

"Hi," she said and quickly opened the door for him. "I saw you coming." She closed the door. "My husband knows . . ." She was going to tell Byron that her spouse knew about their private meeting when Byron interrupted her.

"We were engaged to be married. I know what a dedicated woman you are," he said. He saw a slight blush redden her cheeks.

"And you're always the gentleman. You haven't married?"

"No. Maybe one day, but not . . ." He was trying to avoid the subject.

"You'll find someone one day. You're a wonderful man." She saw him stop in his tracks.

"You painted that?" He was staring at a large painting behind a group of tables.

"Yes."

"We were so happy that day. The snow was hitting us in the face, but we didn't care. We were young and so much in love." He was recollecting a time that now could only be remembered with sadness.

"Painting it helped me resolve a lot of feelings." She looked at him knowing he understood what she meant. "I wanted something to hold onto, but at the same time to let go of. I know you are one person who can understand that, but I truly hope it doesn't offend you or hurt your feelings." She was a caring person to this day.

"Look at us running from the barn to the house. It looks like what I felt back then. You're really a good artist, and from what I've heard, Martha would sure be proud of her namesake cinnamon rolls." He looked away from the painting and saw her staring at him.

"We had . . ." she stopped. "I don't think we should go back to those times." She had a slight blush on her cheeks. "I am happy now, and I pray one day you will be too." "Here, let's take a seat," She pointed out one of the chairs to him, and they both sat down.

"Byron, something that I believe is really important has come to my attention." She came right to the point, knowing the players involved at that time might not be on their side. "I saw my half brother, Walter Striker with . . ." She noticed Byron had an unbelieving look in his eyes.

"Oh God, Professor Striker is the half brother you told Lyssa about. She never really mentioned his name," Byron said. He scratched his head and looked as if he was trying to remember something. "Holy shit, he's the guy I saw messing around with Alyssa. You know, way back when we first went to the club with Lady Godiva." He noticed she did not understand what he was talking about. "Oh God, not you, that was . . ." he stammered and she helped him out.

"I know, it was when Mika was playacting to be me," Madison said. She noticed him nodding a yes.

"But what you don't know, since you actually weren't there, is that Professor Striker was making out with Alyssa outside of the club by the side of the building. When Alyssa saw me coming, she accidentally knocked him in the head and gave him a bloody nose. He knew I recognized him, but he sure didn't seem to care," he continued. "Oh God, the way they were acting I don't think that was their first time. I think those two had something going on before then." He got up from his seat and started to pace around the room.

"Walter introduced me to my husband back then. I think Walter thought my husband's dignified personality held him back from the ladies, so he was glad that we enjoyed each other's company and finally married," Madison said. She tried not to get too personal or hurt

Byron's feelings. "Walter is really not a very nice guy," she then said. She watched him continue to pace. "He has women all over him all the time. He almost wears them like his personal belongings." She seemed embarrassed that she was related to him.

"I'm betting he's the one who got Alyssa pregnant back then," Byron then said. Madison remembered Alyssa's miscarriage.

"Oh God, we have to stop her." There was panic in Madison's voice.

Byron yelled, "I just saw Alyssa, and she wouldn't go near that son of a bitch with a ten foot pole."

"Not Alyssa, Lyssa. Lyssa Yarborough," Madison said. She saw Byron's face turn white. "He took over our loft after . . ." She knew he understood she meant after they broke off their engagement and their lives had changed.

"Let's go . . . I'll drive," Byron said. They grabbed their coats and Madison locked up the café.

"Maddy, I'm really happy for you, and I bet your babies are just as beautiful as you." He was driving through the congested traffic. "When you think about it, it's no wonder we were so much alike."

"I know, because we have some of the same blood." She hoped, as he tried to keep his eyes on the road and with the darkness in the car, he didn't see the tears in her eyes. "You're the only one who calls me Maddy," she whispered.

"Is it okay?" He still cared about her feelings and tried to catch a glimpse of her face.

"Sure," she said.

"I still have my key to the loft. I'm betting he only spends his money on his women and never changed the lock," she said, in a matter-of-fact way. "What's the plan?"

"I guess we'll have to see what we're up against and go from there."

He parked the car in front of the building. "No lights up there, but that doesn't mean anything." He then got out of the car and went to open her door.

"Thanks," she said, remembering him during happier times.

"I almost hope they're not up there," Byron said, as they entered the building and reached the loft.

"It's working," Madison said, as the key clicked and she opened the door. *Oh God, candles,* she thought, *just like before.* Suddenly, they heard moans coming from the living room. He looked at her with compassion in his eyes.

"Lyssa," Byron yelled as four heads popped up from a large mat on the carpeted floor and a naked woman ran toward one of the bedrooms.

"What the hell . . ." Walter shouted as two other women, one over his head and the other sitting on his middle, scurried under a blanket.

"Lyssa get out here!" Byron yelled.

"You son of a bitch," he yelled at Walter and then swiftly backhanded him on the face. Walter fell back on the mat when Lyssa, then fully clothed, ran from the bedroom and out the front door.

"She left," Madison yelled as Walter looked at her in disbelief.

"Not becoming of a university professor," Byron said, looking at the naked older man sprawled on the makeshift bed. "And from the looks of these two, I'd say jail bait," he added as the young girls put their blankets around themselves and ran to a bedroom.

"Get the fuck out of here. And since you're not as opened-minded as your twin you must be Nina; you bitch, stay away from me," Walter was saying, as Byron started for the professor with rage in his eyes. Madison caught his arm.

"He's not worth it, and we have to hurry and find her," Madison said, encouraging him to leave.

"You bastard, you're the one who better stay away," Byron pointed his finger and yelled at the professor as they were leaving the loft to look for Lyssa.

"She was supposed to meet Andy at the hotel by the airport, so I'm guessing that's where she's headed," said Byron as they got into his car and sped off to the hotel.

***

Damn it, why does everybody have to treat me like a kid, Lyssa thought after she directed the cabby to take her to Alyssa's apartment.

"Lyssa, what's going on? You look like shit." said Alyssa when she let Lyssa into her apartment.

"It's your goddamn Puritan brother. You'd think I was still a kid," said Lyssa as she flopped down on a sofa. Alyssa brought her a glass of water.

"What happened?" Alyssa asked.

"God, I'm a big girl . . . no I'm a woman and for pity's sake, I like sex, all right?" Lyssa spit out, not feeling any remorse for what she had been doing.

"Just because your brother has this high-and-mighty idea about waiting until he's married to have sex doesn't mean everybody else thinks like that. He pisses me off so bad." She could feel her blood pressure rising, as Alyssa watched her and let her ramble on.

"You know Byron and I have been seeing each other lately. I've loved him my whole life, but . . ." Lyssa shouted and glared at Alyssa. "God, I have urges that he can't satisfy . . . or won't . . . damn it, why couldn't he just leave me alone?" she yelled. "If he had just put out a little, this wouldn't have happened." She looked completely agitated.

"Slow down. So what happened?" Alyssa asked again.

"I was with Walt at his loft when your holier-than-thou brother walked in on us. Pardon me, but I don't want to wait and Walt's great. Who cares if he's older; he's got the . . ."

Alyssa started to understand. "I hope you're not talking about Wally Striker?" Alyssa asked. She saw from Lyssa's expression that he was the one. "Oh God, that man can't keep his pecker in his pants." Lyssa gave her a stunned look. "That bastard got me pregnant, and who knows how many bastards he's got out there," added Alyssa. She then recognized a look on Lyssa's face that scared her.

"Oh God! Oh God!" Lyssa kept saying until she finally buried her head in her hands and started to sob.

"Don't tell me . . ." said Alyssa, with fear evident in her eyes. She took Lyssa by the shoulders, shook her, and then looked her straight in the eyes.

"Yes, I'm pregnant, and Walt's the father." Lyssa said. She looked at Alyssa and thought she looked as if she might explode.

Alyssa lost all the control she had successfully gained throughout the years after the depressed times when she had lived at the Yasieu Gallery. "It's time that man paid," Alyssa then said. She got up and went for her purse and coat. "I'll find a way. Don't wait up," she said to Lyssa. She walked out of her apartment and slammed the door.

Lyssa felt like she was in shock. She could feel perspiration under her arms and a warm flush fill her body. She felt faint and bowed her head as tears flowed down her cheeks. She stared at the door that Alyssa had just slammed.

∗∗∗

In this part, Christina, you will have to forgive some more of the expletives. Understand that all the facts may never be completely known. From what has been explained in the gossip, Alyssa lost all of her ability to think like a rational woman. She went on a shopping spree and used her credit card to buy an expensive evening gown with all of the accessories, and then she rented a cherry red sports car. I hate to relay this to you, but it is a part of our lives and has to be told because it was about a beautiful woman who lived and loved.

Christy read more of the gossip that explained how Alyssa went to the loft and found Professor Striker alone and then tried to picture it as she continued reading.

"Are you ready?" Alyssa said to the professor when he answered her knock at his door.

"For what, who are you?" the professor asked. He did not remember setting any date or the woman in front of him.

"Don't tell me you forgot, you naughty boy—barefoot and only wearing your pants. Don't tease me. You must've been waiting for me." She patted his cheek and walked into his apartment, as he took a deep sniff of her perfume.

"Hey," he said, as he followed her, "I don't . . ."

Alyssa sat on his sofa and slowly took off the fur coat she had just bought. It covered a sexy crimson, skintight gown that revealed an ample portion of her bare breasts.

"Well maybe I was wrong," he said. He watched her sensually part and lick her thick, red lips. "I'm sure I'd never have forgotten those long, red nails," he whispered, with a heavy pant in his voice. He felt his pulse race when she started to suck one of her fingers as her eyes passionately looked down from his eyes to his chest and then linger on his loins.

"I knew you'd remember," Alyssa murmured, purposely letting one of her long, sleek legs slide through the lengthy slit at the side of her dress. Slowly, she lifted a spiked, scarlet high heal onto the coffee table exposing her naked self to him.

"I see you want some of this," he said seductively. He quickly unbuttoned his pants and stripped, standing fully ready, like the stud he thought she wanted him to be. He then sat next to her and slowly ran his hand up her leg and fondled her until she squirmed and panted for more. "God, you're a horny bitch," he whispered. He watched her pull down her top and get on her hands and knees while he played with her breasts.

"Now," she screamed. She pulled the bottom of her gown up around her waist, and he knew what to do with her.

"Got to . . ." he was saying and started fumbling for a condom in the drawer in the table next to the sofa.

"Forget it," she blurted out, turning her head, as she arched her back and then bending over—forcefully pressing him so hard to her that he was compelled to enter her.

He kept saying, "God, you're the horniest . . ." as she continued to wriggle around until they were both spent and finally fell to the sofa.

"Best fuck you've ever had," Alyssa said, with a confident air about her.

"Not bad, but I still . . ." the professor began while his black eyes looked into hers. "You kind of look familiar, but . . ." He ran his hand through his graying hair.

"Maybe you had too much to drink that night." She noticed he rolled his eyes. "Well, since you don't remember our making this date, I'll remind you that it's all on me and we're going to the best restaurant in town," Alyssa then said. She got up from the sofa and went directly to the bathroom.

Well, I can see you've been here before, so I must know you, he thought when she acted right at home. He stooped to put on his pants. *I must be getting old if I'm forgetting one like this sex craved . . .* He was still thinking when she came back into the room.

She was fully in charge of the situation and took the prerogative to go through his closet and bring his formal suit to him. "Here, put on your tux. Like I said, we're going to . . ."

"I know the best restaurant in town," he interjected, "but could you at least tell me your name? I mean, after all, we did just . . ." He kept talking, as he went to his bathroom, freshened up, and put on his tux.

"Don't you like surprises? I like surprises." She said cheerfully. She took her makeup mirror from the evening bag that perfectly matched her gown, reapplied her lipstick, and tidied her hair. When he came out fully dressed, she purred, "Dressed to kill." She went to him and openly ran her fingernails around the zipper of his suit pants, caressing his forever-stiff manhood. "You're always ready, aren't you, Wally?" She saw a bit of recognition in his eyes when she said his name, so she instantly tried to take his mind off his trying to figure out her name.

"God, you're so horny," he said when she mischievously wrapped her leg around him as he bent down and began to kiss and lick her soft, bulging breasts. When he started to reach between her legs and play with her again, she abruptly stopped him.

"Later. Right now I'm famished, and we have a reservation," she said, in a carefree way, but purposely continued to rub up to him and let him pet her.

"Flirty, prick teaser," he panted as she took his hand and made him play with her until she was satisfied.

"When it comes to being insatiable, I think you've met your match." She smacked his behind and then walked to the front door of the loft. He followed, head down like a dejected paramour, and they left the loft.

"You have excellent taste," he complimented her, as the waiter brought them the wine of her choice and filled their goblets.

"Only the best for you tonight." She licked her fading red lips, tipped the glass of wine his way, and took a long drink of the sweet liquid. "Only the best." She smiled sweetly, while reaching for the chilling bottle and refilling her glass.

"What did I ever do to deserve such attention?" Curiously, he looked at her and only took a small drink of the wine. "You're a classy wench," he whispered. He rubbed her leg through the slit and tried to reach higher when she stopped him.

"Not that I don't go for the thrill to make out in public. I'm just not in the mood right now," she said, wanting to keep up her control.

"Will you excuse me?" She winked. "Powder room," she whispered in his ear. She made sure her breast touched his cheek as she held her glass of wine in her hand and started for the ladies' room. A patron's assistant approached her, and she handed him her glass and he followed her. "Thank you, sweetie," she said to the assistant. She noticed the professor could not take his eyes off of her, as she glided with ease across the floor.

I'm getting another piece of that, he was thinking. He looked around the room and saw many other men and some women also watching her.

"Hello, Mama." Alyssa said to Olivia. She had called her from the ladies' room.

"Alyssa, what's wrong?" she questioned her daughter. "You sound . . ." Olivia wanted to say frantic, but Alyssa interrupted her.

"Mama, I don't have much time. You have to get Rachel and come to my apartment. Lyssa needs her mother right now. I can't explain, but we're not going to make our flight tomorrow. Believe me, Lyssa needs her mother right now." That was all Alyssa would say to her mother. She then hung up the telephone. She looked in the mirror and fixed her makeup. Although she felt sad, she made herself smile before leaving to return to their table.

"Miss me?" she whispered and blew on the back of the professor's neck. She bent low next to him, making certain he got a good look at her wares as she hugged him. She wriggled her behind, while the patron's assistant strained to keep a straight face, keeping his distance until she neared her chair and he seated her. In an instant, the waiter brought her a fresh glass and filled it with the chilled wine.

"We're ready for our appetizers," Alyssa then said to the headwaiter. She felt completely in charge as she watched him snap his fingers and saw another waiter approached with hors d'oeuvres, which included butterfly shrimp, cheese, and fruit. "I'm famished." Her eyes opened wide, as the professor, intrigued, watched her dip the large, firm shellfish in hot butter, slowly lick it, and then devour it.

"I can see you're starting to feel more in the mood," he murmured. He watched her lick the greasy juice from her fingers, ravenously grab another shrimp, and do the same thing. She acted like she could not get enough. "I see you like to eat." He had an eager look in his eyes. "Normally, I don't like to watch people eat, but you make it look so exciting." Passionately, he looked from her breasts to her eyes.

"You know it." She crossed her legs and took the point of her high heal and gently poked him in the groin. "Still at attention I see." She smirked and took another full swig of her wine. She washed her hands in a finger bowl and dried them, as she looked at the waiter and nodded, which cued him to clear the shrimp scraps from the table and bring the plates of prime rib.

"You're incredible," said the professor. He cut into the tender piece of meat. "You know, I don't think I've ever had this much fun in my life." She started to chuckle.

"That's what I wanted to hear." She smiled and watched him completely enjoying himself.

"You're from the university, aren't you?" He could not help but look her over. "You're very beautiful. I know your long, shiny, black hair would cover your naked body in just the right places." He believed he was gaining back control of the evening. "I'd love to . . ." He put his hand on her knee.

"Not yet, Wally," she said his name again. She then slipped her hand under the table and purposely rubbed. Then she squeezed a little harder than he liked.

"Be nice, honey. Don't want to cause any malfunctions with the equipment," he said, as she started to flirt again when the waiter came and asked if they wanted dessert.

"No thank you," Alyssa said, as she winked at Wally, and gave the waiter her credit card. "At least not now," she then added, as the waiter returned and she signed the bill. She rose from her seat and the professor escorted her out of the restaurant.

"You sure like to flaunt it. Like I said before—you're a classy broad." The valet brought her cherry red sports car to the curb.

"I think you actually called me a wench before," she whispered in his ear and then slightly bit it.

"*Huh*," He did not understand what she meant.

"Before, you called me a wench and now I'm a broad. Which is it, Wally?" She generously tipped the valet.

"That usually turns women on." He gave her a bewildered look. He offered to drive but she denied him, so he opened the driver side for her.

He entered the passenger's side. "I can't figure you out. Are you ever going to tell me who you are? Or are we going to eat a sweet dessert at my place?" She put her foot to the throttle and burned rubber when she sped away from the curb. "Holy crap," he blurted out. His head hit the headrest.

"Oh come on, Wally, can't you take a little speed?" She slowed down and pressed the button that controlled the convertible roof.

"Are you nuts . . . its winter." He noticed her looking at him with hate in her eyes. "What's wrong with you?" he screamed, thinking she had lost her mind.

"Come on, Wally, you have to remember me," she taunted. Carefully, she sped out of the city away from traffic.

"You keep calling me Wally, like you know me or something. I only knew one person a long time ago who called me that, but I haven't seen or heard from her in a long . . ." In the limited light, he saw a sign of recognition in her eyes. "Alyssa," he said, as she looked at him with burning tears of fire falling from her eyes. "Oh God, it is you." He looked from her to the window and noticed they were headed for the countryside. "Where are we going?" he yelled, with noticeable panic in his voice.

"We're taking a little midnight ride, Wally," she yelled. A revengeful, bitterness was very apparent in her words. Quickly, she turned up the volume on the radio.

"Wally, you didn't know I miscarried your bastard, did you?" she screamed. They were on a long, lonely country road when she put the car on cruise control.

"What . . ." He could not help but look back and forth from her to the road ahead. "I think you've lost your fucking mind." He saw that she had taken off her seat belt.

"You know, Wally, I do have to give you credit for trying to use a condom tonight," she shouted over the noise of the radio. She then took off her high heels and threw them over her head and out of the convertible. "But you didn't use one when I was young and stupid, did you? No, you got me pregnant." She looked at him and saw the fear she had hoped for.

"I always wear condoms," he screamed at her. Suddenly, he lost control of his bladder and felt the warm urine running down his legs.

"You lie! I know of two times that you didn't—with me and with Lyssa Yarborough." She saw a puzzled look in his eyes.

"Who are you talking about ... damn it. I don't know any ..." She then saw a sign of recognition. "Shit, oh yeah, that's her last name," he said, as she stepped on the gas and he again fell back on the headrest. "Slow down damn it," he yelled, as she laughed and passed a slow moving car.

"You son of a bitch, you got her pregnant and you don't even remember her name. What a bastard ..." She nearly missed a sharp curve in the road. "Oops," she shrieked. She then let out a piercing scream that hurt his eardrums.

"Thank God I lost your bastard," she said with a smirk.

"Hey Wally, Mr. Professor, did you ever hear of Al Capone?" she asked nonchalantly. She thought he looked like he might try to jump out of the car.

"Oh come on, Wally, you're the professor so you must be smart. You know—Al Capone, the gangster. Did you know he died from a sexually transmitted disease?" she prodded and thought he seemed to be in shock. "Poor guy died of syphilis. Did you know you gave me syphilis and who knows whom else?" She thought he looked like he wanted to grab the steering wheel.

"Damn it, I've been clean for over eight years now," he said, as he kept eyeing the steering wheel.

"I wouldn't do that, Wally; we might have an accident." She again let cruise control take over.

"What the hell do you want from me?" he yelled. He ran his fingers through his hair and tried to huddle closer to the seat to shield him against the cold air.

"It's not what I want, Wally. It's what's going to stop," she yelled. "And what's going to stop are your dirty ways of spreading diseases and making bastard babies." He could only stare at her.

He tried to defend himself. "I swear to you, when I found out I had a STD, I always tried to use protection, at least until tonight and back then all those years ago—and then with her," he tried to explain in a matter-of-fact tone that irritated her to her very core. "You both are so fucking horny that I never got the chance to put the damn thing on. So I'd say you both raped me." He noticed her look—so full of rage that robotically she seemed like she could no longer control her actions.

"You tried ... you tried," she screamed. "You bastard ... I hope you enjoyed your goddamn last meal." She rose up on all fours, leaned over the console, and reached for his neck.

"You're crazy!" he screamed, as the car missed the next curve, catapulted into the air, and finally hit a tree, throwing various body parts in many directions.

***

The last thing she remembered was the sound of sirens. When she finally opened her eyes, she could tell she was in the hospital.

"Damn it!" she screamed. She felt like a wrapped mummy. She started to thrash around and tried to pull the tubes out of her body. "I'm supposed to be dead!" she screamed, as her mother stood over her bed.

"Calm down, Alyssa!" Olivia shouted. She pressed the call button and the emergency room nurse came in with a sedative. Alyssa again lost consciousness.

"The doctor said he has to put her in a medicated coma. She's too hysterical right now," Olivia told her family and the Yarboroughs, who were gathered in the hospital waiting room.

"This is all my fault," Lyssa told her mother, Rachel, who put her arm around her daughter to comfort her.

"You can't control what other people do," Rachel said, as she looked at Olivia.

"Your mother's right—this is not your fault," Olivia said, as Ronald came into the room and stood next to her.

"I just talked with a police officer who said they weren't wearing seatbelts, and the car was rented by Alyssa," Ronald said.

Everyone seemed baffled. "We might never find out why she did this," Olivia said, as Lyssa started to sob.

"I'm telling you it's my fault. I told her that Walt, a professor at the university, is the father of the baby I'm going to have," Lyssa said, as Rachel turned and looked at her daughter with shock in her eyes.

"Oh God, Lyssa, you let that man . . ." Rachel began, as she looked at her husband, Cal, who raised his eyebrows.

"I'm not a child mother," Lyssa said. She then looked at Byron and turned her head from his gaze. "You all treat me like I'm still a baby!" she shouted. She got up and ran to the ladies' room.

"Can I go?" Olivia asked, thinking the professor's name seemed like too much of a coincidence to her. Rachel nodded that she could go talk with her daughter.

"Lyssa, we know you're not a baby, and you have to believe that Alyssa did this on her own. She's been dealing with her feelings of trust with men for years. You were young back then, but you have to remember when she had that miscarriage back when Martha passed away," Olivia said to Lyssa, who had locked herself in one of the bathroom stalls.

"Yes, I remember when she had that miscarriage. When I told her I was pregnant with Walt's baby, she went ballistic. So that's why this is all my fault," Lyssa said, with tears falling from her eyes.

"Let me tell you something. This has been coming to a head for a long time. That was one of the reasons Alyssa was majoring in psychology. The class was helping her find herself, and she was getting close to trusting men again," Olivia tried to explain to Lyssa. "She never would tell me his whole name, but I believe it was the man who set her off, not you, honey. Think about it: if you had told her you were pregnant with any other man but this professor, Wally or Walt, whoever he is, she would not have gone off like she did . . . would she?"

Lyssa thought she might be right and came out of the stall. "Probably not, and she did say he was the one who also got her pregnant. She was really angry just talking about him," Lyssa said, starting to believe she did not

RETURN TO RED WINDS

push Alyssa to act like she had and cause the accident. "But the accident killed him and she might . . ."

Olivia took her in her arms. "I know, honey. We just have to pray that she'll be okay," Olivia said. "Now come on, let's go out with the others. You have to know we all love you. Nobody's judging you," she added, as she kept her arm around her and they both went to wait with the others.

After some time, the doctor started bringing Alyssa out of her induced coma. She seemed to have calmed down so he let Olivia and Ronald go in and be with her.

"Mama," Alyssa whispered.

"We're here, honey. Mama and Daddy are here," Olivia said. She caressed her daughter's bandaged head and tried to suppress her own tears when she saw her daughter's swollen, blackened face and missing arm.

"I'm sorry, Mama, but I hated him," Alyssa said, with tears streaming down her battered cheeks.

"You just get better, honey," Ronald said. He took her remaining hand and held it.

"He's dead?" Alyssa asked.

"Yes, honey," Ronald said to her. He could tell his wife was having a hard time talking with their daughter. "Allie, why . . ." he began and noticed his daughter trying to focus on him.

"He was the Wally. Remember, Mama, back when Martha died, when I told you and Aunt Mary about Wally being the father of the baby I miscarried; well, this Walt is the same guy and now . . ." Alyssa stopped when the doctor came into the room and whispered something to Ronald.

"The police officer is outside and has some information for us. I'll be right back," Ronald whispered to his wife and left the room.

"Mama, is Lyssa here? Can I speak with her and Byron?" Alyssa asked.

"I'll get them," Olivia said. She bent and kissed her daughter's forehead and left the room.

"She would like to see you both." Olivia took Lyssa's hand and led her to her son. "Try not to look too surprised because she really looks bad," Olivia then said, as Lyssa and Byron hooked arms and went into Alyssa's room.

"What's going on?" Rachel asked Olivia, as they watched Ronald continue to speak with the police officer.

"I don't know," said Olivia. Ronald shook the officer's hand and walked toward them. "What's that all about?" Olivia asked her husband.

"Well, I hate to say this, but some body parts are still missing," The women cringed. "He also said the professor's full name is Walter Mikail Yasieu Striker." His wife's face went pale and she almost collapsed in his arms. He helped her sit on one of the soft benches. "He was the son of Mikail Yasieu and Junietta Striker." Ronald hurriedly gave them this tragic information.

"Oh my God," Rachel blurted out, as Cal came next to her and they both sat next to Olivia.

"Yasieu, isn't that the same name that Aunt Olivia's daughter, Madison, is related to?" Andy asked, as some shocking information was becoming clear.

"Yes it is, Andy," Rachel said, looking at Olivia with a stunned look in her eyes.

"So that means my sister, Lyssa is going to have . . ." Andy was surmising.

Olivia interjected. "Lyssa's going to have this professor Walter . . . Wally . . . Walt—whatever his name is . . . She' going to have his baby." Olivia stammered. She looked distraught.

"Livi stop. You don't have to go on," Rachel said. She held Olivia's hand.

"Oh God, Rachel, remember how my aunt Junietta tried to seduce my dad? You remember when we were young and they didn't know we were watching from the hayloft . . . remember, we had her stinking nightgown . . ." Olivia whispered for Rachel's ears only. Just then the image of her aunt's naked body slithering near her father filled Olivia's mind and made her shiver. She watched in horror as her father threw Junietta to the floor, disgust evident on his face. Then she remembered how he ordered her aunt off of Red Winds and out of their lives.

"I remember, but you can't talk about that now," Rachel whispered.

"I know Rachel, but I have to make this clear to myself, too." She blinked away tears. "To truly understand this I have to say some things out loud," said Olivia.

Ronald knelt in front of her. "I'm so sorry," he said.

She caressed the side of his cheek. Her sad eyes looked into the eyes of this man who cared so deeply for her. "Me too." She bowed her head.

"Now, Andy, you have to be told something that the rest of us already know, and it's something that will make this even more mind boggling," Olivia said, while Andy stood in front of them. "I know you have been told some of my past, and now I have to tell you that this professor was fathered by Mikail Yasieu, the same Mikail Yasieu who is the biological father of my girls Nina—who we know as Madison—and her twin sister, Mika," Olivia tried to explain. She felt breaking down the exact lineage and history of where and why Mikail Yasieu fit into this scenario could be completely explained to him by Rachel and Cal. She did not want to go into how she felt all those years ago when Mikail forced her to leave her family and go with him.

"But, what you don't know is that this professor's mother, Junietta Striker, was also my mother's sister. This scum of a man—this professor—is also the man who violated my daughter all those years ago." She was desperate to get the foul words out of her mouth and hopefully out of her mind. She saw a look of horror on Rachel's face. She turned to Rachel with uncontrollable tears.

"But we're not related so Lyssa's baby's fine. Come on, Livi, we can't think about that now," Rachel said. She lovingly gave Olivia a sympathetic hug.

"So, if I'm seeing this right . . ." Andy began.

Ronald finished for him. "The professor is Olivia's first cousin," Ronald said. He saw his wife put her head in her hands, so he knew she could not handle saying that at that moment.

Olivia thought if the son was like the father, she could completely understand Alyssa's animosity for the man, but for Alyssa's own sanity, Olivia earnestly prayed that her daughter could find a way to forgive him for what he did to her, the way she had forgiven his father, Mikail Yasieu, for the evil way he had treated her so many years ago. Most of all, she prayed for her daughter's life to be saved.

Byron and Lyssa hurried out of Alyssa's room. "Mom, she's had some kind of a seizure," Byron said. They noticed the crash cart being pushed into her room.

"Oh God, now what?" Olivia shouted.

Later, the doctor came out and told them that Alyssa had suffered a stroke and was again in a medically induced coma.

Months that seemed like years passed, and Alyssa remained conscious but unable to speak or move her upper torso.

"I just don't know, Ronald. Do you think we should go with this therapy?" She looked at her husband. "It seems so farfetched." She looked and felt completely drained from the months of waiting and praying for some kind of a miracle for their daughter.

"She can't speak now as it is, and if we can help her with that maybe the terror will leave her eyes." Ronald sat with his wife in the waiting room next to Alyssa's room.

The doctor came out and sat in a chair across from them. "Your daughter is a very good candidate for this procedure." He had compassion in his eyes. "This is what they call a beta test procedure. It is very new and many are on the list, as a last resort so to say, and Alyssa's name is first. Doctor Wolf, as I explained before, is renowned in this experimental field. Besides his credentials as a neurologist, he is also one of the most astute scientists I have ever met and comes highly recommended." He could see the hesitation in their eyes.

"Steve, you don't have to sell us. You've been at Alyssa's side since the start of all this. You almost feel like family."

Olivia gave him a kind look. "We have trusted her life to you so far and I think if this works, it will help her to know we can understand what's going on with her." She looked at Ronald.

"I agree."

"I kind of thought you both would say that . . . so . . . I have set up an appointment with Doctor Wolf, and if you're ready we can go to his office right now." Steve rose from his seat and they followed.

Doctor Wolf's office was more like a laboratory. He had machinery tucked in every corner of the room. He was sitting at his desk with a computer monitor in front of him. He looked comfortable in his surroundings— more like a kid in a playroom than a scientist at work.

"Doctor Wolf," Steve called out.

They walked toward him. "May I introduce the Browns?" Steve turned to Olivia and Ronald.

"Oh, yes, Olivia and Ronald . . . you don't mind if I call you by your first names now, do you?" He quickly extended his hand first to Olivia and then to Ronald.

"No, of course not." Olivia looked at him with a bit of apprehension in her eyes. To her, he appeared disheveled. His brown hair jutted out, as if he had stuck his finger in a light socket, and the black, dark-rimmed glasses he wore made his eyes look bigger than they should be. He had on a white lab coat, black pants, and leather loafers. She thought he looked more like a teenager than a man with the years of experience he should possess.

"I can see, like many others, you're shocked by my appearance and most likely how old I am." He chuckled.

"Well . . ." Olivia began.

"I am thirty-two and yes, I am a genius. So now that we have that out of the way let's get on to what really matters—Alyssa." He returned to his computer.

Embarrassed, Olivia turned to her husband. "Well . . ." She moved to his computer. "I guess we were expecting someone . . ."

"I know—older and somewhat wiser looking." He chuckled and then started using his keyboard.

Steve began, "Doctor Wolf is the best . . ."

"Adrien, please call me Adrien, and let's not waste time. What I want to show you is important for your daughter. With this procedure she will be able to communicate, and I am sure you know how important that is for you and mostly for her, but she is my main objective." He typed as he spoke.

"Yes Doctor . . . Adrien. Alyssa is always our main concern and objective," Ronald spoke out. "Can you explain this procedure you're talking about?" He stood beside his wife near the high swivel chair where the computer was placed on a tall bench.

"With my assistance, Alyssa will learn a new language, a coded computer language. To break it down, with the aid of wireless computer microchips placed in the occipital lobe of her brain, which deals with sight, her eyes will become her voice, so to say." He did not take his hands off his keyboard or even look at Olivia and Ronald.

"Chips . . . wireless . . . do you mean you want to put these in her brain? That sounds . . ." Olivia's eyes showed fear as she looked at Ronald and Steve.

"Yes, it is a very delicate operation. Of course, many other steps take place, but in my tests, after their placement the nerves have shown a very responsive interaction with the sensors of the chips. In fact, they immediately meld perfectly and interact with the optic nerve. Like you said, it sounds dangerous and it is, but it is not life threatening." He did not stop his work.

"Do these chips hurt?" Olivia asked.

"No, she will not feel them, but since this is my first experiment with . . ."

"With a human." Steve said, sounding calm.

"Yes . . . well . . . even though they meld immediately, I can't say how long the chips will survive. The body might not like the invasion and start to reject them immediately, or they might degenerate in an unknown time." He looked at them for a moment. "But placement is the first step. After that she will learn the code or language to make it possible for her to communicate. Right now she cannot speak or move her upper torso, and she is petrified. Every minute we waste is time she loses to let her thoughts be known." Doctor Wolf always took his work seriously and wanted to help Alyssa out of her pit of despair. He had lost his mother after a stroke and knew the frustration that came with the lack of communication that she had relayed to him with her eyes. After she died, he vowed that his life's work would be to help others with the loss of speech.

"Steve . . ." Olivia looked at him with many questions in her eyes.

"He's the best. He will make it happen," Steve said.

"We will do whatever you ask," Ronald said and Olivia agreed.

"The placement procedure will be in the morning. After a short recovery from the placement, the learning process will begin. Alyssa will need complete concentration for a one-month period. During that time I cannot permit visitors. You may visit right after the implantation, explain to her that school will be in session, and that when graduation day arrives you will see her again." He finally looked at them. "I know this will be hard for you and for her, but I have found if it is to work for her, she has to learn it right away." He turned back to his computer.

Olivia began to question his actions. "But wouldn't our being with her help her to ..."

He swiveled his chair around, tilted his head, and looked at her over the rim of his glasses. "Olivia, tell her you love her and are pulling for her and will see her on graduation day."

"Yes Doctor ... Adrien ... we'll do just that." She looked into his eyes and saw an emphatic compassion staring back at her. "I trust you." She could feel tears welling, so she turned her head and went to Ronald.

"I will visit with Alyssa after I finish these last code applications. If you are still with her at that time, I will see you then." He looked engrossed as he again started typing.

"Yes, we'll still be there," said Olivia as they left Doctor Wolf to his work.

Outside the laboratory Olivia could not help but bombard Steve. "You're sure?" She stepped in front of him as Steve nodded. "But wireless chips, what's that all about?" She was frightened for her daughter and also confused.

"He has explained this to me in detail. I don't know if I can explain it to you without sounding too clinical, but

I'll try." Steve guided them to his office where they made themselves as comfortable as they could.

"Just try to say it in layman's terms, would you, Steve?" Ronald took hold of Olivia's hand.

"Well, like he said, the coded wireless computer micro chips will be placed in her brain. These chips are programmed to stimulate her brain from the occipital lobe and transmit from the lens in her eyes to a receiver in the computer. This is where the language she will learn will come into play. She will turn computer-programmed words into the English language," he explained.

"Oh my God, that's incredible . . . just by looking at the receiver." Ronald looked stunned.

"Well, more has to go on than just looking. From what Adrien has told me, the language she learns is coded in the implanted microchips, and there are many translations for her to choose from. When she chooses a translation, which he will teach her, she will have the ability to transmit it to the receiver." He felt he was giving a good explanation of the procedure.

"But she will only be able to do this with a computer receiver, right?" Ronald asked.

"Yes, that's right, but Adrien's working on a portable receiver. Because Alyssa is what he calls his beta tester, he is willing to provide the expense of his time. Since the hospital has extended him the use of hospital facilities, equipment, and parts, this will be considered an all expense paid procedure for your daughter," Steve said.

Olivia and Ronald looked at each other. "We trust you and Adrien. Let's go tell Alyssa," said Olivia.

Trust was the word for the day and for their daughter's life. They knew the energy inside her was muffled with her silence. They could see panic in her eyes and believed this would release her. Time would tell!

***

The bright green leaves of the Red Winds trees blew in June's warm gentle breeze. Her wheelchair was wheeled down the aisle and placed near the makeshift altar. She was dressed in her bridesmaid gown. "Locked and ready," Steve whispered in her ear, as she looked at him. His crystal-clear blue eyes expressed his love for her. He pulled the brake lever in place.

She smiled. She thought his blonde hair looked like a halo when he bent to gently kiss her cheek. "You're my angel," she relayed on her portable receiver, as tears of joy filled her eyes. Gently, he dabbed her tears and patted her hand. She watched him take his place on the other side of the altar next to the groom.

"You look beautiful," her mother said and patted her shoulder. She then took her place, next to her husband, in the right front row, as the music started. She watched the bride make her entrance on the arm of her father.

"Who gives this woman to be wed to this man," the minister asked.

"Her mother and I do," the bride's father said. His daughter lifted her head and stared into his loving eyes. As the man who had cared for her all of her life, he felt a deep pride. Just then, the memory of another woman came into her father's mind. "You're as beautiful today as your mother was on our wedding day," he whispered to his daughter and kissed her cheek.

"Thank you, Daddy. We love you," his daughter said. She placed her hand close to her stomach and then hugged him. Just then, her future husband joined them. Her father was about to place her hand in his, but his son-in-law to be shook her father's hand and hugged him.

"I'll take good care of her, sir," the groom said. He then looked at his bride-to-be.

"I know you will. God bless you both," her father said, with tears in his eyes, and placed her hand in her future husband's hand. He then took his seat next to her mother.

"Ready?" he whispered to her, as they walked the short distance to the altar.

"Yes, we are," she said, and they both smiled.

Later, as they wound down the reception celebration, the balmy air had a hint of summer evenings to come.

"It was a beautiful ceremony," Alyssa relayed on her receiver. She sat next to Lyssa.

"I thought so too, and without you it never would have taken place. Thanks so much," Lyssa said. A bright smile lit up her eyes as she hugged Alyssa. "I wished my little girl would have been born for the occasion, but I guess she has other plans for us," Lyssa said. "Whoa that was a good one. Here, let me put your hand here," she blurted out. She took Alyssa's hand and placed it where the baby had kicked her.

"Wow! She's sure active. Have you had anymore cramps?" Alyssa relayed. She remembered that Lyssa had told her she had experienced some earlier that morning.

"They've been coming and going all day. Maybe now that the stress of the wedding's over things might start to happen." Lyssa saw Steve and said, "Steve is such a sweetheart." She watched the tall, muscular man in his tailored suit mingle with the remaining guests that were leaving the party.

"He's my savior," Alyssa relayed with a smile and changed the subject. "Lyssa, you're the only one in the family that I told about my condition. I only told you because I love you like a sister, and I needed someone to talk with," Alyssa carefully relayed in her own words. "You know I don't know how much time I have left but . . ."

Lyssa stopped her. "Remember, we don't talk like that. It's always one step and one hour at a time, but I wish you had told me sooner; we could have had the wedding in New York," Lyssa said.

"Oh no, I wanted to watch you walk down the aisle here at Red Winds," Alyssa relayed with a smile. She nodded toward Lyssa and they again hugged, as Byron approached them.

"If you lovely ladies would allow me to show a little bit of my feminine side . . ." he began and puffed up his chest. "I would like to say that this was the most beautiful wedding I have ever attended, and might I add, your husband is a very lucky man." Byron bowed, took Lyssa's hand, and gently kissed the top of it.

"You know, brother, for once in my life I think I can agree with you on something," Alyssa added. Lyssa and Byron laughed as Steve approached them.

"I think we better get back, Alyssa, the night air's not . . ." Steve began in his always-caring way.

Alyssa interrupted. "He's always thinking about me."

"Forever." Steve commented. He released the wheelchair brake.

Olivia and Ronald joined them. "Are you both sure you can't spend the night?" Ronald asked.

"Our flight leaves in four hours," Steve said, with a bit of authority in his voice.

"We understand," Olivia said. She knew her daughter had extended herself by making the trip and for emergency purposes should have stayed close to her hospital and doctors in New York. "But it's sure nice knowing her primary doctor is also her husband," Olivia then said. She hugged Steve and Alyssa. "Love you both."

"Thank you both so much for coming, it meant the world to us," said Lyssa. She reached for Alyssa and hugged her and then reached to hug Steve when a stabbing pain hit at the base of her back. "Oh God!" she shrieked. She stretched to grab at her back. "I can hardly move," Lyssa screamed. She turned fire red and fell back on her chair.

"She's in labor," Steve said as calmly as he could. "We have to get her into the house." The closest men carried Lyssa to the house.

"Here—in here!" Olivia yelled. Lyssa started to thrash and scream, so they had to lay her down on the floor.

"Call 911," Steve yelled and Olivia ran to the phone.

"I'll get some blankets," Ronald said, as Lyssa continued to scream.

"We have to get her gown off," Steve said. While Rachel and Cal helped him disrobe their daughter, Ronald returned with the blankets.

"She's going to have the baby now," Steve blurted out. "Where's my wife?" he screamed. He searched the room for Alyssa.

"She's in here with me," Andy shouted as he locked the brakes on her wheelchair.

"Thanks, Andy," Alyssa relayed. He softly patted her hand.

"The EMS is on the way," Olivia said, as Lyssa tried to control her pain.

"Oh God," Lyssa screamed and started to push.

"Don't push just yet," Steve said, in a controlled manner. "Just take in a deep breath and blow it out." She did as he asked. "That's it," he said, as another contraction made her scream.

"I can see the head. She's coming," Steve said. Olivia held onto Ronald, with Byron close by. Lyssa reached out to her husband.

"Oh God." Alyssa relayed to Andy when they heard the baby cry. "I guess after all these years we're finally related," she relayed to Andy. He hugged her.

"Here you go, Dad," Steve said. He placed Lyssa's newborn daughter in her father's arms. "Congratulations!"

Warm tears of joy fell from Lyssa's eyes as she witnessed the love between father and daughter. "Victoria Marie," Lyssa said, naming her daughter. When she experienced another pain she screamed. "Oh God!"

Steve knelt down to tend her. "She's bleeding. More towels!" Steve shouted. Olivia gave him the towels she had and ran for more.

"I can hear the ambulance," Rachel said, as Ronald ran to let them in.

"I can't stop the hemorrhaging," Steve shouted, as the EMS team came in and took over tending Lyssa.

"Steve, it's Alyssa," Andy shouted from the other room.

"What happened?" Steve shouted to Andy.

"I don't know. Right after Lyssa screamed that last time, we were talking, but then she looked like she was having some kind of seizure. I caught her as she fell over in her chair," Andy tried to explain.

Steve came in the room. "We need a paramedic in here," Steve shouted. "She needs to go to the hospital." Steve then explained to the paramedic about Alyssa's injuries.

"Here put this on her," the paramedic said and gave Steve a blanket.

Olivia and Ronald went to their daughter as the paramedic left the room. "Oh God, is she going to be all right?" Olivia asked, terror filling her heart.

"I don't know. I'm sure it's her internal injuries again," Steve said, fear showing in his eyes. "She insisted, but we really shouldn't have made this trip." He expressed coldness in his voice that Olivia had never heard before.

"I wish she would've told us," Ronald said, as the paramedics returned with another gurney and placed Alyssa on it. "We know her injuries are serious, but she never told us that she shouldn't have traveled." He watched as the two gurneys were loaded into the ambulance.

"They're both in place," one of the paramedics said, signaling the driver to shut the back door.

In the ambulance Steve sat between his wife and Lyssa and explained more of his wife's condition to one of the paramedics, as the other attended Lyssa's profuse bleeding. The baby had been placed in a portable incubator.

With the rest of the family in his vehicle, Ronald drove behind the ambulance. The eerie sound of the siren dulled their senses as they sped to the hospital with the emergency lights flashing.

"It feels like we live here," Olivia said to Rachel as they sat and waited news of their daughters.

"Olivia, you and your family can come in now," Steve said quietly. He approached Olivia where she sat with Rachel.

"Tell Byron when he gets back," Olivia told Rachel.

"Will do," Rachel said. She sat next to Cal, and Olivia and Ronald went with Steve.

"How's she doing?" Ronald asked Steve, as they walked toward Alyssa's room in Intensive Care.

"Not good. She's lost a lot of blood from her internal injuries, but you know your daughter. She insisted on coming to the wedding, and as you know, her injuries are ..." Steve was commenting when Olivia interrupted him.

"Right after the accident we knew her prognosis was not good, but she seemed to have improved. That's why we thought her trip here for the wedding was okay. Now I'm guessing she's back to square one," said Olivia, as Steve just hung his head. "Steve, over these past months you have shown our daughter a love she has been searching for all her life. We can't thank you enough," Olivia said. Ronald, who was holding his wife's hand, nodded in agreement.

"She made it easy for me. She has a dynamic personality and she loves the same way. She'll always be a part of me," Steve whispered. He pressed his hand to his heart. "You know, when I first met her she was very bitter, but then—like a butterfly—a caring, happy woman emerged," Steve said. "She helped a lot of abused women with her community service. The judge was so impressed with her that he let her leave the state and . . ." He tried to control his emotions.

"It was because of you she found herself again," said Olivia, as tears twinkled in her eyes.

"She worked hard to physically come back, but her internal injuries are so severe," said Steve.

"She's a fighter, and it's because of you and the love that you have for our daughter that we got her back again. I thought we had completely lost the spirit of our beautiful girl," said Olivia. "Back then she wanted to die, but you gave her a reason to live. No matter what happens now, we both thank you from the bottom of our hearts for the time we've had with her."

Ronald nodded. He then took Steve by the shoulders and hugged him with Olivia between them. "Yes, thank you, son," Ronald said.

"I love her so much," Steve whispered. Quickly, before they entered her room, he tried to suppress his tears for his wife's sake. "She's so brave." He grabbed their hands and led the couple into the Intensive Care Unit.

"Hi, sweetie," Ronald whispered to his daughter.

She opened her eyes. "Hi." She tried to focus on them. "Can you sit a little closer? Thank Adrien for this contraption," she relayed and laughed as they read what she said.

They noticed the dark circles under her eyes. "You know I had to go, don't you? I would have gone nuts if I had missed this wedding." She seemed to be searching for the right words.

"We know, honey, but if we had known that the trip would be this hard . . ." said Olivia, as she sat next to her daughter and held her remaining hand.

"Mama, I wanted to go home to Red Winds. I had to be here one more time." They could see that the whites of her eyes had turned red. "I only wish I could've seen the autumn leaves one more time. They're so beautiful." She smiled brightly. "Make sure Steve sees them one day." She felt that her time was short.

"We will all make sure he sees them, baby," Olivia whispered. Her tears flowed. While she was kissing the top of her daughter's hand, Byron came into the room.

"Hi, sis," Byron said. He stood on the other side of his sister's bed.

"Hi there, big brother. How's Lyssa doing . . . not quite the honeymoon she had planned." Alyssa relayed. They all laughed.

"She'll have plenty of time for that," Byron said. Ronald and Olivia gave him a puzzled look, knowing that Lyssa was actually in critical condition. "Right now she's holding her own. She's lost a lot of blood, but we have good news; the transfusion is helping."

"Hey, look at this." Byron stood back and unfolded a poster. "I made this a long time ago, but never had the chance to give it to you. I was going to bring it to New York on my next trip." He unraveled a large photograph he had taken of the house on Red Winds that their mother always called Noah's Ark.

"Oh Byron, can you tape it on the wall in front of me?" She had tears in her eyes.

"I'll get some tape," Steve said. He knew he would do anything to bring happiness to his wife.

"It's just beautiful. The autumn leaves are such vibrant colors, just like I remember," Alyssa relayed. Steve brought in the tape and helped Byron place it on the wall. "Mama's Noah's Ark," Alyssa explained to her husband.

"My Mom first called it Noah's Ark Floating on a Sea of Green," Olivia added, as they all admired the picture and thought about the family Olivia had lost so many years ago in a deadly tornado. "My dad always teased Mama about it. He always said he hoped their home was filled with only family and friends and not animals. You should have seen my little brother Jay running and playing. He was such a joy," Olivia added as they quietly enjoyed a loving, family moment.

"Hey brother, remember way back when I acted like I hated to go home?" She had love in her eyes. "I was a brat and said I hated the country life and living in the sticks," Alyssa added. "You know I was just acting back then, don't you, brother?" Her mother then relinquished the spot next to her daughter to her son.

"Yes I knew you were acting, but when haven't you been a brat?" Byron teased.

"Always the big tease, aren't you, brother?" Alyssa's eyesight was dimming when she relayed, "Come and give your sister a hug." He cuddled close to her. "I finally got my big galoot," she whispered.

Byron's eyes opened wide. "I heard you," he whispered to her.

"Don't let on, but I just went blind," she murmured. She held him tight. "Take care of him." She felt for his face and caressed it. "Promise?" she whispered.

"Promise," he whispered back to her. "Allie," he said using her pet name as tears welled in his eyes.

"Steve," said Alyssa almost inaudibly. She let go of her brother.

"Right here, sweetheart." Stunned that she spoke, Steve looked at Olivia and Ronald as Byron let him sit by his wife. "I'm here, baby." He held her hand while Olivia, Ronald, and Byron stood around her bed.

"She can speak," Olivia said as a burst of tears fell from her eyes and down her cheeks.

"Until . . ." Alyssa whispered. Her arm dropped.

Steve lifted her into his arms and shed bitter tears. He sobbed in front of her like he never had before.

The attending doctor came in and pronounced her deceased.

They did not notice the ICU attendants slowly come into the room and unplug the machinery that she was hooked to including her relay receiver.

After the room was cleared and only the family remained, they stood around and hugged each other. Suddenly, the relay receiver started on its own. They all stared at one another when they read: "ICJ" on the screen.

"Jay, my little brother, my godsend," Olivia whispered.

"We always told each other we would let the other know if there is an afterlife and this has to prove it," Byron whispered.

Stunned, they silently stood there taking in the enormity of it all.

During this time, Rachel and Cal were out in the hospital courtyard for a bit of fresh air.

"Waiting is the worst," Rachel said to Cal. They were sitting on a hard concrete bench watching the nurses and doctors walk in and out of the hospital.

"This place has sure grown since we were young," Cal said.

"Yes it has. Look at those two over there." Rachel pointed to a young, pregnant woman with an older woman sitting beside her. "They look so happy. I bet they're just waiting for the baby to come. Why can't our lives be like that?" She did not expect Cal to answer her. "Look at that; I know that's her mother. She's playing with her ponytail. They have so much to look forward to . . . God, they look so happy." She felt an odd feeling in the pit of her stomach. "I'm sorry, honey, I'm just scared." She looked at Cal, and he patted her hand.

"We have to trust that everything will be okay." Cal took her in his arms, and she laid her head on his shoulder.

Just then, a group of nurses passed in front of them. "Yes, it's so sad," Rachel heard one nurse say. "She was so young to go," Rachel heard another nurse say before they were out of hearing range. Then, straining to listen, she heard. "Lyssa . . ." as the group of nurses kept walking away from them.

"Oh God, Cal, did you hear that?" Rachel asked, with a fear so intense hitting her heart she could hardly breathe.

"Hear what?" Cal asked.

"That nurse. I think she said Lyssa died," Rachel said. She tried to get up, but felt weak in her knees and fell back. Cal caught her.

"Come on," Cal said. He took her by the arm and tried to hurry her.

"Oh God, please no," Rachel whispered. Her legs felt like wet noodles.

Cal noticed she looked as white as a sheet and had almost passed out in his arms. "We have to go," Cal said.

He too could feel a panic growing in his chest. They rushed back into the hospital.

"Oh God, Livi," Rachel yelled. She and Cal ran to Olivia thinking it was their daughter, Lyssa, who had died.

"My Alyssa's gone," Olivia told them. Rachel fainted in her husband's arms.

***

Later, they relayed the death of their daughter and the way the receiver acted to Adrien, and he responded in a letter:

In my experience I have dealt with miracles of life and mysteries of death. I could not find any malfunctions in the receiver. Her reaction with the receiver is indeed a true mystery! he wrote. *My deepest sympathy at the loss of life of your lovely daughter.*

Adrien.

They knew life would go on!

Chapter Seven

A warm wisp of breath fogged the glass pane, as the professor looked down to the street below from the third floor window of the office building. It was early evening, but the bright city lights made it possible to see the large white snowflakes falling outside. A quiet peace seemed to fill the room. Suddenly, a warm tear was felt. *I wonder where that came from. This would be a wonderful time for you to be here and share this with me. Sure wish you were here.* The professor noticed the gaiety from the company Christmas party winding down in the next room and went to sit on the sofa.

"Professor," Tess, the professor's assistant, said. She did not want to bother the professor, but knew it was time to leave, so she knocked softly and then called from behind the closed door.

"Yes, Tess, come on in," the professor said.

The petite, young woman walked into the office. The luxurious, leather sofa the professor was sitting on had several comfortable chairs positioned around it near a huge mahogany desk placed close to a blazing fireplace. The spacious room had a homey, inviting air about it. "Settling down I see," Tess remarked. She noticed the lights were set at amber.

"Yes, it's been a very rewarding, yet tiring day," the professor commented.

Tess went to the sofa. "This just came for you," Tess said. She was holding a parcel in her hands.

"Thanks, Tess." The professor could not help but notice that the tiny woman was festively dressed in a bright red pants suit. Her smooth, blonde hair was tied back with a red holiday ribbon at the nape of her neck, which made her always kind, light blue eyes more prominent.

"I know your family must be waiting for you," Tess said. She handed the professor the package.

"Yours too." The professor accepted the parcel, got up from the sofa, went to the desk, and put it down. "This is another special day I will always remember." The professor opened the desk drawer. "And I'm telling you, I couldn't have done it without you." Sporting a bright smile, the professor handed Tess an envelope.

"You have already been more than generous," said Tess and graciously accepted the gratuity.

"Open it," the professor said, wanting to see Tess's expression.

"Oh my goodness," she exclaimed and almost fell backwards. "You are too good to me." Her eyes opened wide and tears fell on her cheeks.

"You're worth every penny, and, who knows, maybe more one day. Now please, get your self home and get that ham you've been talking about in the oven for your family. I know your husband and the kids are waiting for you." The professor started to lead Tess out of the office.

"Yes, I will. Oh my, I hardly know what to say," Tess said and slowly walked toward the door while she stared at her boss.

"Merry Christmas," said the professor while putting an arm around Tess's shoulders and opening the door for her.

"Yes, Merry Christmas and thank you so very much," Tess replied. She then turned and hugged the professor.

"Your welcome, now get out of here." The professor smiled and winked while urging Tess on.

"Okay," Tess said. She turned toward the now empty outer office area where she picked up her coat and purse and started for the elevator. "Don't stay long." The elevator doors opened and from inside she waved a good-bye. "Merry Christm—" Tess was shouting gaily to the professor. Her words faded as the elevator doors were closing.

"Yes, Merry Christmas." The professor returned to the inner office and closed the door.

"I have had many books published, but this one is the dearest," the professor whispered, sitting on the sofa and picking up the newly published book. "I hope I did her proud." The professor had designed the cover and now admired it. Then, remembered the package Tess had brought in and went to the desk. "Linder Law Firm—that's the one across town, who always sent . . ." Quickly, the professor opened the middle desk drawer and took out a pair of scissors.

"Let's see what we have here." An envelope addressed to the professor sat on top of another wrapped package. The professor picked up the envelope and opened it. "After all this time . . . can it really be true?" The professor immediately recognized the handwriting on the envelope.

The front read, My Dearest Christina. The professor unfolded the letter in the envelope and started reading aloud, but tears blurred her vision. She reached for a tissue to blot her eyes and then continued to read.

I knew in my heart one day you would be the author in our family. So long ago, knowing the numbers would not allow me to personally be with you at this time—as you already know—I commissioned Sean Linder of the Linder Law Firm to keep an eye on your career over the years.

In disbelief, she was again reading one of Grammy's letters. *I can't believe this,* she thought; *it's been so long since I received one of these.* She held the letter close to her heart.

> It was his responsibility to have this delivered to you when your book, *Return to Red Winds,* or a title close to that was published, like I always knew it would.

She looked inside the box and again saw a wrapped package with a delicate looking, light pink bow on it. She continued to read.

> Sweetheart, since the day you were born I have loved you. You brought a joy to my life that I cannot describe, and since I cannot physically be at your side right now, know I am there in spirit.

Christina's tears continued to flow. "You always knew when I needed you." She stopped reading. "Oh God, thank you for this incredible woman in my life." She sat at her desk chair and began again to read.

> Christina, with the information you received from Sean, I hope you found the courage to look up your mother. Life is short and should be lived to its fullest. Don't let a relationship that has gone sour put a block in the way and mess up the time you have. Take the first step and get to know your mother again. You know, you only lose when you quit trying.

"Oh my, did I ever meet my mother. You would have loved this gossip." Christina chuckled. She remembered some more of the gossip that Grammy did not live to see, but she felt she was a part of it.

***

Now, it was her turn to graduate from the university, and with that event another letter came her way from Grammy, a letter that would lead her on a life-changing journey. She had the faded photograph in an envelope in her purse. She was good to go in every way except her heart. After a three-hour drive she pulled up in front of the diner where they had arranged to meet. A moment of hesitation plagued her, telling her not to go. She sat with the car running and her hands on the steering wheel. She looked at the flashing neon sign that said Faye's Diner, and the blinking light seemed to shout at her.

I don't know if I can do this, Christina thought. "Oh God, Grammy, even from the grave the gossip continues." She pulled down the sun visor and opened the lighted cosmetic mirror to check her makeup. *Looks the same.* She remembered the letter from Sean of the Linder Law Firm. *Grammy, I hope this works out. It's been over twenty years since I last saw her.* She turned off the car and could feel her hands start to sweat. "Just for you Grammy," she said aloud and opened the car door. "Here we go." She pushed the lock button and the car's horn sounded its familiar beep. *Nice and clean*, she thought as she entered the diner and looked overhead at the tiny bell above the door that sounded her entry.

"Morning," A kind looking, older lady said to her from behind the counter.

"Good morning," Christina said. She came up to the counter and sat on one of the padded, backless stools.

"Not many up this early. The regulars come in around ten thirty, after church. We have a great breakfast special," said the older lady.

Christina cut her short. "I'm supposed to meet someone, so I guess I'll just have a coffee with cream until she gets here."

The nice lady went for the order. "I'm Faye," she said when she returned with the coffee and a small pitcher of cream and placed them in front of Christina. "Sugar's right there." Faye pointed to it.

"Thanks, Faye, but I just use cream." She smiled. "By the way, my name's Christina. I'm meeting my mother here." She felt somewhat relaxed. She poured the cream in the cup and stirred it with the spoon Faye had placed on a napkin next to the cup and saucer.

"That's nice—a mother and daughter meeting for breakfast," Faye said. She rearranged her wire-rimmed eyeglasses and timidly tried to straighten her white apron around her plump figure. She tidied the graying hair she had pulled back in a bun at the nape of her neck.

"Well, I'm hoping it will be nice. You see I haven't seen my mother for over twenty years. I don't even know what she looks like," said Christina and could feel her face flush.

"Oh well, I always liked that old saying about a trip of a thousand miles that starts with one step," Faye commented. She went and poured herself a cup of coffee and took a stool behind the counter near Christina.

"That's true, and this is going to be a big step for me. My mom has had some problems in her life and I was raised by her family," Christina said. She thought it was easy to talk with Faye.

"Oh, I'm sorry to hear that. How did you finally get in touch with each other?" Faye asked, in a caring, non-prying way.

"That's kind of the funny part. You see my Grammy died a long time ago and over the years she's been sending me letters she wrote to me before she died. She has the letters sent to me through a law firm, and that's how I found out how to get in touch with my mother."

She took a sip of her coffee. "I've always loved these heavy white mugs and saucers." She smiled at Faye.

"I'm fond of them too. They make me feel kind of warm and fuzzy and think of fun times when I was young and drank hot chocolate with marshmallow on top," Faye said. She smiled back at Christina. "You said your Grammy has been sending you letters even after she died? That's incredible. She must have really loved you." She looked at Christina with kindness in her eyes.

"I had a really great relationship with Grammy, and my mother and I have been in touch by email ever since I received the letter from Grammy through the law firm. I found out my mother lives close by here, so we made plans to meet at your diner," Christina said.

The bell jingled and a patron came to the counter. Faye got up and headed for the kitchen. "It's all about ready, Ronny. I'll be right back," Faye said. She went to the kitchen through swinging doors.

"Good morning," Christina said to Ronny. She could not help but notice how tall he was. He had a take-charge attitude about him.

"And to you too, miss," Ronny said. He had a smart twinkle in his hazel eyes. He politely bowed his head in recognition of her. "I guess Arlene's not in yet." He looked around the café.

"I've only seen Faye," Christina replied. She watched him stand taller, but he had a calm air about him.

She came from the kitchen through the swinging doors and returned with a bag. "Here you go, Ronny, all ready to go," Faye said. "I'll put it on your tab. You have a good one."

"Thanks, Faye. You too," Ronny nodded toward Faye, smiled at Christina, and left the diner.

"I thought it was her," Christina said. She had a hint of sadness in her eyes. "She should have been here by now."

Faye returned to her seat. "Maybe she's a little scared herself," Faye said. She took a sip of her coffee. "If, like you say, she had some problems in her life, maybe she thinks she doesn't deserve you." She sounded sincere.

"We've had some good talks in our emails, and I thought we got over a lot of issues," Christina said. She started to fidget in her seat. "Maybe I'm being a fool to think she's changed and wants me back in her life." She turned to look out the window at the parking lot and saw only her car.

"Give her a little more time; maybe she's having a little bit of hesitation," said Faye. The bell rang again and a family of three came in and seated themselves.

"Here you go, on the house," Faye said. She put a doughnut on a saucer in front of Christina and refilled her cup. "This won't take long. They always order the special." She went to the customers and then went to the kitchen to fill their orders.

"Church will be out in a while, and I'm expecting Arlene to help me, so if I get busy just wave a good-bye if you take a notion to leave," said Faye, and then the phone rang. "Excuse me a sec," she said.

"Oh no, the church groups will be here soon," Christina heard Faye say on the phone. "Well, you take care of yourself and I'll see you later." Faye hung up the phone and looked worried.

"Trouble?" Christina asked.

Faye sat on the stool again. "I'll say. Arlene's sick and can't make it in. This might be my last time to rest for a while." She put her hand to her head. "Oh boy, I'm glad they all usually order the special." She tried to get comfortable on the stool. "Honey, you stay around and wait as long as you like." She reached over and patted Christina's hand.

"Thanks, Faye," Christina said, and then added. "Wow, do the churchgoers fill up that whole area?" She pointed to a large room lined with long tables draped with white linen cloths.

"Oh no, that's the banquet room. It's used for special occasions," Faye said. She took a big gulp of her coffee.

"You know, I could help you while I wait," Christina said.

Faye looked completely surprised. "Oh golly, I don't know, this can really be a messy job. We always wear these blue cotton dresses, with these thick-soled shoes, and you're all dressed up." The doorbell continued to ring as the churchgoers started to file in. "Well if you're sure." She got up from her seat.

"Just give me an apron and an order pad," Christina said. She felt happy to get her mind off of her mother's absence.

Several hours passed and only a few stragglers lingered at their tables with their drinks.

"We did it. Thanks a lot, Christina," Faye said. She sat next to Christina, but this time it was on the customer's side of the counter.

"What a workout. I'm surprised you don't lose a lot of weight," Christina commented. Instantly, she wished she could take back her words when she saw the look on Faye's face.

"I do have an eating problem, and I like what I cook, so that doesn't help," Faye said. She noticed how red Christina's face had become. "Don't worry about it; I know I'm fat. Never could stay on a diet." She patted Christina's hand.

"I'm sorry. My Grammy always said I never think before I speak." She knew her face had to be beet red.

"Honey, it doesn't bother me about being overweight. Food is one of the comforts I enjoy." The last of the diners motioned for their bills. "I guess you could say food is one of the great loves in my life." She got up and checked out the last customers.

"Faye, I'm truly sorry for saying that."

Faye held an envelope in her hand. "Don't make me feel bad. Like I said, food is one of the loves in my life, and it shows." She started to laugh. "Here you go, your tips and a little over minimum wage." She handed Christina the envelope.

"I can't accept that. I really just wanted to pass the time. Please Faye . . ." Christina tried to give the envelope back to her.

"You really helped me out of a mess, and I'm truly thankful for all you did, so please . . ."

Christina finally accepted the envelope. "If anyone was helped out of a mess, I was. I should have known my mom wouldn't show. I guess she doesn't have the guts to face me yet," Christina said. Her eyes looked sad.

"Oh, honey, maybe you should give her a little more time." She went to the kitchen and brought Christina a fresh handkerchief to wipe her tears. "Maybe you can do that email thing again, and she will have an answer for you." She saw a slight sign of happiness in the younger woman's eyes.

"You're right, I'll do that. I guess I better be on my way." She got up from her seat and started to limp slightly. "Oh wow, I guess I got a blister," Christina said. She took off her right shoe.

"Here take a seat. I'll get some ointment," Faye said and went for first aid supplies.

"I feel pretty stupid," said Christina.

"No, this is my fault. I should have at least taped some gauze on your heels to help cushion your feet," Faye said. She sat across from Christina and held her foot. She bathed the sore areas, applied the ointment, and applied the bandage. "This should help for a while."

"Thanks, Faye, that feels a lot better," Christina said and put on her shoe.

"How's the other foot?" Faye asked.

"It's fine. Doesn't hurt at all," Christina said and got up from the chair.

"Good! And I'm sorry about that. Here take these supplies for later," Faye said. She looked at Christina with concern.

"Oh Faye, that's okay, I'll be all right."

Faye insisted. "Here, please take it, you may need it before you get home."

Christina finally accepted the supplies and put them in her purse. "Thanks, Faye."

"Honey, I was thinking . . . could you tell me what your mom looks like in case she does show up?"

Christina reached into her purse for the picture. "This is the only one I have, and she's younger here, so she might not look exactly like this." She handed the photograph to Faye. "Also, here's my phone number." She wrote her number on a slip of paper she had in her purse.

"We don't have many strangers around here, so I'm sure I'll recognize her." She took the slip of paper from Christina. "So if she happens to show up, I'll give you a call." She returned the picture to her. "And thanks again for all your help, Christina. Stop by anytime you're in the area. Hopefully, Arlene will be feeling better then and you can relax." She chuckled as she walked with Christina to the door.

"I'll be back," Christina said and watched Faye flip the open sign on the door to read closed.

"Like I said, you come by anytime; it was my pleasure to meet you."

Just then Christina surprised her by reaching for her and giving her a quick hug. "Thanks, Faye, I'll be back." She saw the surprised look on Faye's face. She hurried out the door and heard Faye turn the lock.

Nearing her car, she turned and looked back to wave a good-bye to Faye. She had a lonely feeling as the older woman looked at her and waved back. *I hope she has a nice, loving family to go home to,* she thought. She opened the car door and got in.

Returning home, Christina hesitated to send another email to her mother. She believed her mother should be the one to make first contact, but then, after several months, she took Faye's advice and emailed her. She hoped her mother would explain why she didn't show as they had planned.

Weeks went by with no reply from her mother, making Christina think something terribly wrong must have happened to her. Finally, after six months, she felt compelled to return to Faye's Diner on a special day: her birthday. *With all she does, Faye could have lost my phone number and was unable to get in touch with me;* she thought as she drove to the diner early on another Sunday morning. *I don't feel so hesitant this time.* She pulled into the diner's parking lot and again looked at the blinking neon sign. She looked inside the building and saw only one person behind the counter. *Faye,* she thought and went inside.

"Good morning," the young woman behind the counter said to Christina.

She seated herself at the counter. "Good morning. You must be Arlene," Christina said.

The young woman looked shocked. "Yes I am, and you have me at a disadvantage," Arlene said. Then Christina explained who she was and how she had helped Faye out when Arlene was sick.

"I remember that, and you really were a godsend. I hated not to be able to help her. Sundays are so busy and all." Arlene shyly tried to straighten her curly blonde hair. Christina noticed that Arlene stared at her with the clearest, light-blue eyes she had ever seen in her life.

"I was truly happy to help. Is Faye around?" She almost felt transfixed as Arlene continued to stare at her.

"Mom, you have a visitor," Arlene shouted.

"I'll be right there." Christina heard Faye's voice coming from the kitchen.

"Faye!" Christina exclaimed in disbelief.

A slim woman with short, wavy, jet-black hair walked into the room. "Yes it's me, honey," Faye said. She came around the counter and faced Christina.

"But you look like . . ." Christina could not believe who was standing in front of her.

"I am, honey. I'm your mother," Faye said and stood with her head hung low.

"I can't believe this. All that time it was you," Christina said. She was almost afraid to blink as she gawked at her. "I just can't believe my eyes. You look so different. It's like you melted into my mother," she could only think of to say.

"Oh yes, it's me all right. When you left last time, I fell in love with something far more precious than food." Faye appeared openly embarrassed to look at Christina. "It's amazing how losing a few pounds and using a little hair color can change a person's looks. And look—contact lenses." She nervously pointed to her eyes, but purposely did not approach her daughter.

"But why didn't you tell me who you were back then?" asked Christina. "Your weight doesn't matter to me; you're my mother." She then looked at Arlene.

"She told me about you," Arlene said. "You're very lucky; Faye's a wonderful person."

"Victoria, my name is Victoria," Faye interjected and admitted her true identity to Christina. She felt the tears falling from her eyes. "Can you ever forgive me?" She could not hold her head any lower.

"Oh, Mama, I love you and I've missed you." Christina got up from her seat, went to her mother, and took her in her arms. "It's really you. I just can't believe my eyes; you look just like your picture." She held the thin woman at arm's length.

"I almost said something when you showed me the photo, but I couldn't. I didn't look like that woman in the picture, and you're so beautiful. I felt I wasn't good enough for you," Victoria said. She had a pitiful look on her face. "Arlene honey, could you get us a couple of coffees with cream?" Victoria kindly asked her daughter. She had a compassionate look in her eyes when she watched Arlene go for the coffees.

"Let's take a booth," Victoria said.

She led Christina to a booth, where they seated themselves. "Are you going to come home with me?" Christina asked.

"Honey, I am home."

Arlene silently brought them their drinks. "Thank you, honey." Victoria smiled at her, and Arlene left them to give them some private time.

Victoria looked hesitant. She fidgeted in her seat and seemed to be getting up the courage to speak. "I don't know if you are aware of it, but I was in prison for a time." She noticed Christina did not flinch a muscle.

"I knew something happened, but no one would ever tell me anything. They always beat around the bush when I asked questions. So I knew something wasn't right." Christina could not help but stare at her mother from across the table. "You're incredibly beautiful." She saw Victoria blush.

"If you say so, but I don't think so," Victoria said. She looked around feeling self-conscious that someone might be listening, even though Arlene was the only other person present. "I know of Red Winds. I lived there once." She seemed uncomfortable at the mention of the estate.

"It's a wonderful place to live. And your mother ..." Christina was saying. She thought she had to have feelings of love and miss her own mother.

"I guess my earlier years were okay, but my mother never seemed capable of giving me love. My stepdad tried his best, but Mom always seemed a million miles away from me," said Victoria.

She seemed to be remembering other times. "Over the years I've learned I can't put all the blame on my mother. I wasn't your typical run-of-the-mill teenager. I went ballistic. I have more body piercings than I can count, and I'll never show you some of my tattoos. Honey, when I was sixteen, I ran away as far as I could. I got involved with some shady people and in time I was known as the queen of the pole. I made more money in a week at a strip club selling my body than I do here in two months." Suddenly, she thought she was divulging too much personal information when she saw the look in her daughter's eyes. She knew she had to blurt out the truth about her past before she lost her nerve. "Maybe I'd better stop," she said, hesitating.

"No, I want to know it all. It's been too long and I've been kept in the dark forever; it's important that you're truthful. Besides, you might be surprised that I'm tougher than you think,"

Christina said. She sat back and took her coffee cup in her hand and looked completely in control of herself.

"I want you to know that when I became pregnant with you, I took care of myself. I went home, you know, to Red Winds and I was clean," Victoria said. She knew it had been many years since she smoked, but at that very moment she sure wished she had a joint. It was hard to keep herself together when she was looking into the most beautiful eyes she had ever seen in her life —besides Arlene's—looking back at her, but she would have to earn any love or trust from the eyes that now stared at her. "I'm not proud of my past, but it did make me the woman I am today." She had tears in her eyes when she looked over at Arlene.

"She's my half sister," Christina said. She was admiring the younger woman. "She knows more about you than I do," Christina said. She had a little bit of hesitation in her voice.

"I married her father, René. We had the whole bit: a grand wedding and a legitimate child. It actually took nine months," Victoria said, with a slightly embarrassed laugh.

"René." Christina said and grinned.

"Yes, René," Victoria said. "I teased him about his name when I first met him, but it kind of grows on you. He's a kind man, and he knows everything about my past. In fact, he's the real Faye. His middle name is Faye." They both laughed and Arlene looked over at them and smiled. "She's happy for me. She's wanted me to get in touch with you ever since I told her about you," Victoria said, as the bell jingled and Ronny came in for his to go bag.

"I remember him from when I was here last time," Christina said, as they watched Ronny go to the counter. "He's a handsome man." Christina noticed the way he stood by the counter, with a slight tilt of his hips, wearing mechanic's overalls. She remembered how tall he was, but this time she noticed that his black hair was in need of a haircut. Like before, he looked completely in control of himself. She could tell he was flirting with Arlene when she brought him his to go order.

"Yeah, that's Ronny Fiord. He's an auto mechanic who works with his father at the gas station down the road," Victoria said.

"You mean Ford like the auto company?" Christina asked.

"Oh no! It sounds like Ford but its spelled F-i-o-r-d. They're not related to the car company, but thank goodness he has an engineering degree. He's also our area pilot." She watched Christina admire the man. "And, as you can see he's head over heals for Arlene." She smiled, while they watched Ronny flirt with Arlene.

"She knows I want her to finish college before she heads down that road. She just likes the way he teases her. He's been doing it forever. Those two have known each other their whole lives. Poor guy, I know he's been sticking around here until he thinks he can wear her down, but she's made it very clear she's not interested. She even told him she likes a guy at the university. I think my life history has made a big impression on her, and hopefully she will take my advice and wait," Victoria said. She took a sip of her coffee as they watched Ronny try to get a positive response from Arlene.

"He's a pilot?" Christina asked.

"Yes. After he got his engineering degree, he went for the whole bit. He attended a private flying school and passed. He's got more than 1500 hours of flying experience and received his airline pilot license."

"Wow. I thought he looked like . . ." Christina stopped what she was saying. "Well, he just kind of looks like he's out of his element." She felt her body flush.

"You're right—he is. One day it's going to hit him in the head and he'll be out of here," Victoria said. They both continued to watch Arlene and Ronny. "Want a warmer? Mine's cold," Victoria said. She got up from her seat and Christina handed over her cup. "I didn't realize we've been talking this long," she said with a smile, and then went for the coffee.

"Thanks," said Christina. She watched her mother walk behind the counter and put her arm around Arlene. She felt a shot of jealousy hit her in the heart. *Oh boy I wasn't expecting that,* she thought. She rubbed her eyes and ran her hand through her hair. *How much of this did you know all those years, Grammy?*

Her mother returned with the fresh coffee, and a crushed Ronny left with his order. "Honey, Arlene has a great idea. Could you maybe stay with us for a while?" Victoria asked. Excitement was evident in her voice. "We all could get to know each other better." The bell started to jingle and the churchgoers started to file in. "Think about it. I have to get busy," said her mother. She took a last gulp of her coffee, reached over, and patted Christina's hand.

"Well, for right now I'd like my waitress job back." Christina winked at her mother. She stood and walked with her mother to the back of the counter.

"Well, if you're sure, I insist that you wear these." Victoria reached under the counter and pulled out a pair of thick-soled shoes like she and Arlene wore. "I'm pretty sure they're your size," she said to her daughter, as Arlene smiled at them both.

"You should know after taking care of my blisters last time." Arlene also handed her a soft pair of white ankle socks. Christina immediately went to the kitchen to put them on. "I'm ready." She picked up an apron and order pad and returned to the dining room.

"May I have everyone's attention," Victoria then said. The churchgoers stopped their chatter and listened to her. "I would like to introduce my daughter Christina, who is visiting us for a while." She looked at Christina and winked.

"Hi, Christina." The crowd chimed the friendly greeting, which sent a surge of happiness throughout Christina's body.

"Hi," Christina said and waved her hand. Her face was as red as a beet when her mother and Arlene circled and hugged her.

"Oh, and by the way, everyone, today is Christina's birthday," Victoria added.

"You remembered," Christina whispered. She could feel tears rolling down her cheeks. She looked at her mother and Arlene. She could feel herself beaming with a love she had never felt in her life.

"Always," Victoria whispered. With tears glistening in her eyes, she gave both of her daughters a strong bear hug.

"Happy birthday, Christina," The crowd resounded happily.

"Well, ladies, let's get busy," Victoria said to her daughters.

"Counter or tables?" Arlene said. She smiled at Christina.

"Tables," Christina said, as they all went to work.

***

That evening as she drove, Christina thought the gravel drive seemed to go on forever. She noticed that the full late autumn moonbeams either filtered through the forestlands or shined brightly on the long fields that lined each side of the road.

"This is your driveway?" Christina asked Victoria who sat in the passenger seat. She was amazed that they had been on the deserted road for at least two minutes.

"Yes, honey, this is farmland," Victoria said. "Besides his capital investments, René is a land and farm tenant baron."

"Daddy built Hawk's Nest for Mama," Arlene said with pride in her voice. "My friends at the university can't get over all this land either. They're used to subdivisions and condos."

She seemed unconcerned with the familiar landscape, as they approached a well-lighted area.

"Good grief that looks like the airport over there," Christina was saying.

"That's Hawk's Nest. Daddy lights it up to let us know he's waiting for us," Arlene said, as Victoria directed Christina to make a left at the next road.

"Well, I can see why you said you're home. This would be hard to leave behind," Christina said. She looked over at her mother and, in the limited light inside the car; she could see that her mother had a comfortable looking smile on her lips.

"It's the love that makes our home something I could never leave," Victoria said, as they drove in front of a four-car garage just as the door on the far right went up. "That's my René," Victoria said and pointed to her husband.

Christina noticed a large-framed, bald man dressed in denim bib overalls, a long sleeved red shirt, and pants tucked into leather boots motioning her to pull forward. *He looks at least twenty years older than my mother*, Christina thought.

"He's always ready to help," Victoria added, as Christina followed René's instructions and then turned off the car's engine.

"My ladies," René shouted happily. His arms opened wide as both Victoria and Arlene hurried out of the car. Christina watched them hug in front of her car.

Wow, she's right: this place is love, thought Christina.

Arlene opened the driver side door. "Hurry, Christina, Daddy made barbeque," Arlene said, as Christina grabbed her purse, and she and Arlene followed right behind Victoria and René.

"So this is your beautiful daughter, Christina," René said when they made their way into the kitchen.

"Yes," Victoria said. She blushed slightly and put her arm around Christina.

"I think this calls for Champagne," René said. He went to the pantry for four long-stemmed glasses. "You ladies have a seat. I have a couple bottles already chilled."

They sat on comfortable stools placed around a large granite topped counter in the middle of the room. "This is just beautiful," Christina commented. She ran her hand across the cool counter top.

"René wanted to fix up the diner with the granite, but I thought that was a bit much," Victoria said.

René went to her, carrying one of the bottles of Champagne. "I would do anything to make my wife's world a beautiful place to live in, or work in." He smiled at his wife. He then put the bottle down and hugged her waist, as she sat on the stool.

"You spoil me too much," Victoria said.

Arlene laughed and they all hugged. "Daddy can I open the Champagne?" Arlene asked. She looked at him with those eyes that Christina remembered she also had a hard time looking away from.

"Sure. Here's the towel." He watched his daughter open the bottle with ease, just like he had taught her. "Perfect," he said.

Arlene filled the glasses and René passed them around. "To Christina, my sister, may this not be your last visit to Hawk's Nest," Arlene toasted and winked at her sister.

"Here, here," the trio said, looking at Christina. They put their glasses together with a clink and downed the sweet liquid.

"The barbecue is in the oven, and I have hors d'oeuvres," René said. "Let's retreat to the living room."

Victoria and Arlene immediately rose from their seats. "How was your day?" Victoria asked her husband.

They walked with an arm around each other in front of Arlene and Christina into the next room. "They look completely in love," Christina whispered to Arlene.

"They are and they live it every day," Arlene said, with ardent love also showing in her eyes.

They entered the living room. "Happy birthday, Christina," they all shouted.

Christina could not believe her eyes. The entire room was full of balloons, birthday signs, and streamers. "Oh my God, I have never seen so many balloons in one place. This is just fantastic."

They all sang the happy birthday song to her. "You did this all for me?" She pointed to René, knowing he had to be the one, since they all just got home from the diner.

"You know it, and it was fun," René said. "I hope you all have an appetite. Let's eat," He uncovered an array of shrimp, stuffed mushrooms, and what he called beanie weenies wrapped with bacon.

They stayed up into the wee hours of morning eating barbeque and then finishing it off with a beautiful two-layer birthday cake.

"I feel right at home here," Christina said to Arlene.

They were in Arlene's bedroom looking for a nightgown and also for an outfit that Christina could wear in the morning. "My mom has dreamed of this day forever; I'm glad it's here." Arlene said. She showed a couple of her nightgowns to Christina.

"You're a pretty great gal yourself," Christina said to her half sister. "I would think it might be kind of hard to share your mom with me."

Arlene again looked at her with those beautiful, understanding eyes. "Oh no, just seeing my mom this happy makes me happy too. She told me about you when I was around eight years old. She had happiness in her eyes when you started emailing each other. She was beside herself with joy and that is something I would never want to take away from her," Arlene said. She picked up her favorite nightgown. "This is it: nice and snuggly." She held it close to her and then handed it to Christina with a matching robe.

"Oh my, it is snuggly. Are you sure?" Christina asked, thinking it must be her sister's favorite gown.

"Yep, and what about this outfit for tomorrow?" She held up an outfit. "The diner's closed on Mondays so we have the whole day off, but we do have farm chores. I think jeans and this shirt, what'd you think?" Arlene asked.

"Looks perfect, and I'll wash out my undies," Christina said. They both started for Christina's bedroom. "Oh my God, this is just beautiful," Christina remarked when they came into her bedroom. "And look—a candy on my pillow," she said.

They both started to giggle. "That's from Daddy. He does sweet things like that," Arlene said.

She went to the bed and started to turn down the bedding. Christina went to the other side to help. "The bath is over there." She pointed to the room. "Well good night, sister." She gave Christina a loving hug.

"Good night, and thank you for opening up your heart to me—it means the world to me," Christina said.

They hugged again. "I'll come get you for breakfast," Arlene said. She went toward the door, put her arms in the air, and started to yawn.

"Thanks! See you in the morning or should I say later." Christina also yawned. They chuckled.

Arlene blew her a kiss when she walked out, and then quietly shut the door.

Chapter Eight

The humming sounds were getting louder and woke her from her slumber. Quickly, she got out of her warm bed and put on the robe Arlene had given her.

"What's all the commotion?" Christina asked when she noticed Arlene sitting on a bay window seat down the hall from her room.

"It's Mom and Dad. Daddy wants to mow the field before daylight. He wants Hawk's Nest to look beautiful the first time you see it," said Arlene.

Christina sat down beside her. "You have got to be kidding." Christina looked out the window at the scene below with disbelief. "What's she doing?" she asked. "She's in her nightclothes."

"Dad asked Mom to help him set up the brush hog," Arlene said. She had an unconcerned air about her. "Don't worry about it; they do stuff like this all the time. I'm used to it." She looked at Christina, who had a frightful look on her face.

"Holy crap, look at her gown and robe just blowing in the wind. I can't believe this. Maybe I should go help her." Christina started to get up from the seat.

"Don't. Like I said, they do this all the time. Mom's really strong and actually I think she likes the drama. Watch them, they flirt while they work. It's a blast," Arlene said.

Christina noticed her mother slightly raise her gown between her legs, and then try to tie it up to get it out of her way. Just then, René jumped down from the tractor and pulled her into his arms. He ran his leather-gloved hands over the thin material of her gown as they kissed deeply. "Shit, you're right. Look at them; they're acting like a couple of love struck teenagers," Christina smiled and said.

"Yeah, and now Daddy will lift the arm of the brush hog for her, and she'll straddle it. Then he'll get back on the tractor and slowly back up and connect to the hog," Arlene said, as they watched them do what Arlene said.

"Next, she'll run to him, he'll lift her up on his lap, and she'll snuggle in as he drives them behind the barn. See, there she goes up into his lap, and there they go behind the barn. Fortunately, you can't see what goes on back there," she said, as they both looked at each other and giggled. "And then, after some time, Mom will run to the house like she's coming home late from a date. I'm telling you they're hilarious," Arlene said, as they both continued to look out the window.

Finally, Christina broke the silence. "I was wondering about Ronny," she asked nonchalantly. They continued to look out the window, waiting for their mom to make her mad dash to the house. "You've known him all your life?" Christina asked. She noticed Arlene's puzzled look.

"Are you interested in him?" Arlene asked smiling. "That would make me very happy. I've loved him like a brother all my life, but he just doesn't get it."

Her uninterested attitude in him made it easier for Christina to speak of her feelings. "I think he's quite handsome."

Arlene burst into laughter. "Oh God, really, I know he's cute, but I never thought of him as handsome." Arlene could not help but put her hand to her mouth and openly laugh. "I'm sorry. I've just never felt like that about him."

"When he came to the café, your mom told me a little about him."

Arlene looked concerned. "I guess it's kind of hard for you to think of her as your mom too?"

"I do, but . . ." Christina tried to explain her sudden feelings of recognition for her mother.

"I can understand. Don't worry about it. She's a great woman, and in time I know you'll grow to love and admire her, and call her Mom too," Arlene said. They continued to look out the window. "But, now, let's get back to Ronny."

"Mom told me he's an airline pilot," Christina said. She looked at Arlene and they both smiled. Christina had a slight blush on her cheeks. Arlene could not tell if it was because she had finally called Victoria *Mom* or because she was thinking about Ronny.

"Yeah, he is. Now, if he would get his mind off me—like I've asked him to do a million times—and focus on his own life . . ." She noticed Christina blushing again. "Did Mom tell you some of the largest airlines have offered him lucrative career opportunities?" Christina shook her head. "Well, they have, and I have to say this: pardon my French, but he has to get his head out of his ass," Arlene said. Both women looked at each other and started to laugh.

"I get the picture," Christina said. They both giggled and hugged one another.

"Oh look, here she comes," Arlene then said.

They watched as their mother did as Arlene had mentioned before, and ran from behind the barn to the house. They then saw René head out with the tractor's headlights noticeable in the distance.

"The whole barnyard's lit up; don't they think we can see them?" Christina asked.

"I really don't think they care," Arlene said, looking at her sister. "They're in love and they show it." They heard their mother coming up the stairs. "Quick, back to bed; we'll talk about Ronny later."

Both girls jumped up and made it to their rooms before their mother reached the landing.

***

Later that morning, the recognizable, mouth-watering aroma of bacon filled the whole house. *Wow! What a smell to wake up to,* Christina thought. She quickly got out of bed and went to her bathroom.

After showering, she put on the clothes she and Arlene had picked out, but then put on the thick-soled shoes her mother gave her at the diner. "Sure can't wear these sling backs." She put her toeless shoes near a chair by the dressing table. *Farm chores, the dirtier the better.* She wanted to howl, remembering her earlier years of gossip with Grammy, and her times in the barn with their handyman, Wolfgang. She let out a low howl like she always used to do with Wolfgang. *I thought René was a funny name, what about Wolfgang?* She couldn't help but laugh to herself, and then felt a pang in her heart for her lost friend and the times they shared. *We had some fun times, and Wolfgang seemed to understand the oldster kid in me.*

There was a knock at her door. "It's me, Arlene. Are you up?"

Christina ran to the door and opened it. "Who could sleep with the smell of bacon all around . . . I'm famished," Christina said, as both girls started for the stairs.

"All dressed and ready to go." Arlene hugged her sister. "I'm supposed to tell you when we get downstairs to close your eyes. I'll lead you, okay?" She noticed Christina's confused expression. "Remember I told you Daddy wanted your first look of Hawk's Nest to be a beautiful one. Well, he said he also wants it to be one you'll always remember." She smiled. "Trust me; it'll be worth it." Arlene put her arm around Christina's waist.

They reached the bottom of the stairs and Arlene pulled out one of her mother's sleeping masks. "Mama wears this thing when she has to sleep in the afternoon." She gave the black mask to Christina.

"You guys are doing something fun and different around here all the time," Christina said and smiled. "I'm all yours." She put on the mask and hooked onto Arlene's arm.

"We're headed for the southeast family room," Arlene said, as she escorted her sister.

"Good morning, Christina." Christina heard the voices of Rene and her mother.

"Good morning," Christina replied.

"Honey, you can take off the mask now," her mother then said.

Christina did as her mother requested. "What a beautiful room." Christina looked around the dimly lit, gigantic room and noticed René standing in front of a large, draped window. "Nice and warm in here." She turned to her left and saw a huge fireplace with a fire blazing in it. "Wow, I've never seen a fireplace that big. A person could stand on either side of the fire." She looked around in awe of her surroundings.

Everyone seemed to be taking in all that she was experiencing. "We'll roast hot dogs sometime," Arlene said. She squeezed her sister's arm and then pointed to the window where her father stood. "And now for the best part."

René quickly opened the drapes to let in bright, morning sunlight that filled the room. "Oh my God" was all she could think of to say. "It's like looking at a painting of Red Winds." She put her hands to her face, and her eyes filled with warm tears that immediately ran down her cheeks.

"Daddy did it all for Mama," Arlene said. She gave her sister a tissue and continued to escort her to the picture window.

"The leaves are the same reds mixed with yellows just like Red Winds," Christina said. She could not turn her eyes away from the view outside. "It's so bright it almost hurts my eyes."

"Isn't it just wonderful?" Victoria asked, with pride in her voice. She put her arm around Christina and then handed her a jacket. "René wants you to see the pond."

They all put on light coats and headed for a large glass door that led to the back, open-air deck. "Oh my God, you call that a pond, more like Lake Erie," said Christina.

They all started to laugh. "René has a hard time making anything little." Victoria looked at her husband and smiled.

They all gazed at the large body of water. They could smell the scent of the freshly mowed field. The groomed grassland was aesthetically lined with the colorful trees on both sides from the house to the lake.

Christina looked at René. "You're a true artist. This is truly beautiful." She continued to admire the view.

Her mother patted her arm. "He always tells me this is how his love for me feels." She had tears welling in her eyes. "I've been blessed with this man." She went to her husband and wrapped her arms around the large man, as far as she could reach. "My love." She looked into eyes the same color as their daughter Arlene's.

Christina looked at her sister. "Maybe we should leave them for a while." She was not used to their outward shows of affection toward each other.

"Oh no you don't," René then said. He gathered all of his ladies in front of him, and Christina felt like he was coddling them all like a mother hen, protecting them from the world. The feeling was like none she had ever felt from another human being.

"It's love," her mother whispered to her.

Christina looked up at the man and saw his love as he looked down at her and then at the rest of his family.

"And it's for you too," her mother said.

Christina felt as if she completely belonged in their family. She let herself go and accepted their love.

René continued to hug them. "Who's for breakfast? I have bacon and eggs already fixed on English muffins. Any takers?" An enormous smile lit up his face.

"Don't have to ask me twice," Arlene shouted. She grabbed Christina's hand and they ran into the house and then to the kitchen.

"I love you so much," Victoria whispered. She caressed the unshaven, early morning whiskers on his face.

"I love you more." His eyes twinkled when he winked at her.

"You always know what to say." She hugged him with her head on his chest. "Shall we, Mr.?" She wrapped her arm in his.

Yes we shall, Mrs." They laughed joyfully as he led her into the house to join the girls for breakfast.

***

The engine of the old Ford truck purred like a kitten. They turned left from Hawk's Nest onto the gravel road and continued to drive around the lake.

"So you're going to take me to where you and Mama first met?" Christina asked from the passenger side of the truck.

"Yes. Your mother and I have talked about how we wanted to tell you about this, and we both agreed it would be better to show you than tell you, and I felt . . ." René was saying, as they pulled into the parking lot of a small church.

"A church?" Christina seemed confused. She thought, after her mother's shady past, a church would be the last place she could think of where her mother would meet René.

"Yes, a church. Come on in and I'll explain."

René quickly got out of the truck, opened Christina's door, and escorted her to the church.

Reaching the large, ornately carved, double doors, he extended his arm and opened one side. "Let's go up front," he said.

The silence in the church was almost deafening as they walked close to a front pew on the right. He motioned for her to go in first and sit down.

"I almost feel like we're invading somebody's privacy," Christina said. She felt as if someone was watching them.

"Not invading, joining," he said.

At that moment, she thought she could almost understand his meaning. "I think I know what you mean." She smiled at him.

"You see, when I was a baby I was left at an orphanage," he told her. He noticed her eyes widen. "Have you ever seen those movies where the mother leaves the baby in a basket by the door of the orphanage?" She nodded. "Well that actually happened to me. I don't know who my parents are." He looked at her with only kindness in his eyes.

"Oh my, and I thought I had it bad."

He patted her hand in an understanding way. "It's always seemed to me that even if I think life's all against me, there's someone else out there with a situation that's worst than mine." He went on with his story.

"I can agree with that. Did they leave a note on you? There wasn't any way to reach your parents?" she asked.

"No, I was left completely alone. Nuns ran the orphanage, and they were the ones who named me. René came from sister

Mary Jane's father and Faye came from Sister Faye. Faye was her father's name and in his honor she took his name after her vows and then I got stuck with it," he said and chuckled. "Sister Faye was my favorite. We always teased each other about our name."

"Well, when I turned eighteen and it was time to continue my education, the orphanage sent me off to a monastery. It was run by monks, and I learned a lot about life and religion." He tried to get a little more comfortable in the pew. "They want you to suffer in church—brings out the best in you." He knocked on the bench, and they both laughed.

He always has a smile on his lips, and his eyes sparkle with happiness, just like Arlene's. She could not take her eyes off of his.

"I'm just kidding about that," he added.

"You're right, they're not very comfortable." She felt as if they were getting to know each other.

"Well, it's an unusual story, so I guess I better get back to the reason for bringing you here and how and when I met your mother," he said.

She perked up and felt more at ease with her surroundings. "This all seems weird to me after knowing about my mother's past." She could hear the sound of her voice echo in the quiet building.

He gave her a caring glance. "We first met before you were born," he was saying, as she gave him a quick look. "No I'm not your father," he said hurriedly. "Your mom was pregnant with you when I met her."

"Not that I wouldn't wish you to be my father." She tried to hide the hope she had just felt in her heart. "I know my mother doesn't have a clue to who my father is; otherwise, I think she would have told me by now." She lowered her eyes.

"Christina, your mother was a different woman back then. She's made a hundred-and-eighty-degree turn since those days." He reached for her and again patted her hand.

"My life was messed up too, but not in the same way as your mother's. You see I was two weeks away from being ordained a priest when I first met your mother, but I have to tell you that I'd been two weeks away from becoming a priest for more years than I care to say." He saw her confused look.

"You see, I prayed and prayed to follow what I thought was my life's vocation, but at the last minute I could never take my final vows." He knelt halfway down on the padded kneeler and folded his hands on the pew in front of it.

"At that time, I was alone here in this church, or so I thought. I was lying prostrate on the floor up there by the altar. I was praying for guidance, weeping, and asking God to help me finally become the man he wanted me to be when I heard your mother begin to cry from where she sat on the floor—all huddled up—right here in this very pew," he said.

She looked at him and then around her. "She was pregnant with me right here?" She could almost feel her mother's presence.

"Yes she was, and she was a very troubled woman. You see she was contemplating suicide." Christina gasped. "Christina, that is the very reason your mother wanted me to explain all of this to you. She felt she couldn't face you with this information," he said gently.

"Oh God, I'm lucky to be alive," she whispered.

"When I heard her crying I went to her." He saw tears in Christina's eyes. "She was sobbing and it took some time to calm her down. Finally, she told me she was pregnant and being pressured to have an abortion that she didn't want. She was also trying to get off drugs."

She felt completely absorbed in what he was telling her. "She told me she went back to Red Winds to have me," Christina said. She remembered her mom telling her she was clean from drugs when she was pregnant with her.

"Yes, she went back to Red Winds, but first I took her to the orphanage where Sister Faye helped her get clean before she left for home," he said.

"How was she going to . . . you know . . . do it?" Christina asked.

"She had a gun, and she gave it to me before we went to see Sister Faye. Your mother was distraught, but I truly don't think she could have gone through with it. I saw something deep inside her, a kind of strength I believe she got from God." He saw Christina wrap her arms around herself.

"She was a strong woman then and still is, so I don't understand why she didn't stay with her family when she had me, or take me with her when she left." She could not help but believe that as strong as her mother was she could have taken care of her no matter what anybody said.

"Being strong doesn't mean you like who you are. She didn't think she was good enough for you, and she believed her family could give you a better life."

"So then, how did you two get together?" she asked.

"Oh wow! After she left I also did that hundred-and-eighty-degree turn. I was almost forty years old and still without a plan in my life, and when Victoria left I felt alone. She had a fighting, contagious spirit that became a part of me, but I knew she had to get her life together and have her baby with her family. That's when Sister Faye, like many other times over the years, came to my rescue."

Christina felt very close to him, as he poured his heart out to her.

"You see, Sister Faye was the only child of a very wealthy family, who left her their fortune. When she died, I found out

I was her beneficiary," he said. "All of my lands and capital started with Sister Faye's love for me and for the children at the orphanage." He could see he had mystified her.

"I think it might be easier to show you what I'm talking about rather than try to explain it." He slowly got up and reached for her hand. "Come on and get ready for the time of your life." He noticed her raised eyebrows as she let him lead her from the church.

Outside, they walked from the front to the back of the little church. Turning the corner of the church, Christina could hardly believe her eyes when again she saw the beautiful trees that reminded her of Red Winds. He then led her to the forest with the cobblestone path in the middle.

"This is just beautiful. It takes my breath away," she said as she held onto his arm and looked around.

"I planted these trees right after we got married," he said.

She looked at him with amazement written all over her face. "All of this by yourself?" she said in awe.

"Well, I'm about to introduce you to some of those who helped."

They approached a clearing and walked into what she thought looked like a courtyard. "Wow! Fantastic!"

They walked toward a beautiful shrine for Our Lady of Guadalupe. An incredibly exquisite life size figure of the Virgin was positioned protectively in a manmade grotto. "How beautiful, and look the roses are still in bloom."

They walked toward the cave-like entrance that was outlined with raised flowerbeds. Trellises spilled over with an abundance of assorted colored roses. "This is just gorgeous." She could hardly take her eyes from the figure. "I know the story about the poor Indian Juan Diego, who saw the Virgin on a hill in Mexico," she said and noticed that he looked at her with admiration in his eyes. "The Virgin asked Diego to get in touch with the bishop and have a shrine built in her honor."

"Wow! I didn't think you would know the story," he said, looking surprised.

"Oh yeah, the story has always fascinated me. I especially liked the part where the Lady asked Diego to pick the roses that were growing out of season on the hillside and carry them in his cape to show them to the bishop." She continued with the epic legend.

"I think the story then goes that Diego opened up his cape to show the roses to the bishop, and they all fell on the floor. But the real miracle about all of this was that a beautiful image of the Virgin was left on his cape." They continued to look at the figure of the Virgin. "And then after seeing that miracle, the bishop finally believed that Diego really did have a vision of the Virgin, and in the end the bishop built the shrine."

Just then, a soft, red petal, seemingly in slow motion, floated to the ground from one of the roses, and they both looked at each other. "Miracles happen around here all the time," René commented. He picked up the delicate, velvety petal. "This must be for you." He placed it in her hand.

She accepted it. "I will keep it forever, as a memento of this day." She took out her handkerchief and carefully wrapped the petal in it. "Can I call you *Daddy*?" She had a hint of skepticism in her voice, as she looked shyly at him.

"That would make me very happy," He embraced her. "Remember when I told you about meeting your mother in church when she was pregnant with you?" She nodded. "Well, to make a point to her about how important life is, I held her hand on her stomach, and that was when she first felt your life in her." He had tears in his eyes. "It was unbelievable, because at that very moment I also knew how important life is when I felt you too." He was finding it hard to speak.

"Oh, Daddy." She buried her head in his chest.

"Because I felt you, it made me feel like you were a part of me—something to be cherished." They hugged again. "We have a lot to do and if we keep this up, it will be nighttime. There's just not enough time in a day." He took her hand and they walked through another ornately carved wooden door, like the one she had seen at the church, and continued through a foyer.

"Sister Faye would love this place," he said.

They were nearing a room when they heard voices. It sounded like a football stadium. When René opened the side door of the gymnasium, the place exploded with applause and cheering. "Father Harry! Father Harry!"

"Father Harry?" Christina mouthed to René.

He only smiled and escorted her to the middle of the empty floor. "Trees!" he shouted.

She looked around at over a hundred children of varying ages sitting in the bleachers that surrounded the gym floor.

"Please, please . . ." René raised his hands and tried to calm them. This only made the place go wilder, as they stamped their feet and clapped their hands.

Finally, a nun in full habit walked to René and handed him a cordless microphone. "Good morning," he said twice, as they all quieted down and said good morning to him. "May I introduce my daughter, Christina?" He held her hand up and the place went wild again. She looked at him with love in her eyes.

"Ladies and gentlemen," he then said twice. They all quieted again to listen to him. "As you know, Sister Agatha has agreed to call school off this afternoon. We are going to Faye's Diner for lunch." The commotion started again. Finally, he put up his hands to calm them. "So for now, it's back to your studies and we'll see you all later,"

They rose from their seats and started to file happily out in an orderly manner from the gym. "Father Harry! Father Harry!" they continued to say in harmony.

"It almost sounds like they're singing." Christina had to shout for him to hear.

René gave Sister Agatha the microphone.

"They love him," she said and smiled at Christina.

"Who doesn't," Christina added.

"Sister Agatha, this is Victoria's Christina, our daughter."

"I'm so happy to finally meet you. I've heard so much about you," Sister Agatha said. She held onto Christina's hand and gently patted it.

Christina smiled at her. "Thank you Sister, I'm happy to meet you too. And I'm sure we'll be seeing a lot of each other in the future."

"Yes I'm sure. Well I'm off for now," Sister Agatha said, with a wave of her hand. She followed the last of the students that were leaving the gym.

"So now you're also Father Harry?" Christina asked.

"Come on, we have a lot to do," As they left the gym, he waved a good-bye to Sister Agatha. "Sister Faye's maiden name was Harrison, and I was legally given that last name too. Father Harry just kind of stuck," he said. "I never became a priest, but these children like to call me Father, and I like it too." He smiled at her.

They crossed the courtyard and walked toward the woods. "If I had taken my vows as a priest, I don't think I would have been able to do all that I have in my life." They were nearing the shrine when he said, "With my inheritance I built this orphanage in honor of Sister Faye, and it's named in loving memory of her."

"All of those children are orphans?" asked Christina, thinking there were so many. She noticed he nodded yes. "Wow, they all sure love you, Father Harry. By the way, I didn't see a sign on the building," she commented.

"It's on the front; we came in the back way. And you'd never guess by the sign that it's an orphanage because it reads Sister Faye's Home." He squeezed her hand.

"And the trees—the children helped plant the forest?" she asked.

He nodded. "We planted seedlings, saplings, and many large trees. Some of the kids that helped over the years have left, but they come back to check the progress of the forest," he said, with the usual chuckle she had become accustomed to.

"The kids are so much a part of the forest that I like to tease them; I even call them *my trees*," he said, with a twinkle in his eyes. "It's really amazing that over the years, just like the forest has grown, I've seen them grow into strong men and women. Some of them bring their own kids back, and they plant more trees. They love to show their kids what they planted when they were young." His voice displayed a great respect for their accomplishments.

"I will never forget this day," Christina said and looked up at the face of the Virgin. "She's just beautiful."

They stopped in front of the grotto for a moment. "Miracles," he said and bowed his head. Then he took her hand and started for the woods. "Come on, your mother and sister are waiting with another surprise." He smiled at her.

She gave him a puzzled look. "Why am I always surprised when you say something that I don't understand? I don't think I'll ever get used to all the surprises." She shook her head and chuckled. Looking up at him, she saw complete joy in his eyes.

"Miracles, honey—we call them surprises, but they're really miracles," he said, and she believed him.

Chapter Nine

Two years later

The atmosphere in the air seemed tranquil and even the usual chirping of birds seemed muffled. It was a quiet day, but a day filled with joy and happiness.

"Your beauty blew me away," he said and kissed her neck.

"You're tickling me," she whispered. She looked up at him and her heart melted when she saw his love looking into her eyes.

"You're my wife, and I will always love you," he whispered in her ear. She caressed his cheek.

"Hey you two, save it for later," Christina teased her sister and the groom.

A great smile brightened Arlene's face. "I just love this man," She knew Christina did not have to be told that, but she felt she wanted to shout it to the world.

"Come on now. It's time to cut the cake, and Daddy has . . ." Christina began.

Arlene cut her short. "I know it's the Hawk's Nest toast. I'm sure glad you know my Daddy." She squeezed the hand of her husband of two hours.

"Yes, I know, Father Harry," her husband replied.

They stood next to René. "Ladies and gentlemen, may I have your attention," René shouted pleasantly. "I would like to propose a toast." He clanged on his champagne glass. "I feel so blessed this day that my beautiful daughter Arlene has married a man who I feel in my heart can be called my son." He looked at them. Tears filled his clear, blue eyes. "Jeremy came to us when he was just a baby. We have watched him grow to be a gentle, loving man, and now he will go on in life as the husband of my daughter Arlene. Like I said before, I am so blessed."

His wife, Victoria came to his side. "At this time, my wife and I would like to announce that as a wedding gift to these children, we are relinquishing the southern fifty acres of Hawk's Nest to our Arlene and Jeremy, to do with as they please." The guests went wild with cheers. "Please, please let me continue," he shouted. Their cheers subsided. "It pleases me to tell you that Arlene and Jeremy have decided to make their home here at Hawk's Nest and go on with the care of Sister Faye's Home." The guests cheered wildly. "Through our prayers, this was no surprise to my wife or me. My friends, we have a miracle." He raised his glass toward his daughter and Jeremy. "To miracles." he again shouted.

"To miracles!" The guests shouted in return. "To miracles!" they again shouted. The music started to play and the partygoers started to mingle or dance.

"Daddy, that was beautiful. We'll do you proud." Arlene hugged her father and smiled with tears glistening in her eyes.

Her father took her in his arms. "I love you, baby," René whispered through tears and opened his arms. "I love you both."

Jeremy received his father-in-law's bear hug. "You have made me a happy man," Jeremy said quietly into René's ear, "and I don't just mean for the acreage at Hawk's Nest." He looked adoringly at Arlene.

"You don't have to explain to me, my boy," René said.

"We love you both," Victoria added and joined the hug fest.

"Oh, Mama, I'm so happy," said Arlene.

Christina joined them, and René opened up a spot for her. "More miracles," René said. Tears spilled down his cheeks. "We are blessed."

Encircled, they vigorously hugged and kissed. "I don't know who I kissed," Christina said.

Laughing, they broke their embrace. "It doesn't matter," Victoria explained. "You kissed us all."

Sometime later, Arlene, Christina, and their mother sat at a table, relaxing alone. "Mama, have you seen Ronny?" Arlene asked. "You know he's like a brother to me and I wouldn't hurt him." She was trying to explain.

"We know. And now he finally knows," Victoria said. "Honey, he's taking it like the man he is." She remembered his smile as he watched Arlene say her vows.

"I saw him playing catch with some of the boys by the lake," Christina added. "Come on let's go see." She hooked her arm in Arlene's. "You look absolutely beautiful in that gown; white becomes you." As they walked, the trailing veil floated over the green grass and looked like a fluttering butterfly.

Ronny saw them coming; so he tossed the ball, for the last time, to one of the boys. "Hey, I'll catch up with you guys later." He waved to the boys and watched them run off.

"Ronny . . ." Arlene hung her head in front of him. She had a sad smile on her lips.

"What's this? You look like you lost your best friend," he said. He winked at Christina. "You better not let you husband see you looking like that." He took Arlene in his arms.

"Oh Ronny," Arlene cried and buried her head in his chest.

"He's a lucky man," Ronny whispered in her ear loud enough for Christina to hear.

He held Arlene, while looking over her head at Christina, who had tears falling from her eyes. "Come here, you." He opened his arm to Christina, and they all hugged. "And I'm a lucky man too." He was sporting one of his contagious, big grins, as he looked at them.

Quickly, he started to gently guide them back to the reception. "Now, don't take this the wrong way, but I'm leaving town," said Ronny.

They had their arms hooked together, with Arlene in the middle. "You're what? Not because ..." Arlene shouted.

"No, not because you got married, but because it's time. I've got all this education and ..."

Arlene looked at Christina. "Say no more. We know ... too much education for this town," Arlene said.

"Maybe not too much education for the town: maybe just too much of a certain type that the town ..." He was trying to explain without downgrading his place of birth.

"We know," Christina said, with a slight smile. "I live in three states and I still don't have enough education." They all laughed. "And it's not like we won't see each other." She looked at him with sad eyes until she saw that familiar twinkle in his eyes that she was learning to love.

He winked at her. "Oh yes, we'll see each other again." He liked to wink and she loved it.

Finally, they reached the reception area. "Here's your lovely bride," Christina said when the trio approached Jeremy.

"I missed you," Jeremy said and received a loving kiss from his wife.

"Me too," Arlene whispered. She laid her head on his chest and smiled at Christina and Ronny, and they smiled back.

This was a day full of happy tears and growing. Life was changing, but new beginnings were forming, and with this they would all find more surprises. Or, as René always said, "We call them surprises, but they're really miracles."

Chapter Ten

It was a snowy, New York winter day. Flights had been cancelled so the airport and surrounding hotels were packed to capacity. The man was waiting in the employee lounge. He would be ready at a moment's notice. His packed bag was at his feet.

"Don't you look spiffy in your uniform," she said and motioned to the seat next to him, indicating if it was taken.

"Have a seat," he said without replying to her remark about his attire.

"That's why I took this job. I love a man in uniform," she said. "So neat and tidy." She noticed him slightly fidget when he sat up straight in his seat.

"I'm married," he said to her.

"I heard that's what you tell all the girls, but I checked it out and I know otherwise," she whispered in his ear. "You know this snow could delay us here for a pretty long time, and you have to be lonely," she purred. "I'm off duty." She took off her cap and let her long, red hair flow around her shoulders.

"I'm on duty, so ma'am if you don't mind—I'm really into this book." He purposely did not look at her. He was used to women coming on to him.

"Oh, Charlotte Reed, I've read some of her stuff. She writes those sexy romance novels with all that twisted mystery," she commented, which made him look at her. Her green eyes gave him a seductive, penetrating look.

"You have?" He had a look of shock on his face.

"Yes, believe it or not, I like to read." She flipped a tendril of her hair in a teasing way. "You know, I happened to hear another flight attendant say she's stuck in the airport too." She watched him bolt upright and leave. She stood with her hands on her hips. "Well, I never . . ." She walked out of the lounge, stunned at his rejection of her.

"Will Christina . . ." She heard part of what the PA announcer said.

I couldn't hear the last name. Maybe I'd better check. It might be Mom, she thought.

"Excuse me, I'm Christina," she said to one of the information attendants.

"Christina!" a familiar voice shouted.

"Ronny!" she shouted. They embraced. "Sure good to see a familiar face. You stuck here too?" She saw the twinkle she remembered in his eyes.

"Looks that way. I'm on duty, but from the looks of the weather forecast we'll be grounded for some time."

They both looked out the window at the falling snow. "New York," Christina replied and they nodded and laughed.

"Let's see if we can find an empty table in one of the lounges," Ronny said. He went to pick up her bags. "Going to Kansas?"

"I was, but now . . ." She let him take her shoulder bag while she pulled the heavy wheeled bag. "I was texting Arlene, but my phone batteries fizzled out." She watched him for signs of dejection at the mention of Arlene's name, and was overjoyed when he did not show any signs one way or another, except to nod his head.

"Is this okay?" he asked. They found a small liquor bar filled with several, overzealous travelers.

"I think it might be all that's left," she said. They tried to look inconspicuous, as they walked to a far table in the dimly lit lounge.

"What kind of cell do you have? I have my charger," he said. "Do you have your laptop?" If so, they have Internet connection here."

They took a seat and a waiter took their order. "I'm glad they serve food here too; I'm starving," she told him. "Here's my phone," she said and handed it to him.

"Same as mine; let's charge you up." He took her phone and plugged in his charger.

"I was in a hurry and forgot to pack mine." He gave her one of his winks that she loved so much.

"I have wireless Internet, but I was having a problem getting out. Is that the Internet hookup?" She pointed to a jack outlet near the table.

"Yeah, here, let me plug it in for you." He took her laptop from her and plugged the USB cable into the direct Internet connection.

The waiter brought their food and drinks. "Burgers and wine: who could ask for anything more," she said and they laughed. "René would be mortified. He pampers us like queens, and the food he cooks is out of this world." He had a knowing look in his eyes.

"Hey, how did you know I was here?" she asked and started to boot up her PC.

"That's kind of funny. I was in the employee lounge and one of the flight attendants told me you, or should I say Charlotte Reed was stranded here too."

"This thing doesn't want to connect," He stood behind her and watched, as she tried to get the connection. She could smell his musk cologne and smiled. *Nice*, she thought, *not too overbearing*.

They heard a woman ask, "Having trouble with the connection?" It was the flight attendant that had earlier tried to make a move on Ronny.

"Well, actually I am," said Christina before Ronny could reject the woman's help.

"I'm used to this system. You have to know how to work it," the attendant said. She had a slight slur in her voice. "May I?" She slipped in front of Ronny and because of the limited space; she pressed her body to his. "Pardon me," she said, for *accidentally* touching him.

"Here, let me scoot in," Christina said. She realized the woman seemed to be having a difficult time. She noticed that Ronny had bolted like a scared rabbit.

"Take my seat," Christina said. The flight attendant sat and started to peck on Christina's keypad.

"Here we go," the woman said and looked at Ronny passionately. "Yep, just have to know how to work it."

Christina sat next to her. "Looks like you're getting in," Christina said. She looked at Ronny and could see that his face was red with embarrassment. "She's great. Look how she glides through the system," Christina said. "By the way I'm . . ." Christina was about to say her name.

The attendant interrupted her. "Everyone here knows Charlotte Reed. Pleased to meet you. I'm Belle Turner." She offered her hand, and Christina shook it. "I've never flown with your Captain Fiord, but I've heard a lot about him." She gave Ronny another intimate glance. "Here we go—about there. All I need is your password and you're in."

"Oh, a . . ." Christina stammered. "Here let me type it in," she said. She had been drilled too many times not to give out her password, no matter what. "You know, it's not that I don't trust you it's just that . . ." She looked at Belle, with trust in her eyes.

"Oh no, honey, you're right. Here, you type it in yourself," She pushed the laptop in front of Christina.

The waiter came to their table. "Any more drinks here?"

"I'm off duty. I'll have my usual, Hank," Belle said. She had a personal tone in her voice.

"You know a lot of people around here, don't you?" Ronny asked.

"Not as many as I would like to," Belle replied and gave him a lustful look.

"I'm in. Thank you so much," Christina said. She looked at Belle, and then started to type. "Your drink is on me," she then added. "Oh good, Arlene's online." Christina squealed.

"Let me know if I can be of any further assistance," Belle said. She rose from her seat and again slipped in front of Ronny. This time he made certain there was no physical contact.

Christina looked at Ronny. "I think she has the hots for you."

He took the seat Belle had just left. "You have no idea." He wanted to forget about her.

"Oh, I think I have a little idea." She noticed him blush a crimson red. "You're a good looking man, and she knows it," Christina said. "Oh crap, I've made you blush again. Get over it. Besides you're with me." She saw him hang his head. "God, you're so sensitive. We're friends, Ronny, and I really like you. Maybe fate brought us here to get to know each other a little better."

"I just can't stand it when women come on to me. I don't know what to say. I want to talk and get to know them, but it seems all they want is . . ." He looked at her thinking he had never told that to a soul, and now he had spilled his guts to her.

"All they want is you in the sack." She finished his sentence. "I know the feeling."

"You too?" he asked and raised his eyebrows.

"Yep, and what's worse is that they think I'm like the sex-crazed characters in my novels." They both laughed. "Can I give you a little tip?" she whispered. "Just humor them. I've found that when I humor them and start talking about home and things I like, they get bored and go after someone a little more willing."

"That makes sense, and then I wouldn't have to lie."

"Look, Arlene said to say hi to you," She started to read her instant messages. "Oh my God, I'm going to be an aunt." She tried to hold back her excitement.

"Wow, is that right! How great is that? Give her my best."

"Here, you take over—Ladies' room." She got up and headed for the restroom.

"I hate being trapped at the airport," Belle told Christina in the powder room.

"I know what you mean. My family was expecting me," Christina watched Belle reapply her makeup.

"So you and Ronny go way back?" Belle asked.

"Oh yeah, way back." She did not want to get too personal with Belle.

Belle frowned at Christina. "He just ignores me. I think today was the first time he ever looked at me, and that was only because I said your name. How does it feel to be such a famous author? All those men wanting you with desire written all over their faces." She took a small flask from her purse and took a swig.

"It's not like that with me," Christina tried to explain.

"Oh, come on, honey. I may look it, but I'm not stupid. I can see he's got a thing for you." Belle continued. "I waste my time and you come along and he's putty in your hands. Almost makes me sick." She shook her red hair.

Christina could smell Belle's strong perfume. "I'm sorry to hear that." She saw Belle glaring at her in the mirror.

Belle wiped a smudge of lipstick from her front teeth.
"Whatever—but I'm telling you, honey, you'd better watch your
p's and q's 'cause I got my sights set on that man." Belle got up
and put her face right in front of Christina's. "Bye, bye for now"
she added, with a tone of arrogance.

Christina could smell the liquor on her breath. "Bitch!"
Christina thought she heard Belle mumble. "Golly! Can't even
go to the bathroom without getting . . ." Christina tilted her
head, while looking in the mirror, and shrugged her shoulders.
She finished up and left the restroom.

"We lost the connection again, and I got a page to
report back to the employee lounge," said Ronny when she
returned.

"Just when we were getting to know each other better."
Christina pouted. "But thanks for getting me charged up again."
She accepted her phone from him.

"Come with me. I can get you a better weather forecast." He
led her to the bar and paid the bill.

"Later, Ronny," Belle said, from her barstool, and tipped her
glass his way.

"Thanks for your help, Belle," Christina said. She noticed
Ronny only bowed his head and seemed to want to get as far
from the lounge as he could, and away from Belle.

"You know it, honey," Belle replied. "Don't forget our little
talk," she added, looking at Christina. She smiled as she watched
them leave the lounge.

"What's she talking about?" Ronny looked at Christina. "A
little talk, what little talk?" he asked. "You know I don't really
know her, don't you?" He had a complete look of embarrassment
in his eyes.

"Of course I know that. She's just one of those types we were
just talking about. Don't worry about it."

"Wow, I'm such a lucky girl to get a firsthand weather report. I might be on my way sooner than I thought," she said, changing the subject.

"Hey, here's my email and instant message address. Keep in touch. And here, wait a minute . . ." he began, "give me your cell."

She handed it to him. "Now, what are you up to?" She had a look of skepticism written on her face.

His cell phone rang and he handed it to her. "Answer it," he said and winked.

She could feel her body flush. "Hello," she said. She looked into his eyes and smiled.

"Hello," he said. They both started laughing and hung up the phones. "Now we have each other's numbers." They exchanged phones.

The crowd was increasing around them. "Looks like things are starting to come to life again," he said. He put his arm around her and they started for the employee lounge.

They looked like more than friends; they looked like lovers going their separate ways. The crowd was around them, but only one set of eyes watched them from her barstool. Only she cared about the way they looked and the way they acted, as they drifted into the sea of people and out of her view.

Chapter Eleven

"Oh boy, Grammy, you're bringing all these memories back to life. You knew how much I would miss you." Christina again caressed her treasured letter from Grammy. "I hope I live long enough to receive them all." Looking around her office, she could feel Grammy's presence. "I sure do miss you," she said and continued to read.

> I know we didn't have enough time on this Earth together, but I want you to know I am so proud of you. Since you are receiving this letter, I know you have become the success in life you always talked about, and I am sure you have found a wonderful man to love and live with.

"Wow, some more memories," Christina said aloud. She started to remember a time that she knew would always take precedence in her life—a time when not only circumstances in her life changed but also those related to death. *Oh my . . .* she thought as her mind wandered back to a time that she knew Grammy would have thought of as some Earth-shaking gossip.

It was the summer when blight had infected the trees, not only on the Red Winds Estate but also in many spots around the world. The trees were barren and did not produce foliage that year. It was a sorry sight. Bare limbs reached for the sky and seemed to beg for life, but with the help of man's conservation intervention, the trees were saved from destruction.

"Thanks, so much, Daddy, for helping out with this," Christina told René after they had surveyed the foliage problems at Red Winds.

"This is the same problem we're having at Hawk's Nest, but we've been cultivating and feeding the trees. It's not easy, but as you know we have our miracle army." René chuckled.

"Yes, you do," Christina said. "It's sure hard to believe a little mite could cause all this." She looked again at the bare trees. "Do you think we can save the Red Wind trees?"

"I've already spoken with your mother, and she's working it out with Sister Agatha to send a busload to work some miracles here. We'll start with getting rid of the dead foliage. It's a lot of work, but I know it will work." He saw a glint of sadness in her eyes. "I'm sure we can save them. It's working at Hawk's Nest. The limbs are not dying and should produce new foliage next spring. It seems that nature is also taking care of itself." He had hope in his eyes.

"You've learned of something new?" she asked.

"The conservation department has sent out notices that the numbers of praying mantis have been increasing." He saw her puzzled looked. "The mantis is an insect that preys on other insects, and its main course, for now, happens to be the mites that have invaded our forests." He looked pleased. "Miracles . . . miracles, baby . . . always remember . . ."

"I know, Dad. Thanks, you can always cheer me up." She hugged him.

They looked over the land that looked so forlorn. It was not the Red Winds of past.

"Did you hear that Ronny's coming home for vacation?" he asked.

"We've been in touch, but I haven't seen him since last Christmas. He's always so busy with the airlines." She had a shy look in her eyes.

"He's really a nice guy. Your mom and I have always been close to him," René explained.

"Yeah, I know. He is special." She could feel herself flush. Just then her cell phone rang. *Saved by the bell,* she thought. "Excuse me a sec."

"Oh golly, your ears must be ringing. Dad and I were just talking about you." She looked at René. "It's Ronny," she mouthed.

"Honey, I'm going to check the north woods by the chalet and lake," He pointed toward the woods.

"Okay."

"I'm so happy you called. Dad just went to the woods. I guess you know about the tree blight." she said into the phone.

"Yes, and I can see it firsthand right now. Turn around," he said. He walked down the hill behind her. *She is just as beautiful as I remember,* he thought.

"Oh my God!" she shouted and almost dropped the phone. She ran to him.

He almost fell to the ground when she jumped into his arms. "Wow! I wasn't quite expecting such a greeting, but I sure do like it." He gave her one of his sly grins and winked.

"I've missed you," she squealed. "We were just getting to know each other last Christmas when you were called away." She looked at him with sincere eyes.

"I know. Pilots don't have much of a social life. Well, at least not the kind I want to have," he said. They continued to walk with an arm around each other's waists. "You're kind of busy too, with your writing career."

"Phone tag," she related. "We always seem to be on a different time schedule, but we can make up for that now." She put her head on his shoulder and squeezed his waist.

"You bet. But from the looks of this we're going to have a lot of work to do." He was looking over the trees.

"Dad went down by the chalet and lake. He said we have reinforcements coming—or like he always says . . ." They both stopped short.

"Miracles . . ." they said in unison. She resumed walking as she led him through the woods to the chalet and lake area.

"Your mom told me you left Hawk's Nest early. That's how I knew you were here." He saw her looking straight into his eyes. *God she's beautiful,* he thought again.

"You have the most indescribable eye color. You don't know how many times I've thought about your eyes," She blushed and noticed he did too. "God, I don't know what made me say that." She stopped walking. "I don't want you to think I'm like all those other girls."

He looked at her and winked. "I could never think of you like any other girl." He wanted to take her in his arms and hold onto her forever.

"Hey you two!" René shouted. "The cavalry has arrived." He clapped his hands together.

"Just me for now!" Ronny shouted back. They dropped their hold on each other and walked up to him. "The rest should be here shortly," Ronny explained.

"How are the trees by the lake?" Christina asked.

"You might want to take a look," René said. "I'm going to get things set up for the troops." They acted like they wanted to go with him. "I'll be okay. Go check out the lake," he said and turned to leave.

"Call us if you need help." Christina held up the cell phone she had taken out of her pocket.

"You know it," René said. He watched them and chuckled to himself as they walked away. "Love is in the air. Da—da—da—da—da—da—da," he sung, in a whisper, and chuckled.

The lake was crystal clear and the reflection of the chalet showed off its style in the ripples of the water. The small, three-story building was used as a guesthouse. It was a replica of the typical chalets found in many parts of Switzerland. The top floor displayed the familiar tiny windows, but was actually the attic and unusable, except for storage. The second story was a loft, but it still had the tiny windows like the ones on the first floor.

"I love this place: it has so much grace and style," Christina commented. "Don't you just love the broad gables?"

"I know Wolfgang carved the wooden trim under the windows." He explained that he knew some of the history of the chalet.

"Yes, he did. You'd of loved that man," She quickly hid her sadness.

"Pounce, you buzzards!" Christina shouted all at once. She made a fist and punched toward the sky. She looked at Ronny, who glanced up expecting to see buzzards. "Crap, I'm sorry . . ." She started to laugh. "I always told Grammy I wouldn't let any buzzards destroy this property. It's something that goes way back." She could not stop laughing. "Pretending to defend the property now feels so childish, especially when I can't see any buzzards." She continued to laugh and held her stomach.

"You did look a little funny," he said. "I thought I was going to be attacked." He started to laugh too. "Pounce, you buzzards!" he then shouted and started punching at the air.

"Oh my God, is that how I looked?" Tears of laughter fell from her eyes. "This is too much: I might pee in my pants." She ran next to the chalet while he turned his back. "I'm so sorry," she said when she returned, "but I haven't laughed that hard in a long time. I just wasn't prepared," She looked completely embarrassed.

"Good grief, its part of life. Don't worry about it," he said. He noticed she was looking around. "You and Grammy were real close and had some good times?"

"We did . . . I sure miss her. And if she was standing here right now she would have teased me and said, 'If a bean's a bean, what's a pee?'" Christina said. She noticed his baffled look.

"A relief."

She raised her eyebrows. "She had a great sense of humor. I know you both would have hit it off right away." They both laughed"

"I'm sure we would have. It sounds like you're a lot like her."

He came next to her. "You're a very caring woman." He took her in his arms.

She looked into his eyes. "Kiss me," she whispered. "Kiss me before I . . ."

He caressed her cheek. "I'd love to." He bent, touched his lips to hers, and felt a spark, which made him back away. "Don't hurt me," he teased, but did not let her go.

"Never," she whispered. She stood on her tiptoes and embraced the back of his neck. "Never in a billion years." Their lips touched again and they both felt the spark, but they did not pull away.

"Grammy showed me the secret way to get into the attic," she said, with a sly smirk.

"Oh yeah, that sounds mysterious." He slightly lifted one side of his lips to show that grin she was falling in love with. Then, as always, he gave her that cute wink.

"Hell yeah, it's mysterious. Come on I'll show you." She grabbed his hand and looked at him. "You know you grin like Indiana Jones." He just grinned, and she laughed.

They climbed up the hill behind the structure. "See how the chalet's built into the ground?" She let go of his hand and pointed, as they both scaled the slight incline of the mound. "Watch your step. It's kind of lumpy." She led, but still grabbed his hand.

"Trees don't look so good around here," he said.

They both looked around at the crusty leaves that hung lifeless on the limbs of the trees.

"No, they don't." She clung to his hand as she looked around. "Here it is." She took hold of a piece of the siding that looked like a shuttered window. "Step back a bit." She held her arm out. "Oh boy . . . wasp nests; Grammy used to get rid of them by spraying a mixture of dish soap and water on them. I guess they don't like the taste 'cause they don't come back." She noticed the nest was old.

"Sounds like it might work," he commented. "No wasps on this one." He grabbed a small twig and scraped the nest away from the shutter. "Here, I'll open the shutter." He wanted to protect her. "Clever," he remarked. He watched her open the large window hidden behind the shutter.

She put her fingers up to her lips. "It's a secret."

"Cross my heart," he said. He knew from the look on her face that the entrance to the attic would be their secret.

"You have to watch your step. Lots of junk up here." She guided him to a closet and opened the door. A flight of stairs led to the closet in the loft below them that was above the first floor.

"Ingenious," he whispered. "Why am I whispering?" He looked at her like a child about to steal a cookie from the jar. They both laughed.

"Don't get me started. I can't take too much more laughing," she said and held her stomach.

"This place is fantastic." He looked over the loft with the half-railed wall. "It's so homey." He saw the satisfied look in her eyes.

"Grammy and I loved it here," she said, with a look of love lighting up her eyes. "Come here." She guided him to a daybed. "This is mine." She threw off a sheet that protected the sofa.

"And with your permission, also mine." He took her hand and picked her up into his arms.

"All yours," she whispered. She licked his lips to stop the spark. Their tongues played with each other. "I don't know how to say this," Christina said, slightly pulling away from him. "I've read some stuff. I don't think I'm completely stupid. I know males are different than females, but . . ." She was trying to explain her limited knowledge of a man's anatomy.

"You're a virgin?"

"Yes," She felt her body flush. "I better just get this all out in the open right now. I don't exactly know how it works. I know to have babies, the man has to join with the woman, but I actually can't see how any part of a man can be big enough." She knew her face must have shown her embarrassment. When he chuckled, she covered her face with her hands.

"You're not going to believe this, but I've never completely been with a woman. I'm not saying I'm a saint, I've had some fun times, but just not all the way." He gently held her hands in his. "But believe me I know it will work," he explained, with confidence written all over his face.

"I trust you with my life, but we can't make a baby now. We have to wait," she panted. She looked into his eyes.

"I know." He tried to control his passion.

"I love you so much," She felt like she was on fire. Her hormones were raging. "Just kiss me," she begged. He started to unzip her jeans and she let him. "Be gentle with me," she said, with a heavy gasp. She slipped out of her jeans and panties without taking her eyes away from his.

"Always," he murmured. They passionately kissed and he held her close. He unbuttoned her blouse and watched her strip off the rest of her clothes.

"God you're beautiful." He took her breasts in his hands. He could see in her eyes that she trusted him completely. He gently petted her and could feel his passion building. He kissed her breasts, while the soft locks of her hair fell over his face and tickled him like many butterfly kisses. He had to control the fever that was filling his body.

"No babies," she cried. "I love you, but we can't have babies now." She squirmed, yet wanted him in what she thought was all the way.

"No babies," he said. He licked her naked body, but did not disrobe. "I love you," he said softly. He watched her arch her back.

"Ronny," she said, as she tried to hold back her complete desire. He looked at her, and she could feel his love. It was tangible. She could feel herself being pulled into his euphoria, but then she fell to the bed. "Oh God, I'm so sorry." She looked around and felt completely dishonest. "What have I done to you? I was so selfish." She felt ashamed. "This is a special place, and now I've ruined it for us," She tried to cover herself with the blanket.

"No, you haven't; this is our place now." He held her in his arms. "This is our little Heaven." He kissed her lips.

"But ..." She looked at her naked body and then at his, fully clothed. "I still don't understand what there is to be so scared of."

She felt completely satisfied. "I'm so sorry for being stupid about this . . . but how would we make the baby?"

"One day, when it's right, I'll show you," he whispered.

"Can you at least give me a clue," she asked naively. He took her hand and placed it on the front part of his jeans. "Wow! I think I get the picture." She rubbed her hand up and down and saw his passion rising. "I'm sorry." She squirmed away and looked at him.

"Don't worry about it. We both committed our love today. That's all that matters. I love you, Christina, and you love me." They heard voices outside.

"Oh God, its Harry's kids," Christina whispered. She hurried to put on her clothes.

"We can get out through the secret door upstairs," Ronny said. He helped her on with the rest of her clothes. "Come on, hurry," He took her hand,

She finished buttoning her blouse. "What kind of a wife am I going to be?" She tripped and he helped her. "You're such a gentleman, but I can't even control my urges."

"One day, when it's right, we both will let go of all control and give in to our urges." He looked at her and winked. "And if you'll accept me, I know you'll make the best wife any man could ask for."

"Forever," she whispered. "Although, you'll have to teach me some things." She looked at him with innocent eyes.

"My pleasure." They scurried up the steps in the closet and out the attic, and then secured the shutter.

***

"Oh my, those sparks sure did fly. Now I know why they call it sparking. That was a very special time I will always remember."

She again looked at the box. "I want to savor this moment." She could feel Grammy's presence in her office.

"Oh, Grammy, I sure did meet the love of my life, my soul mate." She smiled. "And René and his troops saved the trees on Red Winds." She imagined the beauty of the trees. "But later, the gossip gets better or worse; it depends on how you look at it." She was remembering another time.

"If I hadn't lived it, I would say it was nothing more than just gossip, folklore, or somebody's bad nightmare." She dredged up, in her mind, a time in the past that would always burn in her memory.

***

Golly, I missed a message from Ronny. God, it's always phone tag or something else with us. She shut her laptop and started to drive to her studio apartment. It was raining and she could hardly wait to get home. *I think I'll stop at the deli.*

"Hi, your usual this evening?" Vince, the meat clerk behind the counter, asked.

"Thanks, Vince. Yes the usual. Take your time, I have to check some messages." He smiled and nodded.

She went and sat down at a nearby table. *Let's see what Ronny had to say.* She opened her laptop. *Sure glad I got that new battery for this thing.* She opened his message. *Yippy, he's in town. I wonder why he didn't call.* She pondered this. *That would have been easier than this thing. Oh well, it doesn't matter as long as he finally got in touch with me.* She was still thinking when Vince told her the order was ready.

"Thanks, Vince, I think I'll grab a bottle of wine too."

"Have a nice evening," Vince said and waved good-bye.

"You too," she said, as she grabbed her favorite wine and checked out.

Ronny should have gotten back to me by now, she thought. She was relaxing at home with her deli supper and a glass of wine when she heard a message come in. *He's going to Red Winds this weekend, and wants to meet me there. That's odd. He knows we wouldn't have much time if we have to travel that far. I wonder what's on his mind?*

"You know, to have enough time, I would have to leave here on Wednesday?" she wrote back.

"I really want to see you, and I have a layover. It's really important, and that's the only time I have," he explained.

"I'll do it. For you anything," she typed back. She smiled, knowing she would turn her world upside down for him.

"The chalet by the lake, okay?" he asked.

"Okay," she replied. "See you soon," She signed off. *Our little piece of heaven*, she thought.

Her flight seemed to take forever, but finally—after several hours—she was walking through the woods to the chalet by the lake. It was starting to get dark so she was happy that she brought her flashlight and knapsack.

Looks like Reggie shut off the electric after closing up the main house to visit the family. I guess I could go turn on the power in the shed, she thought. *Nah, this looks kind of romantic.* She started to get some amorous ideas of her own. *This place looks lonely and is locked up tighter than a drum. Looks like he's using the oil lamps and has built a fire.* She looked over the chalet. *What could he be up to?* She neared the door and turned the knob. She was about to call out his name when she was hit from behind, and her world went dark.

"Well, it's about time you woke up," a voice in the distance was saying.

"Who . . . where am I?" Christina asked. She started to cough. "Ronny," she whispered.

"Ronny." The voice in the distance mimicked her. "Ronny, my love, where are you?" the voice then shouted. "Shut the fuck up about Ronny," the voice demanded.

"What do you want?" Christina asked, with panic evident in her voice.

"I've always wanted your precious Ronny, but since I can't have his ass, I'm going to get something that might make my life a little happier without him," the voice said.

"Oh my God." Christina started to recognize the voice. "Belle, is that you?" She looked toward the voice and saw Belle walking toward her. Christina looked around the room. She was laying on a small cot, with a rough blanket thrown over her. The only light in the room came from an oil lamp and a small fire in the brick fireplace. She noticed Belle did not look happy as she came next to her.

"Why did you have to take my man?" Belle screamed in Christina's face. "If you had stayed out of the picture, I know he'd of married me. You bitch." Belle spat in Christina's face.

"He never . . ." Christina was saying when she felt a sting in her left arm and turned to see a large man next to her. She saw him pull a syringe from her arm before her world again went black.

Sunlight filled the room. It hurt her eyes when she tried to open them, but she forced them open.

"Finally. What a twerp. I bet it takes one glass of wine to get you drunk. Next time we'll lessen the knockout drops, Hank?" Belle slurred. She smiled at Hank, who sat next to her on one of the chairs they had placed by a small card table.

"What do you want from me? Where's Ronny?" She could feel a deep panic building in her.

251

"Well, you see. I kind of stole old Ronny boy's Internet protocol address," Belle boasted. "He wasn't anymore careful with his laptop than you were," Belle snarled. "God you look like a stupid bitch. That's how I got in touch with you. You didn't hide your identity like you thought you did," she snickered.

"*Huh*," Christina moaned.

"Look at her. She's so pathetic." Belle took a swig from a bottle of liquor and a puff of a cigarette. "Oh please forgive me. It's not that I don't trust you . . ." Belle mimicked Christina from the time at the bar in the airport.

"At the airport when you helped me . . ." Christina was remembering.

"Yeah, and you helped yourself to my man," Belle shouted. "You're so stupid. I've been making goo goo conversation with you these past weeks, and you couldn't even tell the difference between your lover boy and me. That's how I found out about this place and all the little talks you used to have with your Grammy . . . Oops, I'm sorry your gossip." Belle tried to copy the way she thought Christina spoke. "The sweet, fucking way you talk makes me want to puke; sugar couldn't melt in your mouth," Belle snorted.

When Belle came closer, Christina could smell the rank of her strong perfume mixed with the liquor on her breath. "You're drunk." Christina coughed, trying to get the stench from her lungs. "Belle, come on cut these ropes." Christina tried to get up from the cot and noticed the restraints.

Belle looked at her with hatred written all over her face. "You bitch. You're gonna do what I say, or your lover boy's gonna take a final dip in that pretty lake outside. My Hank here will do just about anything for me, won't you, honey?" She hugged Hank and rubbed him with her overexposed bosom.

"You know it, baby." Hank looked at Christina on the cot and licked his lips.

"Hank kind of has a thing for you too. He's had a hankering ever since he saw you at the bar," Belle cooed, as she openly played with Hank. "That's how Hank got his name; he does a lot of hankering around and hanky panky." She rubbed him. They both started laughing and playing with each other as if they were alone in the room. Christina closed her eyes, but could not shut her ears. She hummed softly to herself.

After some time Christina could feel the cot move back and forth. When she opened her eyes, she spotted Hank sitting on the floor next to her. She wanted to scream, but controlled her urge.

"Not yet!" Belle shouted at him. She wanted to instill a deep, controlling fear in Christina. "Come on over here." Belle yelled out orders to him, and he pretended to obey her. "And get her phone . . . we know lover boy will answer for her," Belle's voice squeaked. She watched Hank play with the top buttons of Christina's silk blouse. His rough hands fondled her breasts in the black, lace bra she wore for the man she loved. He continued to lick his lips. His watery eyes opened wide, as he pretended to frisk her. Slowly, he rubbed his hand down her jeans, and then put his hand into her hip pocket where he retrieved her cell phone.

"Pounce, you buzzards!" Christina yelled. She could see that she gave Hank a bit of a scare.

"Shut the fuck up, or I'll get Hank to pounce. Get away from the bitch; you can play later." She motioned him over.

"Let's figure this damn thing out." He gave Belle the phone and she opened it. "There he is, old lover boy, ready for the picking." She hugged Hank, and in a half-stupor fell into one of the chairs. "We'll have to destroy this phone right after, and use one of the throwaways." She continued to slur her words.

God, they've got this all planned out, Christina thought.

"You just say what I tell you to, or Hank here will not only take care of you, but your lover boy too. You got that straight?" Belle shouted from where she sat.

"Yes, I've got it," Christina whispered. She watched Belle make the call.

"Well hi there." They all heard Ronny's voice on the speaker. "Well hi there," Belle repeated sarcastically.

"Who is this?" Ronny asked.

"Shut up, lover boy, and listen. I have your precious little book writer, and if you want to see her again, you'd better have one million precious dollars in my hands in twenty-four hours," Belle snorted.

"Who is this?"

"Just listen, lover boy . . . I'll get back to you with instructions in ten minutes. If you call in the authorities say good-bye to this one." Belle staggered over to the cot. "Say 'hi Ronny'." She spat in Christina's face.

"Hi Ronny," said Christina.

"Get the picture, lover boy?"

"If you harm her . . ."

"Just wait for my next call." Belle disconnected the phone. "Destroy this and throw it in the lake," Belle ordered. Hank did as she said.

"Okay, our ten minutes are just about up," Belle said and called Ronny's number.

"I want the money wired to this account," Belle said and gave him the number for an account she had set up in a fictitious name in Costa Rica.

"That's a lot of money. I'll do my best, but you're not giving me much time," Ronny shouted with fear evident in his voice.

"I know you can talk your family out of it. No authorities—I'm warning you—if you want to see her pretty face again," Belle again snorted.

"Pounce, you buzzards!" Christina screamed.

"Shut her the fuck up," Belle screamed to Hank. The phone and Christina were shut up.

**

"I should be at the airport shortly," Ronny relayed to René. "Thank God for Learjet." He had a nervous stammer in his voice.

"The car will be waiting. We'll meet you there," René said. He saw the panic in his wife's eyes.

"You know I have to go," Victoria said.

"I know," René said. "We don't have much time." They picked up their gear and left the inn.

"One of my operatives has informed me that your instincts were right. They're holding her at the chalet by the lake;" an FBI agent informed them after they met with him just outside the drive to Red Winds. "This storm might help us," he added.

Victoria rearranged the hood on her poncho. "If they harm her . . ."

"We're experts. Please, you'll have to wait in the trailer." An operative led Ronny, René, and Victoria to their utility control trailer.

"I'll have to show you where the secret door to the attic is," Ronny remarked.

"Yes, but then you'll have to leave it to us," the agent said. His authority was plainly evident in the tone of his voice.

"Of course," Ronny said. "I wouldn't want to cause any problems."

"But first we have to wait for their call," the agent said.

Patiently, they all sat and waited for Belle's call.

Ronny's phone rang. His throat was dry when he answered it. "Hello."

"You got all the money I asked for?" Belle shouted.

"I got what I could, but like I told you . . ." stammered Ronny. He knew he was lying, and if Belle checked, he hoped she wouldn't find out that the Costa Rican government and the US Treasury Department had tampered with fictitious funds.

"People like you make me sick. I guess she just isn't as important to you as I thought," Belle shouted. "Bring the bitch over here," she bellowed.

"Ronny," Christina whispered.

Belled grabbed the phone from her. "Ronny," Belle again mimicked Christina.

"You have to give me more time," Ronny tried to explain.

Just then a bolt of lightning lit up and a blast of thunder clapped. The phones went dead. "Damn thing," Belle shouted angrily. "Blew up right in my ear," she screamed. She tossed what was left of the phone and stuck her finger in her ear.

"Maybe that's a sign," Christina whispered. She looked straight at Hank.

"What's she talking about, a sign?" Hank asked. He looked scared to death.

"Oh you baby, she's playing with you," Belle snorted. Just then another bolt of lightning lit up the room followed by an immediate blast of thunder.

"Shit," Hank screamed.

"Damn it! We'll have to wait out this fucking storm." She looked at Hank. "You baby, get me another one of those throwaways." She went to the card table and took another swig of whiskey. "I should have done this by myself." She gave Hank a 'stupid' look.

"We ought to just take the money. It's plenty," Hank screamed. "I'm sick of this." He looked at Christina. "Let's just keep her tied up. There's nobody around here. She could scream her fucking head off, and no one would fucking hear her." He looked at Belle. "We could take what he has and in a couple days, we'd be sitting on the beach." He was trying to reason with Belle.

"Damn it, I want it all," she screamed at him. "Like I said, we'll wait out the storm and then I'll call him back." In a calmer voice, she said, "I'm generous. I'll give him some more time to come up with the rest." She smiled and took another gulp of the liquor.

Back at the utility control trailer, the group sat waiting word from the operatives near the chalet, where Ronny had explained to them about the entrance to the attic. "What!" the agent screamed. "Right away." He looked at the group.

"What is it?" Ronny almost shouted.

"That last bolt of lightning hit my guys in the field. One's badly burned and the other's having vision problems. We'll have to evacuate them and call in backup." He ordered his remaining operatives to the field to rescue the downed men.

"That could take too long. What if they get wind of what's going on? It will be light soon," Ronny shouted. He was getting agitated.

"Ronny's right," Victoria said. "My daughter's life is at stake. We have to do something now." She knew the agent also believed in what she said.

"You people are not trained for this kind of thing," he explained.

"Sir, as you can see, accidents can and will happen, but Ron here and myself, we're already experts in taking care of other's and ourselves. We can get her out of there," René said, with authority in his voice.

"I know the attic. I can get to the loft above the main floor without detection. I will take full responsibility," Ronny said. He wanted to leap from his seat and go for her, but sat still and watched René.

"After the bout with the trees, I became familiar with the chalet. I didn't know about the secret entrance, but I do know the lay of the land behind the chalet," René said. He looked at his wife.

She looked completely at ease with his decision to help her daughter. "Miracles," Victoria said, with a smile on her lips. "I'll expect a big one." She went to her husband and hugged him.

"You know it, my love." He patted the hand she had placed on his chest.

"This is how I believe it should go down." René began to explain and saw the agent nod when he relayed his hypothesis.

***

"Oh, Grammy, you would love my family," Christina said aloud. She held Grammy's letter close to her heart. She rose from her seat and went to look out the window of her office building. The snow had stopped.

But then, memories of that horrendous time came back to her. "When I saw Ronny's face looking down at me from the loft, I saw so much love and bravery." Her body shivered as she remembered back to that time.

René was waiting on the second floor just outside the stairs in the closet. Ronny had crawled to the edge of the floor of the loft. He had a stupendous view of the main room. He spotted Christina right away and knew that she saw him. It did not please him to see a large, burly man hovering over her, but he knew—with the FBI agent positioned just outside the front door of the chalet—it would soon be over. They were to wait for the agent's invasion through the front door.

"Get your ass over here!" Belle yelled out to Hank. "The storm's letting up. Leave the bitch alone and get your ass over here," she said, the slur evident in her voice.

Drunk, that's good, gives us the advantage, Ronny thought. He looked at Christina and winked. She smiled, which made his heart melt. He motioned for her to stay put. She showed him the restraints.

"Okay," He mouthed and crawled out of sight. He groped across the floor, hitting a chair. It rocked, but he caught it before it fell to the floor. Finally, he reached René.

"I need a knife. She's bound," he whispered to René. Without saying a word, René gave him his pocketknife. Ronny again crawled to the edge of the floor. He noticed the panic in Christina's eyes when Ronny turned to see the burly man coming up the stairs toward him.

Belle spotted Hank climbing the stairs and screamed, "What the fuck?" Just then the FBI agent, with Victoria's help, bashed in the front door. "What the hell . . ." Belle screamed. She caught a glimpse of Ronny nearing Hank on the stairs.

It was happening so fast. The agent entered the room with two guns drawn. Victoria watched as Belle went for her gun. Victoria saw the lit oil lamp and ran for it. She threw it at Belle and it ignited Belle's clothes. Belle screamed and ran outside, but not before she shot off several rounds.

"Ronny," Christina yelled. She saw Hank tumble down the stairs with the agent close to him.

With the storm over and the dawning light, Ronny could see that Hank had been shot in the head, so he jumped over him and went straight to Christina with René following right behind.

"Oh my God," Ronny shouted. He knelt down next to her. He looked at Victoria, who also knelt next to her daughter.

"I'm fine; just get these things off of me." Christina raised her arms the best she could with the restraints.

The agent was shouting, "He's gone. I didn't fire a shot. The woman must've shot him. Where'd she go?"

"She ran outside. I threw the lamp at her . . . she's on fire," Victoria yelled. She caressed Christina's face and held her in her arms after Ronny cut her free.

"I'll go check," the agent said.

When he came back, he said, "She's gone. We'll have to get the coroner. Looks like she drowned trying to put out the fire," the agent explained. "You folks come with me. The less you have to see the better." As he escorted them out the front door, he asked them to turn away from the lake.

"Kind of wobbly?" Ronny asked Christina. "Want me to carry you?"

"No, it feels good to walk. I've been lying down for too long." She put her head on his chest, as they continued to walk to the utility control trailer. "Give me a wink, will ya?" I've been dreaming about your wink and that Harrison Ford smile of yours," Christina said, as her tears fell.

"I love you," he whispered through tears.

"Me too." She stopped and hugged him as hard as she could, and they both turned and slowly walked to catch up with René and Victoria.

Ronny smiled at René. "I'm going to buy a pocketknife."

"I'm getting you one for Christmas," René answered.

They all chuckled and put their arms around one another. They did not look back. Time would heal their mental wounds. They would not allow the beautiful trees on Red Winds to bring back memories of this time. They would only think of it as a travesty that the forest would cover up with a blanket of the colors they loved.

Chapter Twelve

"Grammy, you would love my hero, Ronny, with his Harrison Ford smile." The wrapped package with the pink bow became more of a curiosity to her. She tried to put it out of her mind and started again with Grammy's letter.

> Honey, when you would visit and we had our gossip, you made my day. You were a little bit of sunshine on a cloudy, dreary day. And for that I say thank you and ask God to bless you.

Christina had to blow her nose again and wipe away flowing tears before she could continue to read.

> It was a very sad day when Olivia and Ronald's son Byron lost his life, the day the towers were hit in New York.

Christina could tell that Grammy's hands shook even more when she wrote those words. "Oh Grammy, it's Christmas time, what a great gift you're giving me, and I'm sure now you know about the greatest gift we all could ever have gotten." She started to think back to another time and another Christmas.

***

It was the day before Christmas Eve. That year some of the family had decided to join together at Red Winds.

"Mama, did you and Daddy sleep okay in the family room. I don't know why you two want to sleep on the pullout sofa when there are plenty of bedrooms," Christina asked. They were sipping the last of their breakfast coffee at the kitchen counter.

"We like the open feel of the house. I know it sounds weird, but we both like the wide open space," Victoria said, "and I love looking at the decorated mantel. At first it looked like I just threw all the holly and poinsettias up there, so I took it all down and started over. I think I got it this time. And don't forget how Daddy likes to snack and how nice and close we are to the kitchen." She took her cup to the sink, rinsed it, and placed it in the dishwasher.

"Well if you're happy . . . so you slept okay?" Christina asked.

"Sure, we did, honey. It was so cozy. We enjoyed the quiet of the house and snuggling; the hot toddies were pretty good too. If you ever have trouble sleeping, you should try them— the warm whisky puts you right to sleep," her mother explained with a chuckle. "I know the master bedroom has a fireplace, but, like I said, we like open spaces and the fireplace in the family room kind of reminds us of home. Want a refill?" She asked her daughter, pointing to Christina's coffee cup.

"No, I'm about full up on coffee." Christina got up from her chair, rinsed her cup, and put it in the dishwasher. "Oh, Mama, Grammy would have loved this: you know, all of us here together. Christmas was her favorite time of year," Christina said.

"I know I love it, so I'm sure she would've too," Victoria, replied. "Reggie makes everyone feel right at home. Oh golly, I hope my fudge turns out." Victoria looked worried. "Should we get started?" They gathered the ingredients to start making goodies.

"Only you can make the best Christmas fudge and those to-die-for, no bake, fudgy oatmeal cookies. Mine never turn out like yours," said Christina.

"I had trouble with them when I first started making them, but I guess I've been making them for so long that it just comes naturally," Victoria said and started to stir her fudge mixture.

"I've watched you, but I guess they're just not my thing." She was putting together the makings for an apple pie. "I'm glad we put your batch in the Christmas basket. I bet the Wilsons enjoyed them more than they would've mine," said Christina, watching her mother stirring the chocolate fudge mixture. They both laughed. "Cooking and baking with you is so much fun."

"Wasn't it funny when the three kids were in the tub together getting a bath," her mother said and started to giggle. "When Mr. Wilson yelled out that ho—ho—ho, I thought those kids were going to jump out of their skin. Did you ever hear so much screaming?" They both started to laugh.

"Oh Mama, that's what Christmas is all about—the kids and the love," Christina added. "Mama, Mrs. Wilson told me you and Daddy brought bags of presents the day before. You two just love secret miracles, don't you?" She noticed her mother going about her business as if she had not heard what she said.

"And did you see the look in those kids' eyes when they bundled up in their coats and boots and went outside to look for Santa. René just loves to get them going with that," Victoria said. She seemed to only want to keep up the conversation about the kids, as she continued to stir the fudge. "He acts like he's searching for something up in the sky, and then he points to the planet Mars and makes them think it's Rudolph's nose." She winked at her daughter.

"I know. I went out when Daddy told Evian," Christina said. "I was as excited as she was. He makes it so real." She sounded thrilled.

"Christmas is real, honey. If you believe, you can make it real in your heart and real for those around you," her mother said. "And we certainly can't forget the most important part . . ." She looked at her daughter.

"I know—it's the celebration of the birth of Jesus. You and Daddy make my heart happy, and to me that's the believing," Christina said and hugged her from behind.

"I'm going to burn this fudge if you keep this up," Victoria said and turned to hug her daughter. "Here, you stir." She gave her daughter the wooden spoon. "Just keep an eye on the candy thermometer. Let me know when it bubbles and reads 234 degrees." She went to blow her nose and wipe the tears from her eyes.

Christina started talking about a neighbor who used to live down the road from Red Winds. "You know, Mr. Smithton looked happier than I ever remember seeing him look. After his wife died, I know his family didn't visit him that much when he lived in his small apartment at the assisted-living retirement home," Christina remarked. "We always used to call him Ninety Nine, but then he turned a hundred, and now he's a hundred and one, but we still tease him and call him Ninety Nine." She smiled at her mother.

"I thought he always looked lonely, but when I saw him the other day at the skilled nursing facility, he looked happy. Other residents stood around him, and he was actually laughing. I don't know if he really knew who I was, but I don't think that mattered 'cause he was so happy. I was even afraid to visit him there because I thought he was going to be sad. I remember his wife would never smile; she always had a frown on her face, and everybody always wondered what he saw in her because he smiled all the time. Then, when they celebrated their sixtieth wedding anniversary, she sported the most loving smile when she danced with him. I'm telling you, I never doubted her love or what he saw in her after that," Christina related and continued stirring the fudge.

"That just shows that that old saying is true: love is in the eye of the beholder. It sure is nice that he has so many friends too. Friendly companionship can do wonders for the soul," Victoria said. She finished garnishing a large ham, with a brown sugar and mustard glaze, and placed it in the pre-heated oven.

"I'm glad we had our time with your brothers and their families at Thanksgiving," Christina commented, changing the subject. "We were lucky to have a late autumn. The trees on Hawk's Nest still had some color," Christina said. "It's fun being an older cousin, and the kids are sure cute. We had so much fun playing in the woods. I could smell the acorns . . . and those kids in the leaves." They both laughed. "I don't think the forest was the same after we left it." Christina watched her mother finish placing foil in a large, glass pan while Christina checked the fudge. "It's just about 234 degrees."

"Too bad Ronny couldn't be here," said Victoria and took over the job of mixing the fudge.

"It is one of the busiest times of the year," Christina replied. She watched her mother stir in the chocolate chips and then the marshmallow cream, finishing with the vanilla. "I'm learning your art," she said with a smile.

"I know." Victoria poured the fudge mixture into her prepared pan. "Hey, let me see that rock again," said Victoria, motioning to her daughter to look at her engagement ring. "Beautiful, and I don't just mean the ring." She kissed her daughter's hand. She knew how much her daughter wished her fiancé could be with them.

She gave Christina a spoon. "Here," she said, "we don't want this to go to waste." She watched her daughter enjoy the leftover fudge from the pot. "This is one of the privileges of the cook." She smiled and they both scraped more of the warm fudge.

"Oh, honey, that pie looks so good," remarked Victoria. She was again trying to change the subject, knowing her daughter was still thinking about the absence of the man she loved. "You have the knack." She watched her daughter return to her project of pie making and fluting the edges like a pro,

"I had a good teacher." She looked at her mother lovingly. They both knew her mother had taught Christina her technique for the perfect apple pie. "Just the right amount of tapioca," Christina said and winked at her mother.

"You know it." Victoria laughed. "I get so much joy from cooking. It's kind of my passion," she said. "I still try to watch my diet, but I just love to see people dive into my cooking."

"Besides me, I think I know who's your best customer," Christina added.

"Daddy," they said in unison and laughed while Christina finished the pie.

"I'm glad we bought our tree at the tree farm. I like the idea of preserving the trees and only cutting down enough to thin them out to promote future growth," Victoria said. "And it sure doesn't hurt that they sell hot cocoa and frozen custard either." She looked at her daughter and saw the look of satisfaction in her eyes. "I could've eaten two or three of those frozen custard cones, and the ones double dipped in chocolate . . . to die for." Her mother's eyes lit up.

"I know what you mean. First we eat frozen yogurt and then warm up with hot cocoa. Doesn't make sense, but its fun," Christina said. "And I like the idea of using the leftover greens from the trees; they make beautiful wreaths for the doors and for the fireplace."

"Speaking of trees, did you see all the wood Daddy and Jeremy stacked up on the back porch?" Victoria asked.

"I'm sure we'll need it," Christina said.

"Did I miss anything?" Arlene asked, as she entered the kitchen. She went to the coffeepot on the counter, poured herself a cup of the steaming brew, and sat at the table.

"Not much—just cooking and baking. Did you get her down?" Victoria asked her daughter about her granddaughter, Evian.

"She's so excited. I didn't think she'd ever close her eyes. That warm milk Reggie brought up must have helped," Arlene said. She set the nanny monitor down on the table and dabbed some milk in her coffee.

"Grandma Lyssa and Glenn should be here for supper this evening," Christina said. "I really like Glenn. He's been a godsend for Grandma," she added. She knew it was hard on her grandmother when she lost her husband all those years ago.

"Glenn's a caring man," Victoria replied. "And a vet . . ." She sounded very pleased.

"I know," said Christina. "The business needed a jump start. We all know that her brothers CC and Andy never had an interest in the vet business, so it was a streak of good luck when Glenn took over Papa Cal's practice. I love that they turned the old place into The Yarborough Hospital for Animals."

"Yeah, it was wonderful that they could keep the place going, and it gave Lyssa a new lease on life to see her parent's lifelong business not have to fold. She bloomed when Glenn came into her life," Victoria said and looked at Christina with glassy eyes.

"Are you going to be okay with all of this?" Christina asked her mother.

"Honey, you brought us together again. It was time," Victoria said, as she hugged her daughter. She looked over her shoulder and smiled at Arlene. They all knew it was hard for Victoria to get close to her mother, Lyssa; but Victoria did it out of love for Christina. "You know, right now I kind of wish I could turn back time for just a little while and you were a kid again." Victoria had a slight look of melancholy in her eyes. "I missed so much when I left you. Now that I know what life is really about, I have a deep feeling of regret knowing I missed watching you at Christmastime," Victoria said, again hugging her daughter. She buried her head into Christina's shoulder while trying to control her emotions.

"Oh Mama, I love you, and you make me so happy now. Don't think about the past."

"Gombie," could be heard on the nanny monitor. "Gombie," Evian cried out.

"She wants her godmother," Arlene said and smiled at Christina.

"I'm on it." Christina went to the sink, quickly washed the pie dough from her hands, and left the room.

"She's going to be a good mother, just like you," Victoria said to Arlene.

"Just like you." Arlene stood next to her mother. "What can I do?" she asked, looking around.

"Right now, go sit down and rest," Victoria said, in a loving but stern tone.

"If you're sure," Arlene said when she saw the look of authority that only a mother can give. "Yes, ma'am." She pretended to obey.

"Gombie." They heard Evian's voice again on the monitor.

"My little Gotchie," they heard Christina say. She had left the nanny monitor on the kitchen table. "You don't want your mommy?" Christina asked Evian. "You want your Gombie?" She sat on the side of the bed. "Look at you in this big girl bed." She lay down next to Evian.

"Mommy and Daddy said I'm a big girl." Evian started to yawn and put her arm around Christina's neck. "Gimme a hug," Evian whispered.

"You know it." Christina pulled up the blanket and nestled next to Evian. "Want to sleep some more?" she whispered.

"Want hugs," Evian answered, sounding doubtful. "I saw the nose," she whispered to Christina.

"I know, wasn't it neat?" She saw a little fear in Evian's sleepy eyes.

"I guess," Evian said, with some hesitation.

"Rudolph's bright nose helps Santa find where we are. Santa has a lot of work to do and he has to work day and night," said Christina.

"I know. Mommy and Daddy told me, but ..." She seemed to be having a hard time explaining her fear of the unknown about St. Nick.

"Don't you worry one bit about good old Santa—he loves all of us just like Jesus loves us. Did you know Christmas is Jesus's birthday?"

"Yeah, I know," whispered Evian.

In the kitchen Victoria and Arlene were trying to listen to their conversation. "Oh my, so sweet," Arlene said. She looked at her mother and realized they both had tears streaming down their cheeks.

"Well, honey, Jesus wants all his children to celebrate his birthday, and that means you and me." Christina continued to explain her ideas of Christmas.

"And Mommy and Daddy and Ma Ma and Re Re and ..." Evian was saying excitedly.

"Yes, honey, everybody. And Jesus has all the Santas in the world giving out gifts to all of his children." She saw Evian relax.

"Well, yeah, that's neat, and Santa has to be nice if Jesus sends him to our house." She looked at Christina with trust in her eyes.

"Absolutely." She tenderly caressed Evian's warm cheek and noticed she was falling asleep. When she heard her breathe softly, she slipped out from under the covers and went downstairs.

"Hey, any snacks in here?" René hollered cheerfully, like only he could do. He and Jeremy came in through the backdoor.

"René!" Victoria shushed him. She motioned for him and Jeremy to come and listen.

Just then Christina came into the kitchen and saw them all huddled around the monitor, so she understood they had listened to her and Evian.

"Having some Christmas fun?" She blurted out. "I'm going to tell Santa about you guys spying." She laughed.

They all turned from the table and tried to look innocent. "Well . . ." René slightly coughed. "Me and my number one son here sure are hungry," René bellowed. Victoria gave him a look to quiet him, so as not to wake Evian. "If she's like me, she can sleep through a tornado," he bellowed again. Knowing he was not going to give in, they all just laughed.

"You know us Paul Bunyan types need some grub," he again bellowed one of his contagious bursts of laughter. He put his arm around his son-in-law.

"Thank God for mudrooms," Victoria whispered to Christina. They both chuckled.

"I think it's more like I'm ole Paul here's true blue jackass, Babe." Jeremy jerked his thumb towards his father-in-law and tried to bellow out like him.

"Jeremy . . ." Arlene scolded, as she playfully wagged her finger at her husband.

"Oh, sorry ladies, I mean his overloaded ox," Jeremy remarked. He laughed with his father-in-law.

"Oh come on now, Babe, you're not trying to say you're getting tired?" René teased, with a sly grin. "You should've seen him pull that last tree out of the woods. All I had to do was put it on his back, and my big blue ox here carried it all by himself. What a sight . . ." René was getting into some tall Paul Bunyan tales. He went for a bottle of peppermint schnapps and poured Jeremy and himself each a shot glass full. They sat down at the table.

"Here you go, my lumberjack heroes." Arlene brought them plates of sliced ham and crackers with cheese.

"Thanks, honey," Jeremy said to his wife. She came and sat on his lap.

"You smell like outside," Arlene whispered to her husband after she kissed his neck.

"I know. Ain't it great." He looked at her and gave her a hug.

"Doesn't the deep snow make it hard to cut wood?" Arlene asked.

"Sure it does, honey, but me and Babe here, we can trudge through forty feet of snow and ice." René kept on with his fables. He winked at Jeremy, and they all laughed.

"René you're full of it today," Victoria kidded him.

René took her in his arms. "You know it. Want to check the animals in the barn?" he teased his wife. Victoria laughed, and then with a devious look in her eyes, messed with his hair.

"Daddy!" Arlene said, as she cuddled up to her husband's chest.

"We all know how much Daddy loves Mama," Christina said and winked at her sister, and they all laughed louder than before.

"Come on girls join in the fun." René went for more shot glasses.

"Kind of early," Victoria said, but knew she would join him. He was her love, and she delighted in his knack for getting the most enjoyment out of every minute of life.

"It's Christmastime, a time for celebration and fun," René cheerfully commented. He filled glasses and passed them around.

"Oh no," Arlene cried out. Reggie was standing in the kitchen doorway with her daughter, Evian in hand. "Oh well, it's Christmastime," Arlene said. She picked her daughter up and brought her to her father, Jeremy. "Hot chocolate for my little girl?" Arlene got a cup of the mixture that was kept warm and forever available in a Crock-Pot.

"And a glass of libation for Reggie," René bellowed. He poured a glass and passed it.

The phone rang. "Merry Christmas Eve, Eve . . ." Christina said. "Oh Josh, how nice," She looked at everyone and nodded that she would take his call in the other room. "How you doing, bro?" She asked her half uncle whom she always referred to as a brother. "Adam called earlier. Yeah we're all doing just fine," she said. "Mama said you talked with her earlier. I was making a snow family with Arlene and Evian. This place is really getting festive and not that we needed our spirits lifted, but René just poured us some peppermint schnapps; so it's getting pretty lively around here." She knew he just wanted to touch base and wish them all a Merry Christmas. "You always love keeping in touch with everyone. That's neat. Yeah, you guys have a Merry Christmas too. We love you all," she said and smiled when she hung up the phone.

"Christmas is for the kids," René was saying, as Christina came back into the kitchen. A huge smile lit up his eyes when he winked at his granddaughter and she winked back.

"And for the biggest kid I know," Victoria said. She kissed her husband right on the lips.

"You know it. 'Tis the season for the kid in all of us and miracles to come." René kissed his wife. "What else could we ask for?" René boasted. He tilted his glass toward his family.

"Here—here!" They all shouted and drank to his toast.

"Hey, what'd you say to a card game?" René asked and went to get a deck of cards.

"Sounds like fun. I'm in," Arlene said. She went for another shot of the schnapps.

"Me too. The ham's in the oven and everything else is ready," Victoria said. She sat next to her husband and watched everyone else sit down at the table, with the bottle in the middle of it.

The room was filled with love and the aromas that made them feel warm and cozy. It was Christmastime, a time for family and miracles.

***

A few days earlier, while they had been enjoying their family moments on Red Winds, a Christmas miracle was forming and was about to unfold. The trees that lined the streets twinkled with many colored Christmas lights. The snow left a white winter wonderland for the season.

"I love the snow," Nina said. She was waiting on the last customer in line at her café, Martha's Cinnamon Rolls.

"I know what you mean," the customer said. "Just wouldn't be Christmas without the New York snow." She smiled and took her boxed order.

"Enjoy the rolls—and Merry Christmas," Nina said cheerfully.

"Thanks, and Merry Christmas to you too," the customer said and waved good-bye.

"That man's been in the café all afternoon," Nina's assistant whispered. "He doesn't look homeless, but he only ordered one roll and he's been filling up on coffee. He kept his coat and hat on all the time too. Do you think I should call the police?" Her assistant was leery of the stranger.

"I'll check it out," Nina said. She wiped her hands on her apron and then took it off.

"Good evening, sir. We'll be closing up early today for the holidays," Nina said politely. "Can I offer you a Christmas cinnamon roll, on the house?" she asked. She noticed the man feebly take his badly marred hand and tilt his hat back on his head.

"Maddy," the stranger said.

"Oh my God!" Nina shrieked and held her hand to her mouth. She sat across from the stranger and looked him straight in the eyes. "Stay here," she said hurriedly. She rose from her seat and started to yell out orders in Japanese. Her employees quickly cleared out of the café, and she locked it up.

He watched her with warm tears finding there way down the thick, beaded scars on his face.

She again sat across from him. "Everyone thinks your dead. Your family buried you." She spoke calmly.

"I was attacked and robbed. My identity was stolen, and the man who stole it is the person they buried, not me," he said. He tried to cuddle closer into the warmth of his coat.

"But why didn't you get in touch with your family?" she whispered. She saw that he was fragile and could not take out on him the rage she was feeling. "We all missed you desperately." She sat back on her chair and looked at him sadly.

"I lost my memory and became a John Doe. I'm guessing my driver's license and other items made it logical to assume that he was me." He did not seem to want to explain any further.

"But you know who you are now? You know me?" she asked.

"I was walking past here one day and saw the name on the sign outside. I looked in the window and saw you. You triggered something in me and everything came flooding back." He tried to cover his face with his hand. "You still look at me with love in your eyes," he mumbled.

"Love can't be forced to come or leave; I will always love you. You have a place in my heart that I will always cherish. We have to let your family know." She hoped he would allow her to help him.

"Maddy, there's more . . ." He looked at her with both love and fear written all over his face.

"We'll work out anything . . . together," she whispered. She took his hand and patted it.

***

The sun was setting on Red Winds and twilight, a warm, blazing fire, a few coal oil lamps, and candles lit the family room. They were trimming the Christmas tree.

"I could see you enjoyed watching the girls with Evian as she set up the manger," Lyssa said to her daughter, Victoria.

"Evian's so precious. She loves how René tells the Christmas story about the birth of Jesus," Victoria commented.

"She's so sweet; and the questions . . ." Lyssa chuckled, and so did Victoria. Lyssa noticed her daughter had a look of joy in her eyes, something she was truly happy to see.

"All my girls bring me a joy I sometimes think I don't deserve," said Victoria.

"Honey, just take it in and enjoy it," Lyssa said.

"You know, I don't understand why René was called away yesterday. He left in such a hurry and he's been gone all night, and why did he take Reggie and not you?" Lyssa gave her daughter a confused look. "He didn't say a word?" Lyssa asked Victoria.

"It's Christmastime. I never ask questions around this time," Victoria replied, but she too wondered why her husband left so quickly with Reggie without saying a word, and why he seemed concerned after receiving that mysterious phone call. To be gone all night without a word was truly unlike him.

"Josh and Adam really had a nice time at Hawk's Nest," Lyssa commented about her sons, trying to change the subject. She was stringing popcorn for the tree.

"They have lovely families. You must really be proud," Victoria said about Lyssa's sons and her half brothers. Looking at her mother dressed in a comfy pair of black sweatpants and velvety looking red sweater, she thought she looked completely relaxed and calm in her own skin. It was not hard to believe that she was only eighteen years older than her. Both women looked vital and healthy.

"They're for you to be proud of too. After all, they are your brothers," Lyssa scolded.

"I am," Victoria said. *The spitfire I remember is always lurking,* she thought. She smiled at her mother. *Oh God, I have it too.* She chuckled.

"What?" Lyssa asked. She wondered what made her daughter laugh.

"Oh, nothing, I was just thinking how sometimes I act exactly like you," Victoria said. She noticed Lyssa give her one of her 'I don't think so' looks.

Just then Glenn came into the room. "Nice and cozy in here, great ambiance," he said. He sat next to his wife, Lyssa, on the arm of the sofa, where she and Victoria were seated. "Listen to Jeremy playing the guitar. Evian was so cute when he played 'I saw Mama kissing Santa Claus'," Glenn commented. "She dances around and sings like a pro."

"They sing with her and practice all year long. She's quite the little actress," Victoria said about her granddaughter.

"She's sure a cutie," Lyssa added. Both women smiled at each other.

"Can I help?" Glenn asked, looking at Lyssa.

"I could use some more popcorn," Lyssa said. She took a big, fluffy kernel and popped it into her mouth.

"I think she means the buttered kind," Victoria said. They all laughed.

"I love it, and the smell drives me crazy. More please," Lyssa said, acting shyly. She passed the empty bowl to her husband. "Maybe two bowls." Smiling, she coyly raised her eyebrows and puckered her lips.

"Okay, I never could resist that look," Glenn said. He stooped down and kissed his wife. "One buttered and one for the tree," he said and everyone laughed.

"What's all the commotion?" Christina asked, as she came into the family room and saw Glenn laughing.

"Your mother ate all the popcorn," Lyssa said, smirking.

"Yep, just like me," Victoria teased, going along with Lyssa's fib. She reached her socked foot over and jokingly pushed her mother with it. They smiled at each other.

"I thought popped corn blocked you up," Christina said to Victoria. She watched her mother and grandmother explode with laughter. "What did I say?" Christina asked.

"It's a long story, and would lose its punch . . ." Lyssa was trying to explain, but could not stop laughing.

"Oh well," Christina said. She had that 'are they for real' look in her eyes. "Well, *um*, I see you're working on the white and blue tree lights," she said to her mother.

"Yes, honey, I am, and I'm trying to keep them in line," Victoria explained, still trying to control her laughter.

"I'll get the placement binder if you like . . ." Christina started to say, but then said, "I was just outside, and the house looks so peaceful covered in snow and colored Christmas lights. I remember Papa Cal said the different colored lights looked so jolly." Her grandmother nodded.

"You're right. Mom liked the peaceful look of all blue lights, and Daddy liked the jolly look of multi-colored lights. They both loved the Christmas season, and Daddy would put a multi-colored tree in the window for everyone to see. The one in the family room had all blue lights," Lyssa commented and continued to string the remaining corn.

"I remember Grandpa Cal would do just about anything for Grandma Rachel," Victoria said. She remembered visiting her grandparents when she came home pregnant with Christina and lived down the road from Red Winds, with her mother, Lyssa, and step father.

"Yep, that was Dad, always there for Mama," Lyssa said. "Is it still snowing outside?" Lyssa then asked Christina.

"Just a little, and the cedar Christmas logs from the fire smell great," said Christina, trying to relate her Christmas spirit. "I guess you two are getting into the spirit of Christmas too."

"Of course we are," Victoria said and winked at Christina. "Your Grandma can get me going" She emphasized the word *Grandma*. She was still trying to settle down her laughter. "Could you pass me a tissue?" Victoria asked her daughter. Christina brought her the box, and Victoria blew her nose. "Here, why should I be surprised, you need one too," Victoria teasingly commented to Lyssa. She tossed the tissue box to her mother, and they both exploded into another round of laughter.

"I think I'll go check on Arlene and Evian." Christina looked at them and wondered why they were acting so out of character. She gave them both a puzzled look, as she got up to leave the room.

"Honey, could you bring us another bottle of wine?" her grandmother, Lyssa asked. "This one's about gone."

"Sure," Christina said and left the room. "Like they need another bottle of wine," she mumbled.

"We heard that," Victoria, in good spirits, yelled.

"Crap," she mumbled and ran to the kitchen. "I'll be right back," she yelled.

"Mom and Grandma are really bonding in there," Christina said. She stood next to Glenn and watched him shake the pot of corn.

"It's great. Your grandmother really needed this time," he said, with love showing in his eyes.

"I know," Christina said.

"You know the candlelight vigil at the VFW was really great again this year," Christina said. "I'm sure it's hard to control your emotions when you read the names of all the veterans." She could hear the corn start to pop.

"I do my best," Glenn said, continuing to shack the pot of corn. "Seeing the children dressed as angels and hearing the singing sometimes breaks me up, but ..." He could feel his eyes filling with tears.

"You did a great job," she said.

"Oh crap ... too much corn." Glenn took the pot off the stove. "I'm really not used to making it in a pot. I use the bag stuff in the microwave." He looked for the bowl, as the corn started to overflow.

"Here use this." Christina brought him a roasting pan.

"Thanks." Glenn poured the popped corn in the pan.

"I'll make the next batch. I'm used to making it like this," Christina said.

"I'll butter this batch." Glenn saw the curious look she gave him.

"No, not for the tree, it's for your grandmother. She has a thing for buttered popcorn," he said and Christina burst into laughter. "What?" Glenn asked.

"Those two are just too funny." Christina figured out why they were laughing and grabbed her stomach. She had to run upstairs to the bathroom. "I'll be right back." She left him alone in the room.

This place is crazy—fun but crazy, he thought. He placed a small pot on the cooking range and cut a large slice of creamy butter to melt in the pot.

***

"Here you go, honey." Christina was showing her niece how to place the white and blue lights on a string to then put on the tree.

"How do you know who's who?" Evian, smart for a three-year-old, asked.

"See this list?" Christina showed her the leather binder that held the list of names in order of their placement on the string. "Well, each blue light represents a loved one who's looking down at us from up in heaven," Christina explained, pointing up. She looked into Evian's eyes. *Just like looking into Arlene's clear blue eyes,* she thought. "You look just like your mama." She scooted Evian closer to her.

"Daddy always says that, too," Evian said. "Can you put the white and me the blue?" she asked her aunt about the placement of the bulbs.

"Sure, honey, but I'll have to put in ten white before each blue." Christina screwed the ten white bulbs into the string of lights. "Now, here is yours." Christina handed her a blue bulb.

"Who's this?" Evian asked. She carefully took the blue bulb and tried to twist it onto the string.

"That's for Olivia's mother, Elizabeth," Christina said. She watched Evian struggle to place the bulb. "Want some help?"

"I guess." Evian watched Christina screw in the bulb. "I think I can do the next one." Evian watched as Christina put in the next row of white.

"Okay, here you go." Christina handed Evian another blue bulb.

"Who's this?" Evian asked, holding up the blue bulb.

"That's for Olivia's father, Jason. He built Red Winds with his wife Elizabeth, Olivia's mom," Christina said. She watched Evian quickly kiss the bulb. "You're a sweetheart," Christina said. She watched Evian carefully screw in the bulb. She then added another row of white bulbs.

"You know, I wish we could use the phone and call 'em up in heaven," said Evian innocently.

"Wouldn't that be fun, and I know they all would love it too." Christina caressed Evian's cheek. "You're such a caring little person." She softly pinched Evian's cheek. "I remember one Christmas when Grandpa took me and Grammy to the chalet by the lake. It was snowing just like it is today." Christina looked at her niece and saw she had her complete attention so she continued. "Well, the chalet was real dark, but Grandpa told us to go on in while he put the horse and sled in the barn." She looked at Evian, whose eyes were as big as saucers.

"Weren't you and Grammy scared in the dark?" Evian asked.

"Nah. I always felt safe with Grammy. Well, anyway, Grammy finally found her way to the oil lamp and lit it. You see the electricity was off at that time, and just then we heard a real loud *ho—ho—ho* from outside, and the lights on the Christmas tree came on and music from a CD player started playing." Christina looked at Evian and raised her eyebrows. "I looked toward the door and saw Grandpa in the doorway, so I knew he didn't make that *ho—ho—ho* sound. I just knew it had to be Santa, so I ran upstairs, but he was gone. I'm telling you it was the most exciting thing." She expressed the same excitement she felt back then.

"Wow!" Evian scooted as close as she could to her aunt. "But he didn't scare you."

"Grammy was smiling, so I knew Santa would never want to scare me," Christina explained to her niece. "Want a drink of your hot cocoa?" Christina asked Evian.

"Yes please," Evian said merrily, but she still had a look of skepticism in her eyes. She perked up in her seat and watched her aunt reach for the drink on the table in front of them. "Thank you," Evian said politely and took a generous drink of the concoction. "We call it hot chocolate," she said.

"They mean the same thing," Christina said, noticing her niece's chocolate mustache. "You're so cute." Christina was about to wipe her niece's upper lip, but Evian took another sip. "You look so snug in your footy pajamas. Did you have a nice bubble bath?" she asked her niece.

Evian's eyes brightened. "Did you hear it too?" Evian looked at Christina. "I think I heard Santa just like you did." Evian's eyes opened wide.

"You did?" Christina gave her niece a questioning look.

"I know it had to be him that me and Mama heard outside the bathroom door," she said, with excitement evident in her voice.

"You did? I didn't hear anything. What did he say?" Christina asked. She took the cup Evian almost tossed at her when Evian jumped to her feet next to Christina on the sofa.

"His bells, Mama said. It was his jingle bells, and then he did his *ho—ho—ho*," she bellowed out imitating what she had heard. "I was scared and put the bubbles over my head."

"Oh, honey, Santa wouldn't hurt you," Christina again tried to explain.

"I know, Mama told me . . . but I pooped anyway." Evian looked away from Christina. She jumped a couple more times on the sofa and then flopped down next to her aunt.

"Oh my, I'm sure that could happen when you're not expecting somebody like Santa at your door," Christina said. She hugged Evian, trying to play down the embarrassment she saw on her face.

They both laughed. "I know that's what Mama said too." Evian looked up at Christina. "She said it wasn't pretty under my bubbles." She forgot about it, and to change that kind of talk Evian reached for her hot cocoa in Christina's hand; she took another sip and gave it back to Christina to place on the table. "Another blue?" Evian grabbed another blue bulb. She looked up at Christina with the same question in her eyes about the placement of the bulbs.

"That's for little Jay, Olivia's brother," Christina was saying when there was a loud knock at the front door.

"Golly, is Jay coming down from Heaven to look at the lights?" Evian cried out. She cuddled into Christina.

"I'll get it," they heard Victoria shout on her way to the front door.

Christina hugged Evian. "Oh no, honey, probably just some Christmas Eve visitors, maybe some carolers coming to sing some Christmas songs," Christina said. She saw excitement in her niece's eyes. "Want to check it out?" They both rose from the sofa and met Jeremy on the way.

"René, the door's open," Victoria said. She saw René standing on the front porch in the blustery night air. "Get in here . . . where's Reggie?" She had that caring yet scolding tone in her voice. She looked around, while motioning him into the warmth of the foyer.

"Honey, go get Lyssa and Christina," René whispered.

"What's wrong?" Victoria asked. She had a look of fear in her eyes. "You're scaring me." She knew he was not acting like his normal, boisterous self.

"It's fine, honey, you'll see." René gave her a loving look as he watched her turn and go to find Lyssa and Christina.

Curious, everyone in the house came to the front door. "I'm cold," Evian said. She was in her father's arms.

"Its okay, honey. Here, get into Daddy's sweater." Jeremy saw her chocolate mustache and was about to wipe it off, but she hurriedly opened his sweater and cuddled under it.

"What's going on, Daddy," Christina asked René. She watched her father step to the side of the open door. "Aunt Mary!" Christina shouted.

"Yes, it's me. Bet you never thought this old, retired actress would live this long, did ya?" Mary showed her usual sense of humor. Reggie was pushing her in a wheelchair.

"Hurry in out of the cold." Christina hurried to help them in, but then she spotted another surprise. "Ronny!" she shouted and ran to him. He scooped her into his arms.

"Hi, baby." Ronny kissed her and then looked her in the eyes, as he took her shoulders and gently turned her around.

Christina noticed a man and woman stood huddled behind him. She thought they looked like a homeless family. "Welcome to our home. Welcome to Red Winds," Christina pleasantly greeted the strangers. "Please, come in out of the cold."

They all watched the man, holding a young child, and the woman walk into the foyer. Glenn and René came forward to help them off with their overly stuffed winter coats.

"She's going to have baby Jesus!" Evian shouted out.

They all could see the woman was pregnant. "Evian," Arlene whispered a reprimand to her daughter. She took her daughter from her father's arms. "We can see that. Isn't that wonderful?" She had a puzzled look on her face.

"Oh my God," Lyssa shouted. She put her hands to her mouth and felt as if she might faint. She could not believe her eyes. Glenn went to her.

"Honey," Glenn said and took his wife in his arms. "What is it?"

"Byron ..." Lyssa, feeling completely shocked, stared at him. "Is it you?" She felt she was in one of her dreams. "I always felt you were alive," she whispered. Totally surprised, she could only gawk at him. No one in the room seemed to be able to move. It was like a place in time had frozen them to that spot.

"Grandpa?" Christina asked in a whisper. She looked around the room for some kind of verification.

"Yes," Byron replied. He held the child and the woman beside him as close to his chest as he could without hurting them.

"Oh my God!" Lyssa felt her legs go limp and leaned into Glenn.

"Let's go to the family room," René said and led the way. Everyone was silent as Byron and his family sat on a small loveseat.

Byron looked around the familiar room. Then he noticed Evian's chocolate mustache and smiled at her. She smiled in return.

"How?" Lyssa was compelled to ask. She looked from Byron to the child he held. She looked at the woman next to him and then at Byron.

"That call I got the other day was from Mary," René explained. "Well, Byron's sister, Nina, who you knew as Madison, got in touch with Mary."

"And I got in touch with René," Mary added.

"And René called me. I got an emergency leave, gassed up the jet, and here we are," Ronny said. He continued to hold onto Christina.

"Byron." Lyssa whispered. She could not take her eyes from Byron's. She and Glenn were sitting on the larger sofa—with as many people as it could fit—across from the loveseat. The rest sat on the carpeted floor.

"Madison explained to Mary that Byron has had amnesia all this time," René continued.

"It's impolite to keep your hat on in the house," Evian blurted out.

"Evian," Arlene, again reprimanded her daughter. "I'm so sorry," she said. She could not help but stare and wonder about the man she had only heard about for all these years.

"My husband has been scarred. He always wears his hat in public," the woman next to Byron explained. She felt she had to defend the man she loved.

"Your husband?" A surprised Lyssa asked. She continued to stare at Byron.

"I'm sure we all have many questions, but for now, I think we should let Byron and Lyssa have some private time," René said.

"I believe that is wise," the woman said. "My husband needs to explain a lot." She leaned over and kissed her husband on his cheek and then, with Byron's help, rose from her seat.

René reached down and picked up the now sleeping child from Byron's arms.

Just then, Reggie placed a tiny puppy on the floor that had been kept warm just outside the front door in a large cardboard box.

"A puppy," Evian shouted excitedly, which did not even make the sleeping child flinch.

"That's our Christmas puppy, Rags," Byron said. He watched with a happy heart as Evian picked up the puppy. René then escorted the rest of the family from the room.

Lyssa sat next to him on the smaller sofa and, in disbelief, could only stare at him.

"I know I look frightful," Byron said. He tried to cover his marred face.

"No, that's not it. I just can't believe it's really you," said Lyssa. She caressed his cheek and hugged him. "You can't know how I missed you. Just to hold you in my arms again is a miracle. You're a miracle." She could feel warm tears flowing from her eyes.

"You might say that. All I know is me, this guy," he said, pointing to himself, "hasn't been around for some time." A slight grin formed on his thin, tight lips. His eyes glistened, as he tried to compose himself.

"My grief was unbearable. Without our family I don't know what I would've done." She tried to wipe away her streaming tears. "You can't know how good you feel." She looked deep into his eyes and hugged him again.

"I'm sorry for the grief I caused you." His voice quivered, as he tried to control his emotions.

"Now I know why I always felt you were alive. I'm sure a lot of people who lost loved ones back then had those same feelings," she tried to explain. "It's just that when you lose someone like that . . . I mean so quickly. It's hard to explain except that time seems to stand still." She looked at him. "It hurt me to the core. I had to force myself to live with the real hard facts that I would never see your smile again, hear you laugh, or even argue with you anymore."

"I'm so sorry," He pulled his wool sweater around him.

"It wasn't your fault, but seeing you brings back the grief. I don't know why, but it just does. Out of all the trials in life, I never dreamed I would have to accept you out of my life . . . but I finally did," she cried. With her head on his chest, she hugged him and wept.

After some time, she sat apart from him and decided she had to compose herself and get to know him as the man who now sat in front of her. "You married a Japanese woman?" Lyssa asked about his wife. She thought he seemed so in charge with his demeanor.

"American with Japanese heritage," he explained. "After my mother's situation with her eyes, it's always amazed me about the distinction because of their inherited looks. I don't know your husband's heritage, but . . ." He seemed to be defending his wife.

He noticed, especially since Lyssa already knew of his background, that she understood where he was coming from. "I know what you mean. And maybe because their heritage is so obviously known, the Japanese descendants try to keep up with the traditions of their ancestors," she said. "I think it's great. She seems very devoted to you."

"She was the nurse who treated me when I was brought into the emergency trauma room. When I finally woke up, I didn't know who I was, and I was hysterical. Without her serene personality I don't think I could have made it through the first night." He remembered all those years ago.

"It must've been terrifying," Lyssa said. "She does seem to have a calming way about her."

"I was stabbed and bludgeoned. They kept telling me it was a miracle I was alive." He looked at her for any hesitation. He thought she looked a little squeamish so he quickly tried to play it down. "After my outer wounds healed, we started dating." He started to feel a little uncomfortable talking about his relationship with his wife. He rubbed his eyes and fidgeted in his seat.

"Byron, it's okay. You had no recollection of us. You were trying to make a life for yourself," Lyssa said. "This is just so unbelievable." She scooted over and hugged him. This time they both started to cry.

"Oh my, look around," she said. "I remember once in this house I told you we would marry one day. God, I was a brat." She smiled and wiped her eyes with her hand.

"But you were right," he said. She saw the sparkle in his eyes that she had always loved. "I remember our wedding day . . . also the day we got our Victoria." He smiled at her and she patted his hand. They held each other and shared a silent reflection for that time.

"When this happened, I was so distraught." He lifted his hand to his face. "I didn't think my life was worth that miracle everybody kept talking about." He bowed his head. "I tried once to end it all, but she set me straight." He looked into Lyssa's eyes. "She's a good, loving woman, and a strong one."

"Can you tell me how it happened," she asked. She looked at his face.

"I didn't figure it out myself until a couple of months ago. I've been working as a janitor at a school. I guess something was always trying to get me to remember because I was always going to the school library and looking up artwork. It always amazed Melissa that I knew all the different artist's works." He saw a bewildered look in her eyes.

"Your wife's name is Melissa?"

"Weird, *huh*." He smiled. "I guess something in her name also attracted me to her. Like I said, she's strong and tells it like it is. Just like you," he said. They both chuckled.

"She seems to only have your best interest at heart," Lyssa added.

"You're right, she does." His eyes looked glassy. "Because of her I came back to myself," he continued. "I was walking home one day, the same way I'd gone for many years, but this time when I walked past Madison's café and read the sign Martha's Cinnamon Rolls, something started to open up. When I got home I told Melissa I was starting to remember things, and she urged me to go to therapy, so I did." He had a weary look in his eyes.

"Want a glass of wine?" Lyssa asked. She went to the bar and grabbed two glasses and a bottle of what she remembered was his favorite wine. "I sure could use a drink," she said.

He watched her uncork the bottle and pour the dark liquid into the glasses. "We don't drink much, but right now, I could use something to coat my dry throat." He accepted the glass from her. "You married again?" He noticed she looked a bit embarrassed.

"Yes, I met Glenn after Mama and Daddy died. He took over their vet business. He's really good at it, and I help out too," she explained. "I guess our marriage . . ." She had a puzzled look on her face. "So I'm wondering if our marriage is legal?" She questioned him.

"If you're as happy as you seem to be, and I know I could never leave my family, I guess we'll have to get in touch with a lawyer. Most likely we'll have to divorce," he said. He swallowed the wine in his glass. "That feels good," he said and reached to refill his glass. He watched her only sip the wine in her glass.

"We'll have to let our boys know." She noticed the blood drain from his face. "They have to be told," she then said.

"I know, but this is all so new for me and telling it all to you is just about taking all my strength."

"I'll explain it to them. We'll do it gently. Maybe, like you did, we can get a therapist involved," she said. He seemed to relax. "Both boys enlisted after 911," she told him. "They wanted to do something for you and for our country." She could see a look of pride in him. "Josh joined the air force. They quietly sat for a moment.

"I know my parents have passed," he said. "I've missed so much." He started to scratch his sideburns. "May I?" He reached for his hat.

"Please do. Get comfortable." She tried to prepare herself for the worst. "It looks like you've healed, but I'm sorry for the loss of that great looking head of hair." She did her best to conceal her horror at his many scars. "Oh God, Byron, what did that monster do to you," she cried. "I'm so sorry," She went to him, and he took her into his arms.

"I had to be told when it all happened. I didn't remember. From what I've been told, it was the night before 911," he said. They both refilled their glasses.

"We talked that night," she related. "When last we talked, you said you were at a restaurant with your dad and you were going to walk back to your hotel." She noticed he seemed to remember.

"You're right. I just now remembered our talk. I made a big gallery purchase with Dad at the Brownstone Gallery. Dad was in town for the closing, but he went back to the gallery after we had our dinner," he said and started to shake.

"Stop, you don't have to continue," Lyssa whispered.

"I just realized that was the last time I saw him." He started to sob. "And Mama, she must have . . ." He continued to cry. He reached for her and they embraced.

He tried to change the subject and calm himself. "That little girl, with the chocolate mustache, is she your . . . our . . ." He was choking on his words.

"She's Victoria's grandbaby and my great grandchild." She looked at him and smiled. "She's Christina's niece." She saw him smile back. "After all those years, Christina found Victoria, her mother and my daughter," She saw that he was settling down. "René, the man with Reggie, who brought you to us, is Victoria's husband. He spoke with Madison about you?" she asked.

"Well, actually, Madison first spoke with Aunt Mary and she contacted René, then, after we all met with René and Reggie, Madison went home." He rubbed his eyes and was silent for a moment. "I will never forget how Madison helped me with this. She is a very caring woman." He seemed to be reflecting. "René is also a very caring man," he calmly added.

"Yes, he is, and the little girl with the chocolate mustache is Arlene's child. Arlene is René and Victoria's daughter. The man you saw sitting next to Arlene is her husband, Jeremy," she explained. She could see she was giving him a lot of information. He seemed older than his years and looked terribly exhausted.

"Our boys are happy?" he asked. He scooted from her and reached for his glass.

"They both have married, and yes, besides Christina, you are a grandfather." She smiled at him. "A lot to take in, *huh*?" she asked. She saw him shake his head and rub his forehead. "Can I get Christina?" she asked. "I know she would love to talk with you." She reached over and hugged him.

"Yes, please do."

When she left him alone in the room, he looked around. He felt at home and like a visiting stranger at the same time. He heard a sound and looked toward the doorway to the family room.

"When will Jesus be born?" Evian asked innocently. She went to him and quickly put her arms up for him to boost her up onto the sofa.

"Jesus?" he asked, but then he remembered how Evian had said he and his wife were going to have baby Jesus. "Oh you mean the baby my wife's going to have," he said. "Well, I'll tell you something. It isn't going to be Jesus, but it is going to be a baby boy. And you know what, I'll talk it over with my wife and maybe we can make his middle name Jesus. What do you think about that?" He noticed she did not seem scared or offended by his scarred face or the wild bunches of hair that stuck out from his head.

"You don't have much hair," she said. She stood on the sofa and started to rub his baldhead. "All bumpy." She started to laugh. "I'm Evian, what's your name?" she asked, not letting him answer. "Mama says you're Aunt Christina's grandpa. Can I call you grandpa too?"

"You sure can," he said. "Can I have a hug?"

"Yep," she said. She jumped into his arms and gave him one of René's bear hugs. "Grandpa Re Re loves hugs." She looked at him and saw big tears falling from his eyes. "Happy tears," she said. She wiped his face. "Mama says when I give her big hugs she has happy tears," She spoke to him in a simple, unconcerned way.

"Yes, honey, only happy tears," he said. They again hugged.

***

"Oh, Grammy, we had such a miracle that Christmas. We thought we had lost him forever, but we were blessed. It was one of René's true miracles," Christina spoke aloud. She looked around her office. "I'm glad I had this decorated like this. The fireplace makes it almost feel like home." She hugged herself. "I wish you could've been with us." She looked around again as if someone were watching her. "I can feel you now," she whispered. She clutched the letter to her heart. "You should've seen him standing there." She again remembered back to that Christmas miracle.

"Grandpa Byron was standing near the Christmas tree. He had the Christmas tree, blue-and-white light binder in his hand.

I watched him put his hand to his head and start to sob," she said aloud, as if she were speaking to Grammy.

"Grandpa," Christina remembered whispering to him. She noticed he tried to hide his face in his handkerchief. "Please Grandpa, don't hide from me. I love you no matter what. You can't know how happy I am to see you," she said.

"Yes I can, honey," Byron said. He took the handkerchief, blew his nose, and held his arms open to her. "Oh yes I can," he said again, and they both sobbed openly.

"Happy tears?" She looked at him.

"Yes, only happy tears." He saw her as the child he remembered.

"You're the best Christmas gift ever." She gazed up at him. "I can't help but have a terrible sense of sorrow for all the other people who have lost loved ones. They can't have this incredible happiness I'm having now just hugging you and feeling you in my arms." She started to sob.

"I feel blessed," he whispered. "Thank you God." He lifted his head toward Heaven. "Thank you," he said again. They both held onto each other as tightly as they could and continued to sob only happy tears of joy.

Chapter Thirteen

"I can remember that Christmas as if it were yesterday. Our lives changed after that miracle," Christina reflected, "and I'm sure you now know that Grandpa Byron is still with us." She wished that Grammy could have known, when she was alive, the happiness that they all were blessed with on that miraculous Christmas Eve. She continued to read Grammy's treasured correspondence.

Those were sad days—when Olivia lost her dear friends Rachel and Cal, your great-grandparents, all those years ago.

Christina could tell Grammy's hands were quivering. *Yes those were sad days.* Christina thought, remembering those sad times. She closed her eyes and could almost feel Grammy right next to her. In her mind, when she continued to read, she believed she could hear Grammy's voice.

It was very early in the morning when the call came in to Olivia. "Oh God, Livi, Cal's had some kind of an attack," Rachel was screaming over the phone. "He's on the way by ambulance to the hospital." She could feel a cold sweat on her skin.

"Don't move I'm on my way with Wolfgang. Don't you drive," Olivia demanded.

They arrived at the hospital emergency room and went directly to the information desk. "I'm Mrs. Cal Yarborough. My husband was brought in by ambulance," Rachel explained to the attendant.

"Yes, Mrs. Yarborough. The doctor is with him now. Could you fill out this information for us?" She handed Rachel the forms to be filled out.

"Oh God, Livi, can you do this for me?" With shaking hands, she gave Olivia the clipboard.

"Sit down, Rachel." Olivia led her to a set of chairs where they sat down and completed the information and then returned it to the attendant.

"I think he had a heart attack." Rachel put her hand to her head. "It was horrible. I didn't know what to do, so I just called the ambulance." She looked at Olivia.

Olivia took her in her arms and hugged her. "No matter what, I'm here for you," she said. "Rachel, we've been through a lot together. You're more than my closest friend; you're my sister in every way. We'll get through this together." She reached into her purse and gave Rachel a tissue. They both wiped away their tears, and then spotted the doctor coming toward them.

"Mrs. Yarborough," the doctor said.

"Yes, doctor." Rachel rose from her seat.

"Your husband is sedated right now, but he did suffer a heart attack," The doctor explained to them.

"Can we see him?" Rachel asked.

"Yes, but he is sedated."

"Come on, Livi." Rachel reached for Olivia's hand.

"I'll be just a minute, Rachel. You go ahead." Olivia wanted to speak with the doctor.

"Doctor, can you give me his prognosis?" she asked.

"It really doesn't look good. With his age, I'm afraid there was a lot of damage," he explained. "Let's go to the room. It will help if you are with her." He turned and Olivia followed him.

Oh God, this is going to kill Rachel, Olivia thought. She could feel her legs go slightly limp. Just then the doctor heard a code blue call and raced to Cal's room with Olivia right behind him.

The room was fully lit. Rachel stood as close to Cal's bed as she could. She was holding his hand. "Oh God, Livi, he looks so pale." She took Olivia's hand in her other hand. "We'll have to get in touch with the kids." She looked into Olivia's eyes. She did not notice the beeping machines or the staff coming in the room.

"I'll do it," Olivia said. She put her head on Rachel's shoulder.

Knowing Cal's diagnosis, the machines explained what the doctor needed to know. He did not ask Rachel and Olivia to leave the room. He went to the other side of the bed and physically checked Cal's statistics. His eyes explained it all to Rachel.

"Oh God no . . . Livi . . ." She looked at Cal and then at Olivia. "This can't be. We delivered a colt early this morning." Her tears flowed endlessly. "He was fine . . . he's a strong man . . . he can't be . . ." She again looked at the doctor.

The doctor said, "I'm so sorry. The stress was more than his heart could take."

***

"Oh, Grammy, that was so hard on the family, but then Rachel . . ." Christina remembered with a sad heart.

***

Rachel was never the same after she lost her husband. She had no desire to leave her home. She posted ads for the sale of their vet business. "Too bad CC couldn't take over the business, but we're all so proud of his career as a doctor," Rachel said to Olivia during one of her visits after Cal passed away.

"He's a special man who will bring a lot to this world," Olivia said of CC—Cal and Rachel's eldest son. "You and Cal had a wonderful life, full of love. I didn't understand it when I was young, but it grew on me." She patted Rachel's hand and looked at her with deep empathy written all over her face.

"We both have lost loves." Rachel also knew Olivia's heartache and believed she could completely confide in her. "I woke up one morning, and I could smell his aftershave." She looked at Olivia for signs of disbelief, but saw none so she continued. "And sometimes, I think I hear his voice in the other room. I've been known to carry on a pretty good conversation with him." She chuckled. "Do you think I'm nuts?" She took a slow sip from her glass of wine; she looked at Olivia.

"Well, if you're nuts, then so am I. I've had conversations with all those in my family. Sometimes, I can even feel Jay in the room with me. I know he was a baby when he died, but when I feel him he seems old. I talk to him as the uncle of my kids, and he tells me he's taking care of them." They both laughed.

"If it weren't for my kids, I don't know what I would've done." Rachel took another sip from her glass of wine. "I'm sorry, Livi." She realized Olivia did not have that kind of support.

"I'm happy I have you." Olivia took a sip from her glass of wine.

"When I'm here alone, I feel safe with all our things around me. I don't like leaving, knowing I will come home to an empty house . . . without him . . . the loss is so overbearing. When our neighbor visits, I almost hate her. She listens to me and says she understands, but she . . . she has her husband to go home to. How can she understand?" The wine was not having a good effect on her, but she took another sip anyway.

"I think women have a second sense for that. If she says she understands, she most likely does—to a certain extent, but like you said, unless you live it you really can't completely understand the deep loss." Olivia also took a gulp from her glass of wine. "If you don't mind, I think I'll spend the night." She looked at Rachel.

They both did not realize how pitiful they looked. "Did you even comb your hair today?" Rachel asked. "You look like shit." She started to mess with her own hair.

"Oh, and you look like the Queen of Sheba?" They started to giggle. "Hey, let's try to make some of Martha's cinnamon rolls. Do you have any yeast?" Olivia asked. She slowly got up from her seat and prodded Rachel to do the same. "These old bones sure don't move like they used to. Did you hear that crack?" She stood in front of Rachel waiting for her to follow.

"Yeah, I heard you crack. So what else is new? I crack all the time." Rachel grabbed a hold of Olivia's extended hand, and they went to the kitchen.

Later, they went to sleep in CC's bedroom. With the twin beds, it was perfect for them. It was well into the night when a sound woke Olivia. She looked over at Rachel and noticed her arms were stretched out above her, and she seemed to be talking and hugging someone. For a split second, in the dim moonlight, Olivia believed she saw the figure of Cal.

Quickly, she rubbed her eyes and his apparition was gone. Then, she noticed Rachel was gently snoring and seemed to be sleeping peacefully. The following morning, Rachel appeared refreshed, so she decided not to bring the incident to her attention.

In the months that followed, they did their best to comfort each other. Without their beloved mates, the days were long and the nights were longer, but just knowing they had each other to lean on helped them understand and cope with their losses. They would visit each other often, and kept each other company to live to see another day. But the loneliness became too much for Rachel, and sixty days after Cal's passing she was in hospice. They took care of her every need. It was said she died of a broken heart..

***

"Oh, Grammy, those were sad times for Olivia and Rachel," Christina spoke aloud. For a moment, she held Grammy's letter close to her heart, but then continued to read.

> I also have to put down these words, my sweet Christina, it was a great gift you gave my husband when you stayed by his side until the end.

Christina could feel that day and his spirit.

> We had to live on with our losses, but we helped each other.

"Yes, we helped each other through those hard times." Christina read on.

Later, during our times together I realized I didn't have to divulge all the history to you, as it all would become clear to you in time. You knew me and I knew you, and that was the most important thing. You called me Grammy and I loved it until the day I left this earth.

Christina could almost feel her hugging her.

Sweetheart, I believe in the final myth. I may not physically be with you, but when you believe, I am right by your side. When you see a fluttering butterfly come close to you, or answer the phone and no one is there, that is me saying hello. When the lights blink, that's me."

"Those things have happened." Christina chuckled and read on.

You know, when the Lord looked over the entire universe, he saw Earth. He believed His creation to be a beautiful planet, so, on this rock He built His church. You know I collected rocks. They interested me with their unique age and beauty. If you happen across a rare looking rock, take it home. Who knows how it got there; maybe I left it there for you. It's like when you meet a stranger: you may never cross paths again, so make the most of it. Build a rock garden for your friends; inspire with good examples.

She read Grammy's words of love and her type of wisdom with great understanding. *She was a deep woman,* Christina thought.

Christina, live long and in love and know I will forever love you. Enjoy your gift."

She cautiously lifted the wrapped package from the box. *This wrapping feels like silk and the lace ribbon is such a pretty pink. Of course . . . mine and Grammy's favorite color,* she thought. The lace ribbon easily untied with one pull and fell to either side of the package. Immediately, the silk wrapping slowly slid on top of her desk and the large, brown package was exposed. Another card with her name on it was placed on top. "God, she's full of mystery." She opened the small envelope and read what Grammy wrote.

Christy, it's time. Keep up the gossip! All my love, Grammy.

Christina's tears flowed again, and she felt like a kid again when she read her nickname: Christy. But then she read Grammy's final words.

P.S. Check the envelope under the lid.

She looked to find an envelope taped under the lid and opened it.
"Oh my God, more miracles. René would get a charge out of this," she exclaimed. She had to sit down. "The deed to Red Winds. She left me Red Winds!" She could not believe her eyes. She could not help but hurry to pull out her beautifully wrapped gift. "Just as I remembered it—your beautiful silver tea set." She grabbed another tissue and blew her nose into it. Joy filled her heart. "I wish you were here, so I could pour for you." She caressed the shiny teapot. "I can't wait to show Ronny." She went to her desk and picked up the phone.

"Mr. Fiord, Mrs. Fiord . . ." She could see his 'Indiana Jones' grin, when he picked up his end of the line. "Honey, I got another one of those letters from Grammy. I have so much to tell you, I'm on my way home," She related excitedly to her husband.

"We're waiting for you—and, honey, there's an older gentleman here to see you," Ronny told her.

"Oh yeah, who?" she asked.

"He says his name's Reginald Ti," he said, with a slight laugh.

"Oh my God . . . you're always teasing me. But I thought we had it set up for Reggie and his family to stop by tomorrow for our Christmas visit."

"Well, it just so happens he's received one of those envelopes from the Linder Law offices himself," her husband explained.

"Really, what's it about?" she asked.

"He was advised he could only open it in your presence," he said, sounding vague.

"Honey, can you put him on the phone?" Christiana could feel her building emotions.

"Missy Christina," Reggie said.

"Open it, Reggie. I'm sure it's from Grammy. God that woman's so full of mystery," she whispered under her breath.

"It is from Misses. She wants my family to always have a home on Red Winds. She says my posterity will always have a home.

"Oh, Reggie, she loved you and the Ti family so much, and you will always have a home on Red Winds. Please, stay there with Ronny. I'll be there shortly," Christina said.

"I'll stay. Here's your husband." Reggie gave the phone to Ronny.

"Oh my God, Ronny, that woman lives on." She tried to control her emotions. "I have so much to tell you. I'm on my way; don't let Reggie leave. I love you. See you in a bit," she said and hung up.

"Oh, Grammy, I wish you could see. Your son has inherited Red Winds. I believe you can understand the happiness we feel when we visit." She wiped her eyes. "Grandpa loves the land, and I know when he reads your letter he will feel you as close to him as I do.

"I hope I always make you proud Grammy," she whispered. She again ran her fingers over the coolness of the delicate tea set. "And you can be certain, of course, only when it's time, that I will teach my beautiful daughter how to pour properly." She started to rewrap her gift with the letter from Grammy. "You would love her, Grammy. She's your fourth cousin and your name sake, Olivia Anne. Just like you she enjoys drawing and painting. And I have to say, she loves your signature so much that she uses it herself. Of course, she had to add her own flair by placing on the end of the big A of "OliviA" what she calls her Olivia angel's wings by signing it with our Fiord initial, changing it to "OliviAF." She's full of ideas, has a passion for life, and cares deeply for others."

Christina picked up her newly obtained tea set and placed it back into the box. She held Grammy's letter close to her heart, kissed it, and also placed it in the box.

"You can be certain we will continue to keep the gossip alive, because, as we all do, my Olivia has learned to love the legacy of Red Winds."

Review Requested:

If you loved this book, would you please provide
a review at Amazon.com?

Printed in the USA
CPSIA information can be obtained
at www.ICGtesting.com
CBHW021952201024
16086CB00001B/15